# Laments for the Dead

## Roger Johnson

ISBN 978-1-7364368-7-5 (paperback)

email: rogerj47@gmail.com
website: Roger_Johnson.com

For Cheryl and Jennifer

And mothers and daughters

# ACKNOWLEDGMENTS

My continued appreciation to my small group of readers who offer their insightful critiques and heartfelt encouragement.

**Special thanks to my friends**

Joe DesGeorges: formatting and interior design
Dan Augenstein: cover design.

Books by Roger Johnson

*Laments for the Dead*
*On Point*
*Gifts: The Return*
*Coach Izzy: Full Circle*

# Laments for the Dead

Roger Johnson

IngramSpark

2022

# Laments for the Dead

"Come Fairies, take me out of this dull world, for I would ride with you upon the wind and dance upon the mountains like a flame."

*William Butler Yeats*

"We can't know in this life about the forces that send us on our journeys, but they are mysterious indeed. We are directed by unseen winds."

*Father Tellez*

# I

# DR. OLGA CHERKASOVA

# CHAPTER 1

*Northern Urals, Komi Republic, Soviet Union, late September 1983*

The reindeer do not fear Pyotr, although most are cautious of the boy. He has no apprehension of them at all. They sense that, sense something in his movements, smell, and eyes. Olga worries though--a small boy so close to such large beasts--but she has seen it before and knows Pyotr will be okay. The herd grazes at the edge of the forest, wary. Wild reindeer are rare in this part of Russia anymore, but this herd has migrated to this forest for decades. Four reindeer move into the glen, slowly advancing toward Pyotr. Olga watches carefully as the reindeer near her grandson; she stands and steps closer. The greatest of the herd understands her protective behavior and turns to the approaching animals to warn them to move slowly. The Great One! On this visit to his meadow near the cave, he moves gracefully to greet Pyotr, and even tolerates Olga, although he keeps a clear distance from her. The Great One's antlers spread over three feet from tip-to-tip, and he weighs nearly four-hundred pounds. Soon he will mate, maybe with a dozen cows, and Olga envisions his herds wandering over her mountain for generations to come, long after he has died, long after she has died.

Olga finally feels comfortable with Pyotr's safety. She steps back into the cave, an amphitheater really, and sits at the old, wooden table. *How has Pyotr come into his connection to animals and to the unseen?* She certainly did not give it to him, and she can't remember Ursula having such a gift as her child. Ursula inherited her mother's connection to men. Olga watches Pyotr. He is so small, and the reindeer are not house pets. The Great One looks up to the roof of the cave, scanning it for something. He bellows to his herd, reminding them to be ever vigilant. Olga guesses the bellow signals a message, but she doesn't know for sure. Pyotr holds long grasses up to the snout of The Great One, who eats them slowly. *Why can't life always be so peaceful, always so gentle?* She lifts her camera from the table and snaps a photo. From the top of the cave, she can see Gora Narodnaya, the highest peak in all the Urals. Her majestic mountain. Olga resents the government for its recent intrusion into this sacred part of her world, for digging up part of Gora Narodnaya.

She sets the camera down and straightens a wrinkle in the red tablecloth. Winter is coming at this extreme latitude. This autumn day is a rarity, a gift. The temperature approached nearly fifty degrees earlier in the day, warmer than many summer days in the Northern Urals, but Olga knows. Winter will indeed arrive, sudden and harsh on the wind, just as it always does in Russia; the dark time, the time of loneliness. Today, Olga's chief concern is for her daughter. Ursula hates the cold, but she has a good job in Yamantov, at the excavations as a welder underground, and the job promises to last for several more years. In this economy it is a job to hang on to, but it is hard work and the hours are long. Hours in Soviet Russia are always long for the women.

Olga has made this picnic stop a new summer tradition for her and Pyotr after their once-monthly, mid-week visit to Pyotr's mother in Yamantov. This region of the Soviet Union is sparsely populated except for the towns that hug the rail line from Moscow to Vorkuta beyond the Arctic Circle, a distance traveled not in hours but in days. Olga and her husband discovered the cave quite accidently several years earlier after a visit with her parents. Her husband died the next year in Afghanistan, that useless, heartbreaking war. She continued to come--alone--for its protection; she felt this cave on the western slopes of the Urals could provide a refuge from the world. Olga has never seen another person at the cave, but she knows others have come here. The drawings on the walls of the cave attest to this. They are mostly anti-tsarist sketches from the nineteenth century and pro-Trotsky slogans from the Thirties.

Pyotr runs back to the picnic table for a few more bites of his sandwich, a slice of tomato, and a bit of chocolate. He kisses Grandma Olga on the cheek and runs back out into the meadow with the reindeer. This time, Pyotr runs between several of the smaller reindeer, playing no favorites. Pyotr runs everywhere, such a happy four-year old. Ursula lived in Canada when Pyotr was born. His father worked in Moscow, a diplomat, and he and Ursula traveled to Ottawa on government business. He did not return with Ursula and Pyotr, and once they were gone, he never contacted them again. He defected and disappeared, probably to the United States. Olga did not like him anyway, and he is twenty years older than Ursula, closer to Olga's age. Ursula took the job at Yamantov to be closer to Olga and Olga's parents in Pechora, and it has worked out well.

Pyotr sees more of Grandmother Olga and his great-grandparents than he does his mother. Ursula leaves for Yamantov at two a.m. on Mondays and does not return to Pechora until nearly midnight on Fridays. She lives on-site during the week, building another nuclear facility of some sort. Rumors suggest the facility is a power plant, since the Soviet Union is committed to nuclear power, but it is not on the Pechora River, so that doesn't make sense to Olga. It is probably another military base with accompanying missile silos, only much larger than some of the existing ones. Ursula is not at liberty to say, and she especially cannot speak about the nature of Yamantov to her grandparents. Both of them were exiled to Inta, part of the Gulag, in the Thirties by Joseph Stalin. Olga's parents should have died at Inta, but they refused to give Stalin the satisfaction. Olga was born there in 1937 and lived in Inta until she left for university studies. Yamantov is a closed city, but being so isolated, restrictions are lax, and approved families are allowed to visit. In Pechora at any time, the restrictions of the Cold War are minimal. Her parents may have self-imposed restrictions on travel south of Pechora, but Olga has none. She traveled to Syktyvkar and then even to Moscow to earn her dentistry degree. She had options, but did not like Moscow, so when the job opened up in Pechora, she went home to practice her profession, and she has never regretted it.

In the shade of the cave as she cleans the table, Olga feels a chill, something, however, that feels more than just the dropping temperature of the late afternoon. It is a strange feeling, as if something is being sent to her. She stands and walks into the sunshine, keeping a safe distance from the three reindeer closest to Pyotr, so as not to startle them. She finds a rock where she can sit and lean back. She watches Pyotr with the sun in her face as the afternoon passes. Days such as this make Pechora and the region bearable. This day holds off the long winter. This is her Russia, this mountain and its environs, and she never wants to leave again.

Olga looks up to the bushes on top of the cave to where she heard the crackle of a twig, wondering what kind of an animal made it. Another reindeer maybe? She sees nothing and her eyes return to Pyotr, who now has his hand on The Great One's flank. She shakes her head, marveling at the scene: a three-foot four-inch, skinny, always-talking boy and a six-foot long reindeer that dominates the herd. She will need to take her grandson home soon, before darkness falls. Mr. Borovsky will pick them up at the end of the dirt road where he dropped them off earlier in the day, so they can reboard the bus back to Pechora. The sun will set long before they travel the full distance home, but it will be a day Olga will never forget. The world seems perfect.

§

Twenty-four hours earlier, Olga enjoyed a romp in a stranger's bed at the Yamantov company town. Ursula met Olga and Pyotr at the bus depot, where Ursula hugged her mother and let her go off on her own for the afternoon. Olga went to Yuri's, the local bar named after the first man in space, to find an idle man. She found Gregori, a twenty-eight-year-old iron worker who was between shifts and not yet past his first vodka. He was attracted to her flame red hair and perfect nose. Olga likes younger men; men in the Soviet Union age quickly and are mostly alcoholics. They get past their prime quickly and are full of self-pity. At forty-six, she could pass for her early thirties, a trait she uses to her advantage occasionally.

She rejoined her daughter and grandson for dinner. Ursula had taken Pyotr to the indoor swimming pool which is fed by a nearby hot springs. Swimming is what they always do on these trips. In the evening Olga and Ursula took turns reading stories to Pyotr until he fell asleep in his mother's arms. Then the two women talked. They are close; the only thing they ever seriously argued about was Ursula's decision to take up with an older man, especially the one she did. Olga never trusted him, but he did give them Pyotr. When he took Ursula to Canada, however, Olga hoped they would stay and forge a better life. Ursula had told her mother about the pregnancy while keeping it a secret from the father until they arrived in Canada. That turned out to be a mistake. His plans to defect did not include a child, so after Pyotr's birth, he put them on a plane back to Moscow. The rent on Ursula's apartment there was paid up only for one month. She and Pyotr returned to Pechora nearly four years ago.

Ursula's short life of glamour ended, but she took it well. She began her welder's training and took the job in Yamantov a year later. She never seems to look back, and Olga respects her daughter for her perspective. Olga believes her daughter would probably not have liked Canada and would eventually have worked her way back to the Soviet Union, back to her family and beloved Urals in Komi. She is pretty like her mother, but not as strong. She has her mother's hair and features, and often they are confused as sisters. Ursula says her job will make her more muscular over time, stronger than her mother.

Ursula loves Pyotr but allows the Russian babushka tradition to continue. Grandma Olga and Olga's mother dote on Pyotr, and he lacks for nothing. While Olga works her dental magic in the mouths of Pechora's wealthier families, Pyotr runs his great-grandparents breathless. Ursula thinks it will make them live longer. *If Stalin couldn't kill them, neither can a little Bolsheviki.* It is a close family: an old man, a young boy, and three strong-willed women living in a house built for "enemies of the state" back in the late-Twenties, in a house built to withstand the severe cold of Arctic winters and anything else nature throws at it.

§

Olga yells to Pyotr to say goodbye to the reindeer and come back to the table; it is time to go. She packs the picnic basket, carefully folding the red tablecloth and laying it on top of the uneaten food. What remains can be consumed on the bus over the last four hours to Pechora, although Pyotr usually falls asleep and doesn't eat much more.

The click startles Olga, but she reacts instinctively and looks to Pyotr. An explosion comes from the top of the cave. Olga knows the sound; a hunter has fired a Tiger 7.62 rifle from above her. Olga sees The Great One slump to his front knees and fall headfirst into the ground. She yells to Pyotr to run, but he stands motionless over the fallen reindeer. He doesn't seem scared, but protective in his manner. Olga runs to Pyotr and swoops him into her chest. As she turns, she sees a bearded hunter atop the cave with the rifle. He quickly pivots in the direction of Yamantov, no doubt to return to the path that leads off the cliff and around to the meadow, to the mouth of the cave where he can retrieve his kill. It will take him a few minutes to get to where Olga and Pyotr are now sheltered.

Olga sees the blood on Pyotr's cheek, and anger unlike anything she has ever felt takes hold of her. Suddenly, a complete whiteness consumes her world. There is no sound. Fear replaces her anger; she is confused. She drops to her knees, her maternal instinct trying to protect Pyotr. *What is happening*? Less than a half-minute passes when a penetrating eruption louder than any clap of thunder she has ever heard explodes in the meadow. Pyotr seems pressed into her bosom now. She looks out to the forest and sees small fires. Several trees have been blown down, and the reindeer herd has disappeared, except the scorched carcass of The Great One. Paralysis grips Olga.

Ten minutes pass, maybe more. Olga wants to stay in the cave. She fears going to the top of the protective cavern, which leads back to Pechora, but Pechora is home. Most of the brush fires have been extinguished, but a shower of dust is falling in the meadow. Dusk seems to be coming more quickly than it should be. Pyotr stirs for the first time, his eyes asking, "Babu, where are we?" Olga has no answer. With her finger, she wipes a large drop of The Great One's blood from Pyotr's cheek, and for a reason unknown even to her, she puts it in her mouth and swallows.

Olga places her hand on the back of Pyotr's head and pushes it into her shoulder. "We can't stay here," she tells him. "I'm going to put on your raincoat, and we'll start back up to the road. Mr. Borovsky will be there to pick us up. We'll stay with him tonight if necessary. We'll be okay." She doesn't know if Mr. Borovsky will be at the end of the trail or not, but she knows they cannot stay at the cave overnight. She fears she will never return here again.

Olga wraps Pyotr in his raincoat and puts on hers. She bends down to lift Pyotr onto her back, leaves the picnic basket, and heads out. As they pass The Great One, Olga stoops to gently touch his antler. She utters softly, "Back I send you from where there is no return." She forces herself to turn away and starts up the path. At the top of the cave, the hunter lies motionless, his flesh seared and smoke rising from his clothes, but he moans softly as Olga and Pyotr pass by. She ignores his plea as if she hasn't heard him—she knows she can do nothing for him, but Pyotr looks back. Twenty minutes of determined walking gets them to the road where Mr. Borovsky waits. The winds blow east, toward the Urals and away from Pechora. Toward Siberia. Down from the Arctic Ocean, winter descends.

§

Olga and Pyotr stay the night with Mr. Borovsky. Bus service to Pechora has been suspended. The Soviet Army has immediately closed off all roads to Yamantov for their own use. Helicopters appear first and then dozens of military trucks pass by Mr. Borovsky's house heading east. Olga wonders where the helicopters were based to arrive so soon. Information from Yamantov is restricted, although soldiers stationed along the road indicate no one will be transported out of the accident site and casualties may number in the hundreds or more. Phone service is spotty, but Olga finally gets through to her parents to let them know she and Pyotr are safe. She can't say the same for Ursula. On Tuesday Olga stands by the roadside all day to try to get any news about her daughter. Soldiers in trucks avoid the glares of the townspeople. They utter no words, probably ordered into silence, but their faces speak of a terrible tragedy. Seven women doctors in a van stop at the general store to use the restroom and supplement their lunch, but they have no information to add. A warehouse may have exploded; nothing more. Soviet secrets, a culture of secrecy and obfuscation and paranoia. Men in suits offer encouragement; the fires will soon be contained, and the rescue efforts will begin. The markings on the black cars and vans indicate the officials are with the communist party, not Komi police or fire departments. Not enough time has passed to get troops or officials in from the capital. Strangely, no planes have flown in. If it is a warehouse fire, the runway at Yamantov should be usable. In the evening Mr. Borovsky tells Olga he has found a man who will drive to Pechora the next day and take her home.

Olga is torn. She wants to stay close to Ursula, her only child, but Pyotr needs to return to Pechora. He hasn't spoken since the accident. He mostly sleeps, but when he's awake, he won't allow Grandma Olga out of his reach. Olga knows she can't put him in the car alone. She tells Mr. Borovsky she will accept the ride and return to Pechora. Mr. Borovsky tells her she can stay at his house anytime. "Get Pyotr settled in and come back." Olga nods and then steps in to hug him. Mr. Borovsky holds onto her. "My son is missing too," he says. A few moments later, Olga finally responds, "Thank you," and steps back from the hug. She sees that this acquaintance who has been her patient, always jovial, has become an old man instantly. He seems to be looking to her for answers.

At dinner Pyotr finally eats. Borsch and a boiled potato. Still, he doesn't speak. Afterwards, they sit in the living room to watch television, to see if the one station Mr. Borovsky receives has any information. The news remains generic, saying only that an accident has occurred at a power plant in the Northern Urals, and everything is being done to get medical help to the injured and to contain the fire in the warehouse. Pyotr lays his head on his grandma's lap and falls asleep. Mr. Borovsky covers him with a yellow wool blanket.

"Would you like some coffee?" he asks.

"Yes, thank you. You have been so kind."

Mr. Borovsky goes into his kitchen, returning a few minutes later with two cups. "Be careful, it's hot," he warns. They each sip, and then he asks, "Dr. Cherkasova, may I call you Olga? I fear this event will force us together, but I want this," and here he stretches out his arms as if to mean his house, "to be comfortable."

Olga nods. "And what is your first name? I apologize for not remembering it from my charts."

"You have so many patients, and I have been blessed with good teeth, so they don't stand out. Nor does my name. It is Ivan."

Olga smiles for the first time since the accident. "Where is your wife, Ivan?"

"She makes money in Moscow as an art curator. She likes the city."

"Do you visit her often?"

"No, we haven't seen each other in several years; not since the early-Seventies, I think." Mr. Borovsky smiles. "But she sends me and Gregori a bit of money each month."

Olga doesn't ask. It would be a coincidence. She wonders about such an arrangement, about Ivan's wife, about a man living alone for so many years. *What would cause a man to live alone for so long*? He always seemed happy, but she only knows him as her patient and driver to the cave once a month. She looks at him over her cup while he watches the television, and he appears beaten. Is it more than just the accident? Pyotr stirs with a jerk. He opens his eyes, sees his grandma, and closes them. He pulls himself closer, tighter into her belly and relaxes back to sleep.

"The Soviet government," says Mr. Borovsky, "lies. It lies about the past, it lied about Chelyabinsk 25 years ago, it lies about Afghanistan, and it will lie about this accident. Those of us who live in Komi know this well. Our ancestors knew this. I suspect the rest of the world knows this also."

Olga nods. She was never able to find out the truth about her husband's death in Afghanistan. She allows Mr. Borovsky to continue.

"Gregori is dead. There is no way he could have survived the explosion."

"We can't know that yet, Ivan," says Olga. "We will just have to wait. We can hope."

Mr. Borovsky shakes his head. "Old men can feel their sons. At the moment of the whiteness, I knew. I felt his heart jump into mine without his body. At the same time, I knew I had to go get you and your son. Did you feel the same about your daughter?"

Olga doesn't answer. She didn't feel a jump, and maybe it's a good sign. She hopes Mr. Borovsky's intuition is wrong and that his Gregori survived, but she finds Ivan's premonition fascinating. *Can a parent feel the heart of her child jump into hers? There was something just as the gunshot rang out. Was that Ursula's heart?* The room goes quiet except for the TV announcer's voice. Olga can feel Pyotr's heartbeat against her thigh. "Ivan, you needn't stay up for me. I will fall asleep here on the couch so as not to disturb Pyotr. Why don't you go to bed?"

Mr. Borovsky sighs deeply. "I am tired. Would you like me to leave on the television and the lights?"

"No, thank you. As you say, they just lie, and right now I need the truth. The television announcer will not give it to me. We will have to find it ourselves. Goodnight, Ivan."

With much effort, the old man gets out of his chair, collects the two cups, and walks to the kitchen. He returns and hands her a small cake. "Gregori liked these. You will too. Goodnight." The cake is a deep chocolate, Ursula's favorite, but Olga has no taste for it.

Olga sits in complete darkness and near total silence. Mr. Borovsky's dog breathes heavily in the kitchen, and she can occasionally hear Mr. Borovsky snore, but he is not so loud as her father who drives her mother to another bedroom. *How can he sleep?* For the second night in a row, Olga has not. If Ursula survived, she will be worried about Pyotr. He is a happy, active boy, but fragile at this moment. Being raised by dominant women shapes his personality, and Olga wonders if it will make him strong enough for the coming ordeal.

She wants to walk. She lifts Pyotr's head gently and slides off the couch. She feels the wall for the electrical switch, and when she finds it, she turns it. A dim, naked light bulb gives off an orangey hue, enough to allow her to wander the room without waking Pyotr. She walks to the window and pushes aside the muslin curtains. During the day the avenue was filled with trucks heading for Yamantov, but now there is no traffic. There hasn't been for several hours. *Does the Soviet Army only rescue people during daylight hours? Why the secrecy?* Until she hears from her daughter, there will be questions. Ursula will be able to answer them. Olga turns from the window and wanders to a credenza that has photos. The wood floor creaks slightly. She picks up the first frame, a picture of Mr. Borovsky standing with a younger man. If this is his son Gregori, it is not her Gregori. The younger man wears a military uniform. A second frame shows the same two men holding up a string of fish. *Yes, this is his son.* Olga feels relieved, but she doesn't know why she should be. A third photo shows Gregori in a suit; he's not a welder, that is for sure. She can't make out the items sitting on the desk with him. There are no photos of Mr. Borovsky's wife, of Gregori's mother.

Olga realizes she smells from the long hike carrying Pyotr. She hasn't bathed in nearly three days. She would like to, but she will not leave Pyotr. Tomorrow, when she returns to Pechora and Pyotr is in the care of his great-grandma, Olga will lay in her tub with its clawed feet and relax. She will wash away the sweat and the ash. And cry. *Ursula is still my daughter.*

The telephone sits at the end of the credenza. Olga stares at it; it has worked only sporadically since the explosion. She lifts the receiver and dials Ursula's number in Yamantov. There is no ring, no sound at all. She holds the phone against her shoulder without hanging it up. Has she lost her daughter? It doesn't feel like it. Yesterday morning at the bus station, they hugged tightly as they always do and kissed. Olga rubs her lips with three fingers from her right hand, then kisses them. As a child Ursula would blow three-finger kisses to her mama. Olga puts the receiver back into the carriage and returns to the couch. She lifts Pyotr's head and sits down, returning her grandson's body to the earlier position. She lays her head against the high back, closes her eyes, and falls asleep. A few minutes later, Mr. Borovsky slides his hand around the wall and switches off the light.

§

When Olga wakens, Pyotr is sitting next to her eating sausages and chocolate cake. She smells tobacco. She can tell from the slant of the sun's rays into the east windows that it is early, and now she hears the rumble of trucks on the avenue. She turns her head toward the kitchen where she sees Mr. Borovsky at the stove wearing an apron, a cigarette dangling from his lips. She lifts her left arm and puts it around Pyotr. He scoots back into her body without turning his head or spilling his breakfast.

"Are there any more sausages," she calls out to Mr. Borovsky.

"I think so. You're lucky Gregori isn't here, or he would already have devoured all of them. Would you like some coffee too?" He draws heavily on his cigarette and then puts the stub onto a saucer.

A few minutes later, Ivan brings her a dish with two sausages and a fried egg. He sets a cup of coffee on the end table. "All of the news heads toward Yamantov. No news comes out," he says. He hands Olga a fork. "I don't know what that means."

Olga cuts the first sausage and puts a bite in her mouth. "If there was any good news, it would leak out rapidly." She spears the second half of the first sausage and holds it in front of her mouth. "Is this reindeer, Ivan?" Mr. Borovsky nods. "Another one of Gregori's favorites?" Again, he nods. Pyotr reaches up and takes the sausage off Olga's fork and eats it. Olga breaks the yolk of the egg, stabs another sausage, and puts one end in the yolk. She offers it to Pyotr, who refuses, and then puts the entire sausage in her mouth. "Thank you, Ivan," she says, and hands him the plate. "Come, Pyotr. We are going to the avenue for news."

The main street in Mr. Borovsky's village is the highway to

13

Yamantov. There are just twelve houses in the village, unless houses tucked back in the woods are counted. Mr. Borovsky's house doubles as the bus stop and overnight inn; there is a small general store with a petrol pump, and a library. Olga walks across the avenue to the general store and sits on a wooden bench labeled "Whites." Next to that bench is one labeled "Reds." Her ride to Pechora will not come until noon, and Olga desperately wants information. Pyotr has still not spoken since the gunshot on Monday. Olga imagines that Ursula and Gregori have escaped the blast and are walking along back trails to Ivan's house. If no one is being lifted out of Yamantov, this scenario makes sense to her. She closes her eyes and the whiteness returns. *What was that?*

A young woman wearing a scarf sits down next to her. "They will give us no information because they can't. The power plant has been destroyed; we all know that, and no one who works there survived. We fool ourselves and hold out hope for a miracle, but we all saw the blast. Some of us were blinded for several minutes. It was the reactor. What other explanation can there be?" She leans over and puts her head on Olga's shoulder. Pyotr crooks into her other shoulder. Olga shifts slightly in order to lift her arm around the young woman. She holds them both, the three bodies trying to draw strength from one another. Instead, they seem to grow weaker. Olga lays her cheek on Pyotr's head. Ursula cannot be replaced in his life, not by a grandmother or a great-grandmother. Olga fears both she and Pyotr could be in for a long, hard journey, in search of elusive answers. She looks out over the avenue and doesn't know where she is.

Mr. Borovsky comes later to tell her the driver is ready to go. "Leon is a nice man, very quiet, and a safe driver. He will only talk about the mountains, especially Manaraga, which he believes is the most beautiful mountain in the whole world. He was going to Pechora today to see his family, so he won't accept any payment from you. You will offend him if you even offer. Just tell him thank you at the end. He will take you right to your home; he knows Pechora well. I put some cakes in a handkerchief for Pyotr."

Olga stands. Pyotr lets go of his grandma's hand, turns to the younger woman, steps toward her, and kisses her on the cheek. "I will pray for your mother," she says. She looks up at Olga, who looks so strong in comparison, and says, "And for your daughter. If I hear anything, I will tell Mr. Borovsky." Olga bends over and hugs the young woman.

Olga takes Ivan's arm to cross the street; Pyotr holds her hand to return home to Pechora. There is nothing to say.

§

*The New York Times*
September 29, 1983

## EXPLOSION AT SOVIET MINING FACILITY IN NORTHERN URALS

The Soviet news agency TASS is reporting that an explosion has occurred in the Northern Urals at the construction site of a large coal mine. Details are sketchy, but according to Soviet government officials, the accident happened on Monday, September 26, near the Pechora River on the western slopes of the Urals. The event was picked up by monitoring stations in both Finland and Sweden, but scientists are unable to precisely determine the cause or exact location of the explosion.

Several workers at the site were injured, but TASS reported no deaths. It is unclear whether or not small towns near the blast are in any danger. According to Soviet reports, the explosion occurred in a warehouse away from the site where critical materials are being stored. The mine has not yet become operational. The facility will supply energy needs to the Komi Republic and to the industrial cities farther south in the Urals. The Komi Republic is an important coal and timber region for the Soviet Union, but it is sparsely populated. Most of the population lives in towns strung out along the rail line that extends from Vologda to Vorkuta, which is north of the Arctic Circle.

TASS reports conflict with accounts from several European

nations. Western journalists believe the explosion was much greater than TASS is reporting or the Soviet government is admitting. Casualty rates could also be much higher than TASS is reporting. There has been no comment from the White House. The Deputy Press Secretary Larry Speakes said the White House will monitor the situation carefully.

§

*The New York Times*
September 30, 1983

## SOVIET EXPLOSION BRINGS INTERNATIONAL CONCERN

Evidence from outside the Soviet Union continues to mount that the explosion that occurred at a coal mine on September 26 was more severe than initially reported. Radiation counts drifting into the Pacific indicate that the blast did involve a nuclear reactor. However, since the location of the site is extremely remote, danger to large population centers both in the Soviet Union and beyond its borders seems slight. This does not preclude the possibility that there were substantial casualties at the blast site.

Unnamed sources at the White House have said that it is possible the Soviet Union is minimizing the effects of the explosion because it does not want to further damage its international standing after the downing of the Korean Air Lines passenger jet on September 1 that caused the deaths of 269 passengers, including a U.S. Congressman. President Reagan continues to refuse comment on the current situation. He has voiced strong condemnation over the downing of KAL 007 at nearly every public appearance over the past month.

The mine is being built on a tributary to the Pechora River on the west side of the Ural Mountains near the village of

Yamantov.  Other spellings are Yamantou or Yamen-tov.  The closest city to the site is Pechora, but it is over 100 miles away. Western journalists have been denied access to the area.  The Komi Republic played a prominent role as a destination for prisoners of the Stalin-era because of its severe weather conditions and isolation from Moscow.  Many of its towns and villages were a part of the Gulag, or Soviet prison system from the Thirties, Forties, and Fifties.

*The Times* will continue to update this story as information is obtained.

# CHAPTER 2

*Komi Republic, Winter, 1983-84*

When Olga returns to Mr. Borovsky's village, she drives her own car. At four points along the way, Soviet soldiers stop and question her. She explains her work as a dentist and has appointments to keep with the village people. This is the only time she can break away from her busy schedule in Pechora. The soldiers are trying to prevent journalists and curiosity-seekers from getting too close to the accident--and information from getting too far. She promises to check in with authorities at each village. As she drives, she gets angrier. Such secrecy in Russia! Komi and especially the regions north and east of Pechora were exempt from the intrigue of the Cold War. All that began to change when Premier Brezhnev began the secret excavations near Mt. Narodnaya in 1979. Four years of secrecy and the loss of some of the Polar Urals most beautiful areas, forests where she and her husband and father would hunt each autumn. At the edge of Mr. Borovsky's village, at Uralansk, the town limits sign has been removed.

Despite the Army's attempt to stifle information, rumors abound. Some say Yamantov is a super-site for intercontinental missiles, a place where the Soviet Union can launch multiple missiles at the United States if the need arises. By building this site closer to the Arctic Ocean, it will give America less time to respond. The excavations mean the silos will be buried deeper into the permafrost and be more secure against a first strike by America. Another rumor says Yamantov will be the first of several nuclear power plants to be built in the Pechora Basin to supply all of Russia with energy for the rest of her lifetime. Olga knows the Komi. They have never been fully locked into the Soviet nation and will find conspiracies in every action. So many of the men and women who were sent to Komi as prisoners hated Stalin and his successors. Like her parents, many stayed to avoid interaction with Moscow. All of Russia has harsh weather, but Komi's winds are especially difficult, and they harden the Komi people—in both good and bad ways.

Mr. Borovsky has no concrete information, nor does the younger woman from the bench. They are both fatalistic about the fate of the workers at Yamantov. Olga has brought along a small dental kit to at least check and clean the teeth of some of her patients; she will not be able to provide any substantive work. She will see patients in Ivan's kitchen in the mornings. She has also brought along some books. As a teenager she read constantly, but now she has little time between her work and Pyotr. Olga has insisted on paying Ivan a small amount of money for her room and board—and for taking over his kitchen as her office after breakfast. He resisted, but she knows he needs it, since the buses are not running. She can easily afford it.

"Olga," says Ivan, "the winds have been good to us here. They are protecting us."

Olga harrumphs. She thinks of Ursula and Gregori. She finds it peculiar that she includes the unseen, unknown Gregori in her thoughts. There is that other Gregori, but he is of little concern to her. She wonders where the winds will decide to deposit Yamantov's ashes.

That evening, after serving dinner to Olga and the younger woman, who seems more lost than the others, Ivan brings out the cards and poker chips. Olga gives him a look. "We could sit and stare at one another, but that would do no good, so I think we should gamble. Do you want to play twenty-one or regular poker?" Olga doesn't care, but the younger woman prefers twenty-one. They play for a half-an-hour and the young woman loses all her chips, but no money transfers hands. She thanks Ivan, hugs Olga, and leaves.

"She has very little," says Ivan. "She and her husband rent a cabin just off the avenue with two friends who also work at the plant. She does the cooking and cleaning and is paid a small fee by her husband's friends. All of them moved from Gorki looking for work. She sleeps alone now in the cabin. So few of the workers at Yamantov are from Komi. They are strangers to our land. They have no regard for Narodnaya and her beautiful sisters."

"Do you think she will stay?" asks Olga.

"I have no idea. Would you like some coffee?

"Yes, I would. Not so strong as last time, if that pleases you." Ivan leaves for the kitchen, and Olga pulls a book from her purse and settles on the couch. She doesn't open it, but instead drops her head and starts to cry softly. Ursula. Her baby. Her daughter. Her best friend. Ursula. No additional information about Yamantov comes from the television that night or the next or the next. The snow that falls on the Northern Urals, on the slopes of Gora Narodnaya, buries the scar at Yamantov, and the ground becomes quiet again.

§

Over the next several months when the weather allows, Olga travels to Mr. Borovsky's village even though she has mostly given up hope Ursula survived the accident. The Army cordons off the area around Yamantov at a distance only four kilometers from Mr. Borovsky's house. It removes all the signs with the town's name, so now the town has no name. A few bodies are removed from the site, but Ursula's and Gregori's are not among them. Without a body Olga refuses to have a memorial service for her daughter. She tells Pyotr to pray for his mother and to hope for the best, but he outwardly refuses to pray or to talk about his mother. He clings to his great-grandfather, Olga's father, whose health seems fragile. The two of them play chess, watch hockey on television, hike, and read together. Grampar begins teaching Pyotr to draw. Olga and her mother are comfortable with this drawing together, an old man who is nearly deaf and a five-year-old boy who seldom speaks. Grampar's toughness and independence are being transferred.

Yuri Andropov, the Soviet General Secretary, dies in early February, about four-and-a-half months after Yamantov disappeared. He is replaced by Konstantin Chernenko, another ailing Bolshevik from the Stalin era. When Grampar hears the news of Andropov's death, he walks outside and says a few choice words expressing his disdain for the Soviet leader. Grampar uses Andropov's name, a symbol of bad luck for the passing leader. Pyotr asks Babu Olga why Grampar has taken off his shirt and pants and is shaking them out. Olga says Grampar has no grief for Premier Andropov and is angry the leader never explained to the Soviet people about the accident where Ursula worked. Pyotr runs outside and strips naked next to his Grampar.

After dinner Grampar reads to Pyotr and then takes him to bed. He returns to the living room where Olga reads, pulls the rocker over next to her, and takes the book out of her hands. "When the weather gets a little better, maybe at the end of March, I want to go with you."

Olga asks, "Go with me where?"

"To Gora Narodnaya, to Yamantov. I need to see."

§

Olga and Grampar arrive at Mr. Borovsky's inn just before noon. Olga has arranged for them to stay for two nights. Grampar picked this time because the weather for the first week in April has been unseasonably warm, warm enough for the trails around Yamantov to be open, although snow drifts still make the hike imposing. From his hunting days, Grampar knows the terrain well, and he wants to hike to a spot where he can see the accident site. He has brought along his binoculars and his drawing pad.

"The young woman left," says Mr. Borovsky. "She stopped by last weekend to say goodbye. She's going home to Gorki. There was no point staying here, and there was no money either." He brings in soup and sandwiches to Olga and her father. He reaches for a bottle of vodka on the credenza and pours a small glass for both of his guests.

Grampar lifts his drink in a toast. "To Chairman Chernenko.

May he die as quickly as his predecessor." Mr. Borovsky smiles and nods. They all clink glasses.

"Olga tells me you want to go for a hike to the hills. I can drive you part of the way tomorrow. The good weather is supposed to hold, and you will be able to see the excavation site." Ivan is speaking loudly. "I will pack you a lunch. We'll have to take a bit of a diversion so as not to arouse suspicion. The Army tries to keep sightseers away."

For the rest of the afternoon, Olga sees patients in the kitchen. They are becoming fewer and fewer. Her attention to the patients wanders as she checks in on her father frequently or looks out the window to the avenue when trucks pass by. Ivan and Grampar sit in the parlor and tell stories from their past. Both are former prisoners in the Gulag, and both have strong feelings against the communists who supported Stalin. Ivan was sent to Vorkuta at the end of the railroad line. He left "that god-forsaken hell" in 1957, a year after Khrushchev denounced Stalin to the Communist Party. Ivan lifts his shirt to show Grampar a scar in his side where he was shot by the secret police as a teenager. Neither man was allowed to fight during the Great Patriotic War against the Nazis. Both worked in the mines delivering coal to the cities.

After dinner Ivan puts on a record with traditional Komi music, and they all drink coffee with a shot of vodka. Grampar has a spot of vanilla added to his. After a few minutes, Olga gets up and takes Ivan's hand to get him off the sofa. They dance a bouncy fling that requires a good bit of fancy footwork. Grampar claps to the scene, and they all laugh at the end of the song. Olga kisses Ivan on both cheeks before he flops onto the couch.

§

Grampar hikes slowly but deliberately in his snowshoes; he knows his path. He stops frequently to rest, and his breathing labors. Olga is patient with her father. She looks for any traces of reindeer, but there are none. At one of their stops, she asks her father what he hopes to see from the bluffs.

"I don't know for sure. The government tells us Yamantov was a coal mine, but I know that is a lie. Ursula indicated as much, even though she wasn't allowed to tell me what it was. The Cold War stretches its tentacles to the extreme boundaries of the empire, and I need to see Yamantov for myself."

"The locals say there is nothing left to see."

"Then that will be something to see. I owe it to Ursula—and to Pyotr." Grampar drinks from his canteen, screws on the cap, and starts up the path again for the last leg of the hike. A few steps from the top of the designated bluff, Grampar stops and turns to Olga. "Promise me you will not give the details to Pyotr. I will tell your mama." Olga promises. Grampar nods and walks to the open spot where the slopes of Mt. Narodnaya can be seen, where Yamantov once lay. He and Olga are shaken. In time they both survey the accident site with the binoculars. A large area of the lower mountain has caved in upon itself, as if an extremely large lake was drained leaving only its basin, or that a million dump trucks stole the soil Olga and her family once walked. The forest trees in all directions have been blown down like so many matchsticks. Neither speaks. What can be said? Grampar quickly sketches the outline of Narodnaya at its highest levels, but he leaves out the foot-hills below. As they prepare to leave, Grampar picks up a stone and throws it as far as he can in the direction of Yamantov.

After scraping away a small bit of snow, Olga takes a small, brown-paper bag and fills it with dirt. She stands, looks north-east to Gora Narodnaya, holds the sack over her head, and says, "Descend down from the tops of the trees my sun-faced and sweet daughter. We send you to the place where the road is not becoming shorter, to the place of which my ears and your ears have not heard of." She repeats her words and then puts the bag into her pack.

§

In his bed two nights later, Grampar holds his wife. "They were moving the living world underground. It was not meant to be. The underground world should be reserved for the dead. God created the permafrost to keep us above ground, even during the terrible winters here in the Komi." The old couple holds each other tightly.

Grampar cries softly. "There are no bodies to bury. What will happen to her soul?"

§

A month later Olga's mother dies unexpectedly. Grampar is devastated. "It isn't supposed to be like this," he tells Olga. "She was the healthy one." He sits down with Pyotr, who found Grandmar on the kitchen floor just after breakfast, to tell him why it should not have happened this way. "I fell in love with her on this day back when we were proud to be communists." Olga has heard this story before and always loves it. Her mother and father stole away to a friend's dacha in the central Urals, a secret at the time, and pledged their undying love. Their life together since that day over fifty years ago is the love story of fairy tales, and Olga is proud to be the offspring of that tale, proud to be the daughter of these two survivors.

§

The funeral takes place a few days later. Neighbors have been bringing food daily, and there will be more food and gatherings in the days to come. Grandmar has not practiced her Russian Orthodox faith in decades, except to attend church to hear the music occasionally. She and Grampar got swept up in the atheism of communism in their youth, accepting the scientific and materialistic creed of the Party. Recently, however, she has talked about God and Heaven, so Olga and Grampar include some prayers to be said at the gravesite.

A small brass band leads the procession to the cemetery, followed by two men carrying the casket lid, and then the open wooden casket carried by six pallbearers. Grandmar looks like a wax figure from a museum. Behind her walk Grampar, Olga, and Pyotr. Then come the neighbors and friends. Since the death was unexpected, there is much crying. When the lid is nailed on the casket, Grampar collapses to the ground. It is lowered into the grave, and a Russian Orthodox priest says a few prayers and makes hand gestures that Pyotr wonders about. Olga holds his hand and tells him she will explain later when they return home.

A man in a tight-fitting black suit says the eulogy. He focuses mostly on the sweet nature of her character and that she was a loving wife and mother. A small birch tree is planted and consecrated: "a new beginning." Olga wonders what new beginning can occur amidst the tragic events of the past year. She is confused; there is anger and sorrow, and she begins to cry. Pyotr turns to Grampar and asks, "Where are we sending her?"

# Chapter 3

*Komi Republic, Spring/Summer, 1984*

Olga studies Pyotr constantly, looking for signs of depression or disorientation, but except for his diminished talking, she senses nothing. He continues to run everywhere, played hockey all winter, and competes ferociously against both her and Grampar in board games. Pyotr goes to sleep at bedtime, doesn't take a nap, and never complains of any headaches. Olga experiences all these symptoms. In addition, Olga's work suffers. On some days, she calls in sick, and many of her patients have complained about her inability to concentrate. Olga doesn't care. Nine months has passed since the accident; three weeks since her mother's death. Grampar sits more in front of the television. He draws and reads less; only Pyotr wakens his senses. Pyotr tells Babu that Mama lives in the mountain now, and still much work remains to be done there. "She's a builder, and when she finishes the power plant, she'll come home to us."

"When do you think that might be, Pyotr" Olga asks.

"I think before I grow big." He changes direction slightly. "Can I sleep in her bed until she comes home?" he asks.

Olga has been going into Ursula's bedroom late at night and crying. She touches her daughter's things, smells her clothes, and sits in the rocker next to the bed. She can cry in her own room, so she consents to Pyotr's request. "Do you want to move your things into your mama's room?" asks Olga.

Pyotr says he doesn't; his stuff will remain in his room, but he just wants to keep Mama's bed right while she's gone. "She misses me. She'll be very tired when she comes home, and I want her bed to be ready." Ursula's room has an unobstructed view of the river and the sky. Pyotr brings in his telescope that Grampar bought him for Christmas and erects it in Ursula's dormer window. The Soviet government banned the holiday, but many Christians in Komi ignore the ban, and some even give presents. Besides, telescopes are science, and the Soviet government can't object to that. Grampar instructs Pyotr to tell anyone who asks that it is a late birthday present.

§

Two days after Pyotr begins sleeping in Ursula's bed, he asks Olga if his daddy knows his mama works beneath the ground. Olga hasn't even thought about that. Ursula and her husband Melor didn't correspond once she returned to Russia, and Olga has no idea where he might be. "I don't know," she answers truthfully. "If I knew where he was, I would tell him."

"We should go looking for him. Mama told me he lives in America."

"I think Grampar might be too old to go to America, Pyotr."

"No, Babu. Grampar will stay here and take care of the house. Besides, when Mama comes home, someone needs to be here to let her in."

Pyotr's expression disarms Olga. For the remainder of the day, she thinks about Melor. One image keeps coming up: Melor winked at everything and everyone to the point of irritation, although Ursula was captivated by it. Pyotr cannot know his father, and now he is asking to go look for him.

§

Pyotr is a sheltered boy for Pechora. Most pre-school aged children in the Soviet Union attend daycare, but Pyotr never has. Ursula, Olga, and Grandmar decided not to send Pyotr; one of them would always be home to tend to his educational preparation. He has one year left before formal school begins, and Olga wonders if she should look for a kindergarten. The accident skewed everything. She watches Pyotr as he moves chess pieces on the kitchen table. He holds the knight and practices all its possible moves around the board. He stops to pick his nose. When he gets what he so diligently searched for, he holds it up for inspection. He looks over to his Babu, displays it with a smile, and says, "Ta-da." Olga smiles back, and tears well up in her eyes.

Grampar comes into the kitchen, bends over to say something to Pyotr, and asks how long until dinner. Olga hasn't started it yet. Grampar pats Pyotr on the shoulder and tells Olga that they will go for a walk to the park, maybe for a half-hour or so. Pyotr takes Grampar's hand, and they leave out the back door.

Dinner. Olga has lost her appetite and about fifteen pounds since the accident, but she tries to cook proper meals for Pyotr and her father. Leftover stroganoff sounds good if she has some extra sour cream and noodles. There is a half-box of noodles in the pantry and an unopened tub of sour cream in the refrigerator, enough for the boys, but she can't remember buying either. She starts heating the leftover sauce and puts a pot of water on the stove for the noodles. From the pantry, she takes the bottle of vodka, pours herself a small glass, and sits at the table waiting.

Pyotr flies in the back door with a commotion. "A dog bit Grampar at the park, Babu! Come help him!"

Olga follows Pyotr out the door trying to keep up. Her thoughts are of her father lying on the grass with blood pooling nearby. She can't catch Pyotr to ask. A block up and a half-block over, she spots Grampar limping back toward her. Pyotr has already taken Grampar's arm and put it around his shoulders to help him walk. Olga is out of breath, but she asks where he was bitten and if he needs a doctor.

"No, no. I don't think it pierced the skin. Pyotr ran him off quickly," answers Grampar.

Olga makes Grampar sit on the curb in order for her to examine his leg. Redness seems to be the only sign, and there is no blood, but Grampar's pant leg is torn. She touches Grampar's leg and asks if it hurts. "Were you bitten anywhere else?"

Grampar shakes his head. "No, Pyotr scared the cur away quickly before it/ had a chance to do real damage. He ran at him waving his arms and warned him not to hurt me." Grampar's eyes and voice reflect his amazement at Pyotr's action. "He told the dog he would be sent away to a silent place if he hurt me. I don't know what he meant, but the dog seemed to hear him and ran away. Then, he ran to get you. When I realized I wasn't hurt badly, I started walking home." Grampar shakes his head, looks over to Pyotr, and asks, "What did you mean, Pyotr? What did you say to the dog?"

Pyotr has no answer for his Grampar; instead, he looks confused, as if he doesn't understand what he did. Olga helps Grampar stand, and they walk back to the house where the stroganoff has bubbled over onto the stove and the water continues to boil. Olga makes her father soak his leg in the bathtub before dinner, then, covers it with mercurochrome. Pyotr sits on the tub's rim the whole time. Any question about the event seems to confuse him, so Olga and Grampar let it go. Pyotr asks if they can take the telescope outside after dinner and "get closer to the stars." Grampar reminds him that it won't be really dark until very late but promises to wake him after midnight if he goes to bed right after dinner for several hours of sleep. Grampar looks to his daughter and asks her to wake him at midnight so he can get a few hours of sleep himself. As tired as Olga is, she will need to set her alarm clock to do this.

§

Olga shivers, but she wants to hear her father's explanation to Pyotr about the constellations. Grampar sets the telescope's tripod on the fence for balance and so Pyotr can look into it while stand-ing straight up. "Let's start by finding the Big Dipper without the telescope." Grampar points to the northern sky. "See it there. Four stars make up the pan and three stars form the handle. We can look up in the sky every clear night and see it. It never falls below the horizon, so once we locate it, we can find lots of other stars and identify them. We won't notice it tonight, but it rotates counter-clockwise around the North Star." Pyotr asks what rotates means, and Grampar uses his hand to explain a circular motion. "Look into the telescope at Polaris—the North Star." It is easily visible, and Pyotr smiles. Grampar continues. "When Grandmar and I lived in Inta, we believed the Big Dipper watched over us. People up there told us the Big Dipper protected the Northern Urals and the Arctic Ocean from the southern devils." Pyotr asks if wolves are devils. "No, the devils were not animals, but tribes of people from Moscow back when your mother was born." Grampar looks over to Olga and touches her side. Pyotr looks through the telescope again, but Polaris has vanished. "Since the earth is turning, we have to adjust the telescope constantly, sort of like our lives." Grampar sights in Polaris again and lets Pyotr see it. "Anyway, the Big Dipper is part of a whole bunch of stars we call a constellation. The Big Dipper's constellation is named Ursa Major." Grampar pauses to watch Pyotr's face.

Pyotr's mind races, and both Grampar and Olga notice. They wait. Finally, Pyotr looks to Olga. "Did you name Mama after those stars?"

Olga starts to explain that Grampar said "Ursa," not Ursula, but she catches herself. She began her sentence with "No," so she needs to adjust. "It was your grandpa who died in the war who named your mama after those stars. See how they sparkle? So did your mama."

Grampar takes a step into Olga's shoulder and puts his arm around her. "Your grandpa wanted to name her Ursa, but Babu Olga thought Ursula was a prettier name, so your mama was named Ursula."

Pyotr thinks. Finally, he responds, "I think Ursula is a prettier name too. Can we look at Mama's stars again sometime?"

§

After Olga tucks Pyotr into bed, she sits with Grampar at the kitchen table. "That's a remarkable boy we have, Papa. I wonder if he realizes the family constellation is missing some stars."

Grampar sips his cold coffee. "We look to the skies to view things that may no longer exist. We only see the light from something that once lived, but has long ago burned out, probably with a bright explosion. I think Pyotr knows what's missing in this family—how could he not—but maybe now we can explain to him the great whiteness that occurred at Yamantov."

"But he believes Ursula still works inside Narodnaya."

"We'll allow him to believe what he wants and explain things to him as he asks. Who knows, maybe Ursula still has work to do inside that mountain. Maybe it's what you and I should believe too." He reaches over and takes his daughter's hand. "I think Pyotr is handling this much better than you or me. He sees things that don't exist too, and yet he makes them sparkle." Grampar gets up and kisses his daughter on the top of her head. "Goodnight, my sweet Olga. Pyotr will be all right."

Olga sits for a long time looking into the darkness before going to bed.

§

In early summer, the Soviet Army shuts down Uralansk and moves the remaining villagers farther south. Ivan Borovsky has decided to live in Kiev rather than move to Moscow to live with his wife. In Kiev Mr. Borovsky has in-laws who will welcome him. He stops in Pechora to say goodbye to Olga, Grampar, and Pyotr. He has brought a few of his son's things for Pyotr, the most important being Gregori's hockey equipment.

"It's all too big for him now, but you can cut down the stick, and he'll grow into the skates when he becomes a teenager." Mr. Borovsky gives Pyotr a Red Army sweater, the white, visitors one with the red star on the front. The name on the back is Tretiak. "Vladislav Tretiak is my son's favorite player, even though he is a goalie and my Gregori played left wing. We met him once when they played an exhibition game here." Pyotr puts the sweater on over his shirt. It touches the ground, but Pyotr beams. He knows of Tretiak, and the gift will be worn for the remainder of the day. Mr. Borovsky pulls a helmet from the large bag and slips it on Pyotr's head. Grampar taps the over-sized helmet with his knuckles and everyone laughs. There are pads, pants, and socks in the bag, all of which are too large for Pyotr, but which will be stored in his closet as prized possessions. "Your teammates will be jealous of your sweater, so keep a close eye on it." He hands Pyotr a plastic ball that Gregori used for summer practice when there was no ice rink and tells him to go out into the yard and practice his slap shots. Grampar goes to Pyotr's room and brings him his own stick which fits his hands better, and the two of them head out to the back yard to arrange a goal. Grampar senses Mr. Borovsky has news for Olga.

Olga brews coffee and heats two scones. They sit at the kitchen table, lean their heads forward, and speak in whispers.

Mr. Borovsky shakes his head gently. "The Army bulldozed all of the houses. Some of the soldiers say it is not safe to be so close to Yamantov, that the radiation spread farther out than they earlier predicted. None of the soldiers want to work on the clean-up; they are afraid. They want to bury it beneath as much dirt as they can move. One of the soldiers told me no one will ever be able to return to the site, at least not in our lifetimes."

"I can't imagine never hiking the slopes of my Narodnaya again," says Olga. "Grampar hopes to take Pyotr there someday and show him the places where our family hunted and fished, where we picnicked and camped. This will devastate him." They sit in their own thoughts for a moment, holding hands across the table. "It was no warehouse fire," says Olga bitterly. "The reactor had to have exploded. Why didn't they just come out and say so?"

"Because they lie. They need to be perfect in this war with America. I think Yamantov was a part of that struggle in some way, but in the end, we killed our own children."

Olga gasps. To this day, she has not said aloud that Ursula died, even though she believes it to be true. In this house Ursula lives, whether or not she lives outside the house. Olga will not admit it today even in the face of this new information. She lets go of Ivan's hand, puts both her hands around her cup, and raises it slowly to her mouth, but not to her lips. "Do you still feel Gregori's heart?"

"No, not for several months. He left me one night and never returned, but he allowed me to grieve. He must have known I needed to hold him one more time. Olga, how do we go on?"

Go on? Olga asks herself. I struggle to live each day, struggle to get out of bed, struggle to go to bed, struggle to eat, struggle to work.  I have an ulcer and constant headaches.  I scratched my daughter's initials into the palm of my left hand, and I dream about her every night.  I wake up to a white flash and see The Great One's burned carcass.  Go on?  Olga lifts her eyes and takes Mr. Borovsky's hand again.  He looks so old and beaten.  "Grampar was imprisoned in the Gulag by Stalin.  He told me he and my mother survived to spite Stalin.  Maybe we find the strength to go on to spite those fools in Moscow.  We spit in their faces and live another day.  We find courage to tell our children one day that we lived to be with them in the mountain—no, on the mountain, on our Narodnaya."

"But you have Pyotr," answers Mr. Borovsky sadly.

"From this day forward, Ivan, you will be Pyotr's uncle.  You will send him birthday cards, and he will send you cards on your birthday.  When he passes each grade, you will call and tell him congratulations.  I will take pictures and send them to you."  Olga squeezes Ivan's hand hard and gives it a jerk.  "Look at me!  It is time I do something for myself, and you are stronger than me.  Go on?  Yes, Ivan, we will go on and find some answers."

"I don't even know the questions," says Mr. Borovsky.

"Maybe our answers will tell us the questions, but we will never again stupidly ask what happened while we wait for the government to provide an answer that we can't believe."

Grampar has been listening at the door.  He walks to the table and stands over Olga and Ivan like their minister.  "This will never be okay, but this will be.  Ursula and Gregori are gone and won't be coming back, but the bonds remain.  Let go of the pain but hold tight to your child's hand.  Our children are our blood, and it courses through our bodies with each beat of our heart."

Mr. Borovsky manages to whisper, "I'll try."

Olga jerks his hand again, and Ivan lifts his head.  "Listen, Uncle Ivan, you'll do more than try.  You'll go on."

Pyotr walks back in holding the ball in his left hand.  "I scored," he says with a toothy smile.

§

Olga's red hair has grown out, and she has not dyed it again.  It is brown with several strands of gray that are quite noticeable to her when she looks in the mirror. I've aged rapidly, she thinks to herself, more like a forty-six-year-old babushka. I put up a tough front yesterday with Ivan, telling him he must go on, but God knows whether I can follow my own advice, whether I am strong enough. I have always been the dominant one, even in this strong family, but now I cling to Pyotr. No day dawns brighter; the grief endures. It seems as if I want to hold on to it, to never let go. Would there be closure if I could recover my daughter's body? Olga moves out of the bathroom, but her image in the mirror stays. I should go find a man for a night; then I would take care of myself again—at least on the outside. I might put on makeup and fluff my hair. Except, and here Olga sees her reflection again, I have no desire in that part of my body. She places her hands over her breasts and squeezes. She returns to the bathroom and locks the door. It is a deliberate action, a thoughtful action, and a needed passion. I need to do this, she thinks. She unzips her dress and lets it fall to the floor. She removes her panties. She puts the lid down on the toilet, sits, and draws moisture from her mouth onto her fingers. She has not visited this place since the accident. She takes her time and tries to remember someone, anyone. Slowly, deliberately, she arouses herself. I must go on; I must get myself back, she tells herself. Feelings return, and as she continues, she finds that spot in her vagina where she so often went to pleasure herself. She leans back against the toilet and pushes deeper inside herself. She draws out her own moisture and feels a return. Her fingers remember and take over, doing the same thing they did almost daily for decades, and the flood occurs, washing over her hand and spilling onto the floor. Olga's body finally relaxes and her left-hand slides gently over her right, as if to provide support after the fact, feeling the blood as it pulsates through her pubic area. She is both spent and rejuvenated, and a bit embarrassed.

§

Later in the morning, Olga butters a piece of toast and watches Pyotr in the yard. He seems to be having a serious talk with an unseen friend. He gestures with his hands, tucks his head, and kneels during the conversation. The shade tree obscures Pyotr's facial expressions, so Olga can't determine his mood. Children and their fantasy friends; Ursula had them, and so did she. Pyotr doesn't have lots of friends his age yet; he has always had the family and its adult friends, but he never complains. Still, Olga wonders. Growing up in Inta, she had lots of friends. It seems as though the Gulag prisoners were a prolific bunch, although she no longer keeps in touch with her childhood gang.

Pyotr comes in the back door and stands in front of his grandmother. "Who were you just talking with in the yard?" she asks.

"The hunter," he says.

A shudder goes through Olga's body, and she doesn't respond immediately.

"Do we have anything for his burns, Babu? His skin hurts."

Olga squats down to Pyotr's eye level. "The hunter who shot the reindeer?"

"Yes. He hurts." Pyotr's eyes lock on to Olga's. "He's crawled a long way to say he's sorry for shooting my reindeer."

Tears form in Olga's eyes. She reaches out and grasps Pyotr's shoulders. She asks a question she immediately wishes she could take back. "Did he bring his rifle?"

"No, Babu, he doesn't want it anymore, so he left it on the cave. Do we have any salve?"

Olga bites her lip and nods. She stands. "I think we have something in the medicine chest. Stay here while I get it." She goes into the bathroom and brings back a tube of balm. "Do you want me to go with you?"

"No, Babu. He's mad at you for walking past him and leaving him alone."

Pyotr returns to his invisible victim and performs a healing rite while Olga watches from inside. She wishes Ursula was standing next to her so they could watch him together, as they once did. She wishes she understood what he saw in his mind, and today, where his vision of that terrible day came from. Pyotr doesn't talk about that day directly, but she knows he thinks about it constantly. Olga senses his anger at her, especially in times of his silence, but she doesn't know why exactly. Is it because she lived and his mother didn't, because she didn't protect his mother? What? Her sorrow for Ursula, for her own mother, for all the dead at Yamantov is not her only sorrow. She has lost a life too--her own--and it will never come back as it once was. She remains a solitary soul, but no one grieves for her.

When he's done, Pyotr hands Olga the salve and walks to Grampar's room. Pyotr wakes his grandfather up around ten each morning. He sits on the bed and listens to Grampar tell of his recent dreams, almost like a sacred ritual. Olga stays out until the stories are completed and Grampar has dressed and done his bathroom routine. Usually, she just waits until they come to the kitchen and want breakfast, for Pyotr, his second. They never discuss Grampar's dreams outside his room.

§

Early on Thursday Olga drives to Mr. Borovsky's old village, or at least as close as she can. She is stopped by a gate on the highway twenty kilometers from Uralansk, where four Soviet soldiers stand guard with Kalashnikovs. They look young and nervous. Olga asks permission to park and walk toward the village, but they deny her access and order her to turn around and drive away. Instead, she pulls off the highway, takes a cooler from the backseat, and walks to the guard station where she offers the soldiers colas and iced tea. They seem reluctant, but Olga persists in her offer. Besides, she has anticipated this and made herself up to be more appealing. Maybe for her next trip here, she will dye her hair red again. The junior officer, a lieutenant, brings her a chair.

"I lost my daughter in the accident, my only child, and I like to drive here to view the mountain. I live in Pechora with my parents and her son, my grandson. Narodnaya gives me comfort." The facts are true, but the emotion of comfort stretches that truth, and the soldiers relax a bit.

"I'm sorry for your loss, ma'am, and I'm sorry I have to ask you, but can I see your identification please." The lieutenant fumbles his duty by saying the government wants to restrict sightseers to the tragedy. Information has also been limited to prevent information from leaking out. The soldiers are not from Komi; two are even Muslims from one of the southern republics near Iran. The lieutenant comes from Prypiat, a new nuclear city near Kiev in the Ukraine, and he does all the talking. He is glad the restricted area has been moved farther from Yamantov and the radiation. He has heard stories.

"We are all subject to the rumors, I'm afraid, and will be for a long time to come. My grandson and I were picnicking nearby when the explosion occurred. Fortunately, we were protected by a cave. Sadly, my daughter was working. The whiteness never leaves my memory." Olga hopes she can gain sympathy in order for the soldiers to relax their guard and allow her to hike away from the highway to an elevated spot so she can get a glimpse of Narodnaya.

"Too many were at Yamantov that day," says the lieutenant. "The private lost a brother who drove a truck for the Army. They discovered his truck at the company town a short distance away beyond the excavations of Yamantov."

Olga hesitates to ask, but she can't help herself. She looks to the private. "Did they recover his body?"

He shakes his head and looks down at his boots.

"I don't know why the Army sent him here," says the lieutenant. "This place became his brother's coffin, and the private has to stare at the coffin every day. He could serve his duties in many other places, but the generals don't seem to care. I try to keep him here at the guard shack as much as I can, where the mountain can't be seen. Unlike you, he finds no solace in that mountain."

"He didn't grow up here. My family did. From every direction Gora Narodnaya was my backyard. The private's coffin is my daughter's haven, her starry sanctuary at night and her new playground by day. I hope someday to be able to kneel at ground zero in Yamantov and say a prayer," says Olga.

"With the radiation, you may not live long enough to enter the city."

The soldiers drink their colas in silence for a while. Olga studies the lieutenant. She wonders how he would be in bed, if she could arrange such an escape for them both. It wouldn't matter if he was married; he's a soldier on active duty, and Russian women understand such things. The soldiers lift the wooden barrier and wave through an Army truck with a canvas cover. The telephone in the guard house rings and the lieutenant takes a message. In the half-hour since she arrived, no private vehicle has appeared. She clears her throat to get the lieutenant's attention. "Would it be okay if I took a short walk to the top of the bluff to see my mountain, to see my daughter's playground? I won't go farther or stay too long. If you want, I'll leave you my car keys and identification."

The lieutenant hesitates, but one of the Muslim soldiers tells him Olga can do no harm. "Park your car in the trees away from the guard house so it is less obvious and leave me your keys. We will look the other way when you head off down the trail."

§

Olga sits on the knoll with her knees drawn into her chest. She can't see Yamantov, but the upper slopes of majestic Narodnaya spread out before her. She slides an envelope from her breast pocket and carefully unfolds the note from within. It is a prayer given to her from one of her patients, Rabbi Weil. "You have gone from me, but the bond which unites our souls can never be severed; your image lives within my heart." She senses another behind her, but she doesn't turn. She keeps her eyes on her mountain and invites the other to sit with her.

"I heard you coming," says Olga.

"I hope I didn't disturb you."

"No, you didn't. Have you been to this hill before?"

"No. I've been afraid."

"There are lots of emotions to be experienced, but fear shouldn't be one of them." Olga reaches over and takes the private's hand. "Was your brother older than you?"

"Yes. We are from Stalingrad, so far from here. He came to earn better pay."

"Ironic. Komi and Narodnaya and our small towns were the

prisoners of Stalin, as was your city, and so many people died in each place."

They sit in silence for a time before the private speaks again. "It is also ironic you and I both have a journey ahead of us. I don't know how I know about your journey; I just do."

Olga keeps her eyes on Narodnaya. "Where will you be going?"

"Down there."

"You won't find your brother."

"Maybe he'll know I've come, though. I wrote my parents and told them of my decision."

"Do they approve?"

"They never replied. I don't intend to die there, just go in and call for him, maybe say a prayer." He pauses. "Do you know where your journey will be taking you?"

Olga nods, mostly to herself. "America, if I can get there. My son and I need to look for someone too."

# II

# The Key Man

# CHAPTER 4

*Ouray, Colorado, December 1983*

A dozen or more common, brass keys lay on the workbench. Another is held tightly in the vice while Samuel files down the jagged edge. A hundred more, recently smoothed and now useless, sit in an old pickle jar at the end of the workbench. Two more, also filed, hang on a silver chain adorning a crucifix hanging on the pegboard holding tools. He leans into his task; he tries to demolish at least a dozen each morning. A visitor might wonder where he gets all these keys and why he labors so diligently to render them unusable, but there are no visitors to his garage.

Later in the morning, he works on a poem, the same poem he has been writing for nearly two weeks. He almost has it, but now he puts it into the present tense.

> My walks along the wooded path
> Often take me past the old man's cabin.
>
> Today, under a cloudless sky,
> The old man sits half-naked
>
> In a folding chair reading poetry aloud,
> Probably to himself and the trees.
>
> I slow my pace to listen, then stop.
> He re-reads a passage until he gets it right,

It seems.  Then he looks up
And recites the verse to the trees who stand

At attention and listen carefully without
Comment, but sway in seeming approval.

In these vast woods, he seems not alone,
But surrounded by an audience respectfully awaiting

His next words.  Like all intimate friends,
They accept his gift as it is offered,

With quiet appreciation and humbleness.
I smile and continue my walk.

I bet that the old man
Bundles up on chilly nights

And sits in his folding chair among
His trees, who are no longer his audience

But his guardians, and gazes up at the night sky
Wondering about mortality and shooting stars.

And I wonder about his thoughts,
About his solitude near the end of his life.

This is the only poem Samuel has ever written, and he has no plans to write another.  Tinkering with it has become a part of his morning ritual.  It just came to him one day when he saw a half-naked, old man sitting among some trees near the river.

Samuel ponders the last two lines of his poem.  Does anyone know about the thoughts of others?  They sure wouldn't know about his. He pushes the poem aside and opens a letter from the library. They want him to return the books. He should since he doesn't read them; they seemed interesting when he browsed through them at the library that first day back, but none of them keep his attention.

Samuel wonders what has kept the half-naked old man in Ouray all his life. He wants to talk with him, to learn if the poem's assumptions are true. Maybe the man isn't a native; maybe he moved to Ouray recently. Maybe the old man isn't even lonely. Maybe the old man has a wife. Maybe, maybe, maybe. Samuel doesn't know, and he doubts he'll have the time to find out. He closes the lid on his pen, done with the poem for today, stands, and heads out the door to walk to the post office. He could go earlier, but he has established a minor routine to get him through each morning. It doesn't get him much further. And he has a plan.

Samuel Elkington stays alone in his parents' house in Ouray, a tiny town in southwest Colorado. When his parents divorced, neither wanted the cabin, but they didn't sell it. His mother moved back to Illinois, and his stepfather remarried and went to the central California coast, up near Cambria. His mother returns every summer for a month to escape the sticky Illinois heat. Samuel will be leaving shortly; he only has another eight or nine days. For most of his life, he was Sam or Sammy or Elk, but now he is Samuel. When he met with the psychiatrist, Sam seemed too familiar, so he asked to be called Samuel. It gave him some distance. He may become Sam again, especially if others have a say in it.

As a boy, especially during his teen years, Samuel loved Ouray. He knew most everyone, jeeped the four-wheel drive paths through the steep mountains, fished, and had a fun girlfriend. Now he feels trapped in this box-canyon town, especially since winter has come and the days are so short. Direct sunlight lasts only six hours at his place, and clouds obscure much of that. Sunlight has been a rare commodity the last several years, and the darkness has limited his vision. The everyday snow drizzle supports his going; he needs a full measure of sunshine.

The post office is three blocks away on Main Street. Samuel

walks with his hands in his pockets to shield them from the biting wind. His left hand fondles the silvery, gray rock he always carries, a gift from his girlfriend over eight years ago. Its meaning has changed over time, but he goes nowhere without his stone.

Samuel has two letters at the Post Office: one from Greg Benson's mother and one from the psychiatrist's secretary. He stuffs them into his coat pocket and heads back to the cabin. He stops in the sporting goods store and buys a box of .45 shells, exchanges small talk with the clerk, an old friend of his mother, and glances at the newspaper on the way out. The last of the U.S. troops in Grenada are being withdrawn, Lech Walesa's wife accepted the Nobel Peace prize on his behalf in Oslo, and Cabbage Patch dolls are in short supply for the Christmas shoppers. He shakes his head about what the front page omits. Instead of going back to his parents' house, Samuel walks to a bar. He wants a beer.

Samuel stays much longer than he intended. Hell, he thinks, I never even intended to go to the bar. It's not part of my routine. The huge Regulator clock chimes six o'clock. Outside, darkness has descended, like only a box canyon in winter can be. The shortest day of the year comes next week; Christmas just five days later. No presents. He's drunk. He shouldn't have talked so much to the stranger. Why did the man ask so many questions? Samuel can't remember his answers, but the man was there before he was, and he couldn't have known Samuel was going to show up. He tries to clear up the chronology. The man was in the bar first, wasn't he? Samuel, you dumb shit, you can't make any stranger your friend now.

Back in the house, he boils water for spaghetti and finds a can of tomato sauce to heat. Eat, walk around, stay alert. He loads his .45 and peeks out the curtains.

§

Samuel inserts a key into the vice, puts a work glove on his right hand, and begins to file. This one is an old door key, a Yale brand and tough. It takes him a few extra minutes. The second key comes from Chicago Lock, another quality key. The third has only a four-digit number and no other identification. It was made for a special situation. Samuel pauses and

studies it before inserting it into the vise. It contains an alloy to harden it, designed never to fail, bend, or get jammed. He puts it into the vise and pushes the file forward slowly. He repeats this action over and over, a determination in his actions. He has strong hands and large forearms, signs that manual labor has always been a part of his being. When Samuel finishes his fourteenth key, he puts the file back on the pegboard, takes off his glove, and goes into the house.

He changes into khaki slacks and a blue, button-down shirt to head off to St. Daniel's Catholic Church. He is mostly oblivious to the words of the priest during the service, and he doesn't take communion. Because of the ritual service, he likes this church, even though he is not Catholic. He can sit to one side and not be disturbed. He tries to communicate with the second spirit living in his body, and it seems to be trying to get comfortable in him. For the past few months since it joined him, churches have been the best environment for these attempts, almost like safe houses for souls. How apropos, he thinks.

Greg felt it first, on the way back to Washington, calling it the "something," and was angry it was in him. Sam dismissed this "something" as stress, but he too was shaken. When Greg told the psychiatrist about the spirit, the doctor recommended a temporary suspension from duty—and hospital care. It was obvious to Greg that the doctor didn't believe him. Sam understood Greg's suffering, so he listened. What Sam didn't understand was Greg's last request, for Sam to take care of it. That night, Greg hanged himself.

Sam thought the spirit wasn't real, even though he began to feel it after Greg's death. When the psychiatrist questioned Samuel about it, he denied its existence. The shrink declared Samuel fit for duty and signed off on him, and he left Washington for Colorado on leave. Now, he feels responsible for this second soul, although he doesn't know why.

Outside the church after the service, the priest asks Samuel if he would like to talk. Samuel thanks him but says no, not at this time.

Maybe down the road. Down the road, he thinks, everything now is down the road. The priest doesn't make him feel uncomfortable like the psychiatrist did. The priest seems to be patient. Samuel guesses he is in his mid-forties, about a dozen years older than himself. He wears heavy black glasses from a previous generation, but they go with his robes. He looks like a Catholic priest. Samuel wonders if he still would over a beer or cribbage board. He'll never know.

At the house Samuel changes back into jeans, sweatshirt, and boots. No poetry today; he has to write Greg's mother. He knows why Greg committed suicide, but he won't tell her; she doesn't want to know the reason—the real reason. So he'll continue the lie he has concocted to help her understand. Greg's fiancée broke up with him—true—and he didn't get the promotion he was expecting—false—and he didn't have anyone to talk to—again, false. Greg and Sam talked continuously. Over-talked. But they were unable to understand, and the guilt overtook Greg. He said he wasn't strong enough to have the second spirit.

§

At the Montrose library forty-five miles north of Ouray, Samuel searches the national newspapers for any new information. As always, nothing has been disclosed. He absolutely knows it to be true, but without verification, doubts creep in, especially about the details. He clenches his teeth hard, which shakes his face. He remembers his captain telling him not to expect too much truth from the world if it comes from the mouths of leaders--or in this case, not spoken. Two small town boys, Greg Benson and Sam Elkington, were ordered to remain silent, along with several others. It remains his secret now, but Samuel wonders if it should be. The second spirit stirs.

He drives the hour south back to Ouray over a snowy highway. He will leave Ouray at the end of the week to seek the truth, and he knows they will come to Ouray to keep him from revealing that truth. He has a week before the chase begins—for both. He mulls it over. Yes, for them, it will be a chase, a hunt, but for him it will be a search--and hopefully an escape.

His classic LeMans fishtails on the ice, but Samuel corrects it and drives on. It has never been a good winter car. Too front heavy. He will leave it in the driveway when he leaves and take his mother's reliable Chevy station wagon. Samuel has already loaded fifty-pound bags of sand in the back of the wagon to add traction if the roads are icy. He remembers when he let Delany drive the LeMans that winter so long ago, and she lost control and drove into the creek up near Ridgeway. They were lucky and the car wasn't damaged. Sam's stepdad came with the truck and pulled out his car. Then they went for beers. Good times; real good times. His dad called Delany a keeper that night. She wasn't, but she would have loved the upcoming flight. She just couldn't wait for him when he was away. Young people shouldn't wait and lose their youth; let older people wait. Of all the people Samuel knows, Delany would be the one who would believe him about a second soul, believe him about the event. Believe in him. But she couldn't wait.

§

The next key tightened in the vise this morning is labeled 25safe. Samuel assumes the key fits someone's safe, but he has no idea what the 25 stands for. It does pique his curiosity though. What if it was a date, a day of the month? No matter. He takes his file and pushes forward with his gloved hand while his left hand provides top pressure and guidance. Another reads Do Not Duplicate. A Master key has the numbers 1248 stamped on the back side. The next number in the sequence should be 16, but then the number would read 1-2-4-8-1-6 and that wouldn't hold to the pattern. The last two keys for the morning are both labeled Made in the USA. So am I, says Samuel, so am I.

Samuel can't recall the face of the old man in his poem, not that he should—he didn't get that close--but it bothers him. He remembers the man had thinning gray hair parted to one side and kind of shaggy. Was he wearing a hat? If he was, then Samuel couldn't have remembered a part. It's been almost three weeks since he saw him. At the time it seemed as though he was a grampa, but then, aren't all old men grampas? Samuel's own grampa, his mom's dad, taught him to shoot, to fish, to ski, and a little about politics. When Gramps died, Sam gave up painting. He wonders how to get in touch with the old man in his poem.

His mother's *Better Homes and Gardens* is the only mail. Samuel will take it the house and stack it with the rest of her mail in the flowered box to be picked up next summer. Anything of importance gets forwarded either to Illinois or California. He's curious about the man in the bar from a few days ago; he wonders if he would be there again today. And a cold beer always tastes good, even on a cold and snowy December day.

The Outlaw staff has changed since Samuel first started drinking there a dozen or so years ago, and he doesn't recognize them. The stranger sits at the bar in the same stool, and Samuel takes the one next to him. It occurs to Samuel that maybe he is the stranger and not the other way around. Maybe the stranger belongs here, but he doesn't look like it.

Samuel nods, orders a beer, and asks. "Been here long?"

The stranger nods. "Since about ten. Too early for a responsible citizen."

Samuel laughs. "No, I meant have you lived in Ouray long?"

The waitress slides a beer in front of Samuel and stares at him. The stranger lifts his for a silent toast. "Off and on, more in Ridgeway. When we talked the other day, you looked familiar, but I didn't want to pry."

Samuel feels a bit more at ease, not completely, but he takes a chance. If the stranger has been looking for him, he would know some of the information anyway. "I grew up here but left for the service a while back. I'm Leroy Elkington's boy."

The stranger smells of Old Spice cologne. He leans closer to Samuel's face, studies it, and nods. "Nah, I don't see a resemblance today. You must look like your mom. Haven't seen your pop for some time. Where'd he go?"

"Aw, my parents split up and headed out." In his mind he says to himself, they headed on down the road, of course. "How'd you know my dad?"

"When I got back from the service, he gave me a job at his rental shop. Only stayed on for a few months before I started working on a ranch over in Ridgeway, but he seemed like a good guy. Must have been almost thirty years ago. I'd see him around occasionally. You don't look like you'd been born then."

Samuel shakes his head. The two men sit in silence for a moment in their own thoughts sipping beer.

The Old Spice man asks, "What branch?"

"Navy," answers Samuel.

"What kind of ship?"

"Pigboat," says Samuel. "I didn't catch your name."

"Arnold," he says.

They go quiet. Arnold doesn't seem as inquisitive as he was yesterday. Samuel asks, "You wouldn't happen to know about an older fellow who might live down by the river who sits out half-naked and talks aloud to nature, would you? I saw him this last month, and I'd like to ask him a few things."

Arnold nods, "You probably mean Professor Abbott. He's sort of the resident philosopher around here. Nice, old guy who used to teach over in Gunnison. History, I think." The waitress concurs.

"Know where I might find him?"

The waitress shakes her head. "Check the phone book. If you can't find him there, just ask at the courthouse. Shouldn't be too hard." She asks if either man needs another beer. Samuel shakes his head, puts a ten on the counter, and then holds up both hands indicating keep the change. He nods over to Arnold and the waitress turns to get him another. Samuel stands, shakes hands with Arnold, and leaves.

§

*Esse est percipi* is etched on a wood plaque over the front door at Barkley Abbott's house, which is located just a block from the river toward the open end of the box canyon. Snow has been shoveled from the main sidewalk up to the porch. A homemade, wooden bench and table sit on the covered porch next to a set of wooden chimes hanging from fish line. No one answers Samuel's knock, so he walks around back. The old man is hanging clothes on a line that stretches between two metal poles. Flannel shirts and jeans predominate. A large cottonwood tree lies fallen along the north side of the property. Samuel watches silently and waits for the old man to notice him. At least he's not half-naked, thinks Samuel, but he isn't dressed to be outside long on this windy, cold afternoon. Samuel blows into his hands and realizes he wouldn't have recognized the man if they passed on Main Street. In time the old man turns back to his house and notices Samuel. "You the one who called?" he asks. Samuel nods. "Well, follow me in and we'll get a cup of joe and talk." He stands a full six inches taller than Samuel.

Light from numerous skylights floods the house. The old man rearranges a chair so Samuel can sit at the kitchen table, a spot mostly covered with African violets. The coffee was brewed earlier, and the old man pours two cups and sits down adjacent to Samuel. He rubs his scruffy hair, wipes his face, and looks at his guest. The older man has giant-sized, puffy hands. "Can I call you Sam instead of Samuel? When are you going to shave that beard?"

Samuel smiles and realizes he has been put at ease. "I wrote a poem about you and wondered what you were saying to the trees?"

"It's going to be a short conversation if that's all you want to know. Trees don't disagree with me, so I tell them whatever I want. They don't talk back, and after twenty-five years of dealing with college administrators and students, especially those pricks in the late-Sixties, silence can be a blessing. I write bad novels, but my trees, especially those in the park, seem to like them." He stares at Sam over his coffee.

"What should I call you?" asks Samuel.

"Let's be equals here. Call me Barkley."

"I understand you taught at Western State. I did some part-time work over in Gunnison before I joined the Navy. Colder there in the winter than here."

"That's when I left. It was January of sixty-eight and the temperature hit forty-four below and stayed below zero until March. I finished the semester and moved into this place." Barkley pauses. "I'm eighty, I think, maybe more, but after seventy, it doesn't matter anymore. You get old and life's painful. I'm always uncomfortable; back hurts, feet hurt, arthritis. It's why I live alone. No one would put up with my complaining." The old man smiles. "Anything I've said that can help your poetry yet?"

"I'm no poet. Just this one, and it just came to me the afternoon I watched you talking to yourself." Samuel doesn't add that he talks to imaginary objects too.

"To the trees, remember?"

"To your trees." Samuel doesn't really know what to say or where to go with the conversation, but he's been carrying the old man around for nearly two weeks. During this time his new companion has been a good listener, different from the spirit, but an ear to his silent voice. Samuel has spoken about Greg's suicide, his own guilt, and the events leading up to his return to Colorado, and the half-naked old man of his poem listened and nodded. He somehow understood. Samuel even broached the subject of his second spirit, and the old man didn't reject the possibility. Now the old man has a name and a face. Samuel sits across the table from Barkley, who now asks him about his thoughts, and Samuel is unable to speak.

"How about this, son? Let me talk. People around here tell me I'm good at it. Unlike you, I write a lot. I'm working on a book about the early settlement of western Colorado--have been for fifteen years. You might say it's a work in progress. When you saw me, I was reading poetry. I write quite a bit of it, but it's never any good. I have a girlfriend. She lives over in Gunnison, still teaching American literature at Western State, but that's mostly just a telephone relationship. Seems to work better for both of us that way. She's quite a bit younger than me, which is fine, but I'm quite a bit older than her, and that's a problem." Barkley laughs at his little joke. "Feel free to jump in when you have something to say, Sam." He then asks, "How'd you get my name?"

"I was sitting having a beer at The Outlaw talking with a guy at the bar, and he thought it might be you."

Barkley nods. "What was his name?"

"Arnold."

Barkley thinks for a moment and shakes his head. "Doesn't ring a bell, but I forget a lot of details nowadays. First name or last?"

"He didn't say. I assumed it was his first."

"What does he look like?"

"Older than me by a generation, but younger than you. His big ass devoured the bar stool. Flat top. Kind of military-like. And reading glasses down on his nose."

"Hmm." Barkley stands up and gets himself a drink of water. Samuel refuses his host's offer. The old man wanders the kitchen for a few minutes, checking plant leaves and straightening the counter. Eventually, he refills Samuel's cup of coffee and returns to his seat. "What're you doing back here, Sam? You seem to be looking for something."

Samuel's mind races, yet each thought is compartmentalized: that Barkley doesn't know Arnold, that he has a girlfriend who doesn't live in town, and that Barkley sees into him. Yet he doesn't mind. Samuel doesn't answer Barkley directly. "Where were you from originally? Not many of us Ourayans are natives."

Barkley nods. "Back in Old America. Syracuse. But that was so long ago. The East of my childhood no longer exists. I came out here during the Depression to teach and never left. Taught high school in Denver for few years and got my Ph.D. at DU, then moved over to Gunnison during the war. Spent nearly twenty-five years there. It was a good gig. Good friends. As I said, my bones couldn't take the cold any longer, so I moved over here. You'd think I would have gone to Texas or someplace warm, but these mountains get in your soul. Besides, there is Lizzie, and she's kind of buried herself in my soul too." Barkley goes away for a moment. "This is a good town to wind down in, to tie up loose ends before it's over. People leave me mostly alone."

Samuel remembers the last lines of his poem. He lifts his butt off the chair slightly to get to his wallet. He takes out a handwritten copy of his poem, unfolds it, and passes it to Barkley. He stays quiet and allows Barkley time to read it. Samuel knows now that the old man in the poem wasn't sitting by his own cabin, but he thinks he got the last part of his poem right.

"How old are you, Sam?"

"Thirty-three, sir." The mood has altered, for the better.

"I suspect this decade will be my last, and it does give me pause. Not death and the Great Beyond, but the fate of my mind." A knock at the front door interrupts him, and someone enters along with a blast of cold air. "That's Henry. He comes by most afternoons to pass the time. Another old man."

Henry is short, maybe five feet-four, but he's wound tight like he jogs five miles every morning before breakfast. After introductions Samuel excuses himself. Barkley offers the poem back to Samuel, but he says to keep it. Barkley asks him to come by tomorrow morning. Samuel tells him it will be closer to noon and asks if that will be all right.

§

The next morning Samuel shortens his routine in order to go to the library before he visits Barkley. He can't find a translation there for the sign above Barkley's door, but he knows it's something like "what is perceived." Without a question mark on the phrase, he knows his translation is inaccurate. A bright sun warms the day, almost like the day he watched Barkley sitting half-naked.

Barkley insists they sit in the sun with their coffees. Samuel asks about the sign. "I learned a long time ago that a little philosophy can get you through the day and into the evening where it might get you laid," says Barkley. He waits to see if Samuel notes his humor. "It means, 'To be is to be perceived.' I'm not very deep, but I like philosophical quotes. I guess my sign means that things exist only when someone, like you or me, has the idea of it. If no one knows about something, it's not real. Living alone—in solitude—makes you think about stupid shit like this." Both men laugh. "I like your poem."

"Thanks. That's all you're going to get."

Barkley gets up. "Bring your coffee. I want to show you something." They walk through the house where Barkley warms both coffees. Out back, Barkley points to the fallen cottonwood. "That tree fell over last spring while I was in Gunnison visiting Lizzie. I like to go over during the week and sit in on her classes; she always has something to teach me. She was teaching a lesson on the power of language, something about dirty words that Steinbeck used in his books. Cussing up a storm to her students. Anyway, when I got back, my tree was down. Luckily, it fell away from my house and my neighbor's. He must have been in town, because he didn't hear it go down, which goes to the saying about if a tree falls in the forest. No one was here to hear it, so I guess there was no sound. Just a backyard event."

Samuel shakes his head. "Is this going somewhere?"

"Yep, you seem to have been knocked down a bit. Just wondering if you're here to take up my space and drink my coffee, or are you going to make a sound. If you got something to say, start talking."

Back in the kitchen, Samuel runs his fingers over the edge of the table, his eyes following their path. He reaches into his pocket, withdraws his rock, and places it on the table between him and Barkley. "Know what this is?" he asks. The old professor shakes his head and stays quiet. "It's a birthday present from Delany Herrera. She was my girlfriend before I joined the Navy, and for a time even after." Between each thought, Samuel pauses, measuring his words. He hasn't spoken to anyone in depth since Greg's suicide, not even the psychiatrist. Samuel stonewalled him. "Delany's family owned the motel across from the swimming pool as you come into town. They sold it and moved to Durango. I think they bought another one there." Samuel's fingers stop at the seam in the metal that wraps the table. He scratches out some old food with his thumbnail. "I didn't know what it was because it didn't matter. Probably millions of years old, but for me it's only ten years old. We broke up a few years later, but I keep the rock." He picks it up and examines it. He hands it across the table to Barkley. "See, nothing special." He allows the old man time. "I know who Henry is. I didn't recognize him yesterday, but it came to me last night. When I was a kid, about ten, he was a Little League baseball coach. He did something at the junior high too, but I'm pretty sure he wasn't a teacher."

"Part-time art teacher and volunteer deputy sheriff," says Barkley. "It paid his bills for a while. His real calling is an artist, painter mostly, some sculpture. That's what he does now."

"I didn't continue with baseball after Little League. And I didn't take art. Does he still work at the school?"

"No, not for several years. He and I became friends shortly after I moved here. Can't remember how, but now we're best friends. We check in on each other, drink beer together, and cuss at old age." Barkley is speaking softly.

Samuel extends his hand for his rock. "Uranium. It's unstable and a bit radioactive. Its half-life is somewhere between one billion and four billion years. It's slowly committing suicide." Samuel rolls his tongue behind his lower lip. He doesn't know where he's going. "My friend, Greg, committed suicide just over ten weeks ago. We had a pact, but I didn't hold up my end of the deal." Samuel stares at his rock, looks into his stone, and sees Greg's body hanging from a rafter too high for him to pull down. The firemen had to do it. "We were supposed to go together, but I think he saw my hesitancy and went out on his own." Samuel places the rock down gently and rubs his nose. "In his note he told me it was okay, that he understood. Understood what?" says Samuel more forcefully. "I fucking don't understand anything!" His breathing is rapid, and he swallows hard. The room goes silent as neither man moves.

"Camus said suicide was the only serious philosophical question. He died in a car wreck. Old people think about suicide a lot; Henry and I talk about it. We won't, I suspect, but we talk about it." Barkley pauses. "I don't suppose you want to tell me what your guilt is about yet, do you?"

Samuel shakes his head no.

"Henry checked up on your bar-buddy Arnold. He doesn't live here. Yeah, he did some work up in Ridgeway on a ranch, but nobody seems to know what exactly he does. A lot of people sort of know him; he comes and goes. Henry said he'd keep digging. If you don't mind, I'd like to have him sit in with us on these talks. He's a good dude, a bit of a busy body, sees things differently than me, and real imaginative. Only if you're comfortable with it though."

Samuel puts the rock back in his pocket. "I was planning on leaving here in a few days. Ouray is closing in on me. I just stopped in on my way out anyway."

Barkley lets out a soft laugh. "Son, do you have any idea about what you just said? I sure don't." Samuel looks up with a tired face, something Barkley notices. "I'm hungry, Sam. How about we go downtown and get a burger. Maybe I can talk you into staying for a few extra days."

§

"Did you hesitate?" asks Barkley. He dips a fry in ketchup and drops it into his mouth.

Samuel nods his head. He is about to divulge a secret, but he isn't sure how to do it. Sam was right to dismiss it, but it saved his life and continues to urge Samuel toward something. *Esse est percipi,* Samuel says to himself. But start small. "For the last two and a half months, I've had this feeling as if I'm carrying around another person inside me. Just sort of popped into me. Now," Samuel pauses. Just come out with it, he tells himself. If Barkley laughs, I'll laugh too, finish my burger, and head out. It's what I planned to do anyway. "Now, I talk to this person a lot. What do you think about that?"

"You're not referring to your conscience, are you?" Barkley is speeding through his meal.

"It sort of acts like my conscience, but it's not that. It's not of me."

"Did you ever have this feeling before?"

"I can understand if you don't believe me, if you have doubts. I haven't been able to make sense of her either," says Samuel.

"Her?"

Samuel starts to say he misspoke, but he nods instead. "Yeah, it usually seems like a her. It has to sound absurd, but to me, she's real. She's unsettled about something, God knows what, and she's hiding in me just now. Like me, she's lost. My best guess is that her hiding in me is part of her lostness."

"There's no such word as lostness, but I get your meaning. Son, there's no ending to life's absurdities, but this doesn't sound, to me, like one of them." Barkley reaches over and puts his hand on Samuel's shoulder. "I'm not a religious guy, you know, Christianity and all.  Too many Christians cherry-pick their faith, but I do believe in God, because He answers some of my stupidest questions, at least in a round-about way."

Samuel tilts his head to the right and purses his lips as if to say, I can accept that.  I can lie to the rest of the world, but I better not lie to myself.

Barkley pulls his hand back and eats another fry.  "No matter what I do or think, God works ahead of me, so when I wonder about the noise of the tree falling, I know God heard it.  Having said all that, all that nonsense, I think He makes me find the answers to my dilemmas.  Never has He appeared and given me the answer directly."  Barkley smiles.  "He's running out of time too.  My death will precede His timetable to answer any of my questions."

"I hesitated because I didn't want to kill her too."

"So you saved her life?"

"Not life.  Spirit.  She's not a life; she's a spirit—or soul."  Samuel looks in the eyes of Barkley for confirmation.

"That makes a little more sense," says Barkley.  He takes the last of his hamburger bun and wipes up the ketchup on his plate.  Samuel still has half of his burger to go.  "What about Henry?"

"He's ex-military, right," says Samuel, not really making it a question.  "Why don't you ask him over tonight, and I'll show up.  I'll tell him what I told you."

§

Samuel plans to leave on Friday before the sun comes up.  He tells Barkley and Henry he hopes to get as far north as Sheridan, Wyoming, if the roads are dry, and then into Canada by Saturday afternoon.  He will drive his mom's station wagon and leave his LeMans parked in the driveway for anyone to see.  For Arnold to see.  Henry reluctantly agrees to move the Pontiac occasionally, and an automatic timer has been installed for the lights in Samuel's house.  A neighbor kid will shovel the walk when necessary.  None of the three men believe this will be the best long-term solution, but it will give Samuel the needed time to get out of the country.  Henry thinks it's not the best plan, though, and he still doesn't believe in the second spirit who inhabits Samuel's body. The trio finishes off one six-pack and starts on a second. When Samuel explains it to Henry, he tries to stifle a laugh, feigning serious introspection, but it doesn't work. Samuel is not offended. Instead, he turns to Barkley and tells him that was how he should have responded.

"Ah," says Henry, "a shaman in our midst. Bark, you told me this kid had a real problem, but you didn't tell me he was a soul retriever." Henry turns back to Samuel. "I'm sorry, Sam, but the professor and I are not always in agreement about life. He's a naïve believer in all world views, and I'm a bit of a skeptic." Samuel doesn't know about shamanism. "A shaman is a magic man in some religions, but I didn't know Bark was a parishioner in any one of them." Henry shakes his head at Barkley. "Shamans are supposed to be able to make contact with the invisible forces that exist alongside all of us visible people. He can also be a healer, and if that's the case, you better work your magic on my old friend here."

"I'm no shaman guy," says Samuel. "I just have this other soul kicking my insides, trying to escape, I think." Samuel pops open his beer one-handed. "Henry, when I told the Navy psychiatrist, he pretended like it was important I let it out, since Greg committed suicide. He didn't believe me, so I went along with him and told him the feeling was gone. Then he signed off on me and let me go on leave." Henry doesn't believe in the value of shrinks either. On that, Samuel and Henry agree.

Barkley bends over and rubs his old legs. "You don't have to go, you know. You go AWOL, and the Navy will find you eventually. Even in Canada. How about you call them and tell them you lost track of time, and you'll be a few days late." He looks up from below to check Samuel's response. It's a no. "Well, then, how about you move in with Henry. He has a big house—too big for one little old man. I'm sure you could hide out there for a while."

This is the first Henry has heard of the plan. "No risk to me, of course," he says.

"What are they going to do, lock you up at your age?"

They drink in silence for another round, each thinking his own thoughts.

§

Thirty-five minutes later, Barkley is asleep. Henry takes a blanket from the barcalounger and covers his friend. He pats him on the shoulder and turns to Samuel. "How you are holding up?"

Samuel shakes his head. "Being AWOL won't be my problem. I'm running to get time, time I didn't want just a few months ago. How am I holding up? Not worth a damn."

Henry moves closer to Samuel, pulls up a chair, and sits. "Understand that I'm an artist and retired lawman, and like my friend over there, I don't know much of anything." Henry tries to get Samuel's eyes, but they stay hidden. "Except that I care about Barkley, and he cares about you. Your poem spoke to him somehow, and now he wants to help you. I get that. Bark's a broken man, and he isn't quite what you've been led to believe. He doesn't own this house; I do. He lives here free. He didn't retire over there at Western State; he was forced out with no benefits. We maintain a lie, in a sense we live a lie, to keep his dignity. Lizzie doesn't exist, well, not anymore. Lizzie is an English professor in Gunnison, and a damn good one. Maybe the best, but he has nothing to do with Bark anymore. Lizzie was Bark's pet name for him when they were lovers, but the college couldn't accept a homosexual couple on their staff back in 1967, so Bark made them a deal. He would leave, totally and clean, if they would allow Lizzie to stay, to get him his chance. They agreed. He moved over here and rented this house from me. My wife and I got to know him. Before I learned he was that way. Just in case you're wondering, I'm not a queer. Just a widower who got very lonely when my wife died. So Bark and I sort of lean on each other." Henry takes a deep breath and lets it out slowly. "Bark's like a big puppy sometimes; he just wants to please, but he's not looking to find another partner. You aren't a love interest for him, so put yourself at ease there. Bark's more full of shit sometimes than anyone I've ever known, but it's never in an arrogant way. He just has all this knowledge that was once taught to college students, and now he has no use for it, so it just comes out. I suspect you've heard a lot of his philosophy already."

Samuel starts nodding and lifts his head. He bites the inside of his cheek. "So what do you think about my second soul?"

"I believe you think you're carrying around this spirit, but I don't accept those ideas. Doesn't matter though. You believe it and so does my friend. That's all that matters to me. We both want to know why you feel so guilty, but we're pretty sure you're not going to tell us." Henry pauses to be proven wrong. Samuel gives no response, so Henry moves on. "Bark knows about guilt. He tells me no amount of time will cure him. Here's my question to you. Can you be cured? By going to Canada, you'll just be breaking the law and giving up on your country."

Samuel shakes his head before he says no aloud. Fatigue, especially in the evenings, consumes him; he can barely keep his eyes open. It happens every evening. His morning routine is important just so he can function. The key ritual, mail, groceries, planning, but then he hits the wall. He wants to sleep and never wake, but she won't let him, and he can't let her down.

§

Henry Taluse sits at Barkley's kitchen table and does some pencil sketches. It's past midnight. Samuel somehow found the energy to go home, and Barkley snores in his lounger. Henry covers several pages with drawings about a young man with a beard carrying a young woman in his stomach. None of them satisfy his artistic sense. He pushes aside his sketches and pulls a road atlas to him. He calculates it will take Samuel about thirteen hours to drive from Ouray to Sheridan, Wyoming, even in the best of conditions. The weather forecast for tomorrow is foreboding to the north. Maybe Samuel can get to Casper, maybe not even that far. Most likely, Samuel will get only to Rawlins. He won't get into Canada until Sunday. Henry mulls over his options and doesn't like any of them.

§

Someone at The Outlaw recognized Sam Elkington and called Delany Herrera. Guess who's back in town, said the voice on the other end of the phone. Now, Delany drives from Durango in a heavy snowstorm to see her old boyfriend. At Silverton she realizes her folly and finds a motel.

§

How many brass keys are there in America, especially with all the antique stores in every little town? Too many for Samuel to conquer in a lifetime. This will be his last morning of slaying the dragon's children. He has killed enough. After the dozen he has smoothed this morning, he puts away the file, sweeps up his work area, and tosses the useless keys into the pickle jar. He reaches over to the pegboard and takes the silver chain with the two dead keys and slips it around his neck. He unhooks the crucifix and puts it in the pickle jar. He notices a spot of blood on his left forefinger, licks it off, and presses his finger against his jeans. Samuel will change the oil and antifreeze in the station wagon, pack a cooler of food, and maybe stop in to see Barkley. Then he will sleep in preparation for his early start. He wishes the second spirit could communicate better, because it seems unsettled today.

§

On the night before Samuel leaves Ouray, he drives his red Pontiac to Henry's house. There, he enters through the front door and walks out the back door. He returns to his house, entering the back door, goes to the garage, and drives his mother's white station wagon two blocks away. It's packed for an extensive journey: clothes, food, and a metal box. He parks it and returns to Henry's house, where he gives a set of keys to Henry, before driving his Pontiac back home. Samuel sets his alarm clock for four a.m. and sleeps in his clothes. He wakes to the night, moments before the alarm goes off, ending his dream intentionally. He moves through the house in darkness, as invisible as possible. He exits through the back door, walks to the alley, and makes his way quickly to the station wagon.

Samuel drives north out of town towards Ridgway, in the direction of Canada. He is not anxious for the sun, for light. He wants to be invisible, to drive in the darkness for as long as possible. He pulls off the road and parks behind a grove of trees just before town and watches. Three cars pass by and continue north toward Montrose. Satisfied, he gets back on the road. In Ridgway he turns west on Colorado 62 to Placerville, where he turns south on Colorado 145, which will take him the ninety miles to Cortez. The weather breaks south and no snow falls on Lizard Head Pass. In Cortez Samuel takes U.S. 491 and drives due south into New Mexico down to Gallup, where the temperature registers thirty-four degrees, forty-one degrees warmer than it was in Ouray six hours earlier and two-hundred and fifty-eight miles back. On the west side of town, Samuel stops at the Route 66 Gas and Grits to fill up the wagon and get breakfast. He's a bacon and eggs guy with tomato juice and coffee, one sugar. He takes his time; the mostly night driving has been tense, and the restaurant atmosphere relaxes him. The patrons are Navajo or Hopi Indians, men with cowboy hats. He looks at the postcards on the revolving rack and picks one with cacti and coyotes on it. Samuel leaves six dollars on the table and heads out, west on Interstate 40/Route 66 toward Flagstaff.

In Flagstaff the temperature has dipped to twenty-eight degrees, according to the sign on the bank building, but it's sunny and the road remains dry. Flagstaff, where he spent his first two years of college, could be a nice semi-mountain town to settle in; he's comfortable here--but not at this time. He catches Interstate 17 for the next leg to Phoenix. He plans to arrive by four-thirty. Nowhere does he exceed the speed limit. Draw no attention, talk to no one unnecessarily.

The spirit has been silent for the entire trip. Samuel wonders what this means. Is his passenger still with him; does she approve of his decision; was she really in him in the first place? Has this been a delusion based on Greg's suicide? There are no answers from her. Regardless, there are the other answers he must find.

He pauses in Phoenix only for gasoline and a pop. I-17 melds into Interstate 10, about two hours to Tucson, where he will stop for the night before completing the trip to Mexico tomorrow. Nogales should be fairly easy to pass through, fairly easy for an American to get lost. His fake driver's license reads John Samuels, age thirty, hometown Denver. He pulls into Tucson before seven and looks for an inexpensive motel. He finds a rustic one just off the interstate, but there are several to choose from. It crosses his mind that many of the people in these motels could be on the run. He'd like to talk with someone, but now is not the time, and he's tired from his long drive. He pays in cash.

His room reeks of smoke. He should have asked for a non-smoking room, but they probably don't have any of those. He won't go back now; it would just raise a flag in case he has been followed. Unlikely. As far as he knows, no one has a clue where he is. He feels a little guilty about not being clean with Barkley and Henry, but something Henry said last week sent a warning to his antenna, something about desertion being unacceptable. And about Arnold.

Samuel doesn't want to sleep just yet, so he brings in the cooler and makes himself a ham and cheese sandwich. He noticed a newspaper stand at the office, and he walks back and buys the *Arizona Daily-Star*. There is nothing new about the nuclear power plant accident in the Soviet Union, but a discotheque fire in Spain has killed nearly a hundred dancers. Samuel wonders how many workers died at Yamantov. He bites open a bag of potato chips and pops the tab on a Coors. He turns on the TV, where the Dukes of Hazzard just jumped through their windows and drove away. Dallas begins before he finishes his sandwich. The TV is still on when Samuel awakens at eleven-thirty-five. His beer is warm, and Steve McQueen races a motorcycle along a double fence in The Great Escape. She woke him to tell him someone wants to see him. Samuel knows there are several people who want him, but he's unsure what she is saying. He wonders who this new person might be.

Saturday morning breaks warm and sunny. He eats the same breakfast as yesterday at the IHOP, for a little more money. He has a two-hour drive to Mexico. He sheds his pea coat, puts his paper coffee cup in a makeshift holder, and drives south out of Tucson. On the American side of Nogales, Samuel stops at one of the many shops to buy Mexican car insurance. At the checkpoint a guard asks for his driver's license, asks how long he plans to stay in Mexico, and waves him through. The border guard doesn't bend over to look at him in the car. Samuel's destination is Hermosillo, and if that doesn't work, he'll drive on to Guaymas. He'll stay until he has a few answers, the ones he can glean himself, and has a handle on the next few months of his life . . . but not much longer than that.

§

"Our boy is on the move. Yeah, Canada. Two or three days. Access going into either Regina or Winnipeg should be easy for him. He shouldn't be hard to track. He's in the white station wagon; he left his Pontiac LeMans here in Ouray. We need to get him before he gets permanently lost."

§

Delany Herrera isn't Mexican; she's a combination of Hopi and French. That's the family joke. No one speaks Spanish, they've never been in Mexico, and two of the children have blue eyes, Delany being one of them. Sam fought a kid in high school who called her a beanerita, but until then the word had never been a part of her vocabulary. She laughed, but Sam protected her honor. She later asked him if he was embarrassed to be dating an Indian. She doesn't remember his answer, but they didn't stop dating. One summer they made up Indian names for each other: he was Alo and she was Cha'Risa, Hopi names. At the time they thought they were so clever. When the high school put in a cement loading platform at the back of the boiler room, they wrote their Indian names in it—with an arrow underneath. She named her family's motel in Durango the Broken-Arrow Inn.

She visits Ouray a couple of times each summer, but seldom in the winter. The drive over Red Mountain Pass is too harrowing, just like last weekend when she was stranded in Silverton. From the last hairpin turn above Ouray, Delany sees Sam's parents' house. Why didn't Mrs. Elkington sell it when she divorced?

§

"I'm looking for Sam Elkington," says Delany after knocking on the door.

"He's gone," says Henry.

"I was going to be here last week, but the snowstorm shut down the pass."

"He was here; you just missed him. Stayed for a few weeks and then drove off a day ago. Didn't say exactly where he was going. I just stopped in to check on the house." Henry studies the woman. Small town attractive, but not beautiful, although to old men, most young women are pretty. She would be challenging to sketch: dark hair, blue eyes, ruddy-brown complexion, roundish face with high cheeks, and about five-three. "I'm Henry Taluse, and who might you be?"

"I'm Delany. I knew Sam pretty well back when, but then he went off to the Navy, and we sort of lost track. I just heard he was in town and thought it might be fun to get together. He was always fun and a little crazy."

Henry invites Delany inside to get out of the wind. It is a familiar house to her; the furniture is the same as it was when she and Sam dated. Henry tells her to have a seat, and she selects the couch where they spent so much time making out. Along the hallway wall are four boxes containing various papers and small items. Flowers decorate one of the boxes, but the other three are plain brown shipping boxes about two feet by eighteen inches by twelve inches high. The flowered box is labeled "Mom," next to it is one labeled "Leroy," another has "NAVY" written in black magic marker, and last one has no label.

"Will you be staying long?" asks Henry.

"I guess not. I only came to see Sam. Maybe I'll drop by The Outlaw to say hi to a few old friends, but since the weather's good, I'll probably head back to Durango while the roads are dry."

Henry senses a disappointment in Delany's tone. She is not wearing a wedding ring, but she did make herself up for the visit. "I don't know Sam well; just met him a week or so ago, and he asked me to keep the house looking lived-in for another few days. By the end of the week, I suppose I'll close it up." Henry pauses. "Unless he comes back."

Delany looks past the old man to a photo on the wall, a

composite of Sam that includes his high school graduation picture and one of him when he finished basic training for the Navy. These are the Sams she remembers. Henry's last sentence brings her back quickly. "He might come back?"

"I don't know. His leave time has run out, but I just sense his naval career holds no interest for him any longer."

"I can't imagine Sam not being gung-ho for the Navy. It's what broke us up. Once he decided on things, he pretty much went all out, and I decided we were done." She purses her lips and shakes her head gently. "You probably didn't know him well enough to realize what a stubborn stubborn man he can be, which is okay since I'm so tolerant and forgiving."

"So, you're pretty stubborn too, huh?"

"Maybe more so than Sam, but it's a woman's prerogative." They both smile. Delany gets up and goes to the kitchen for water. She knows in which cupboard the glasses are stored. She doesn't ask Henry if he wants a glass, but she brings him one anyway. "Sam's a pretty patriotic guy, not so much different from other boys in Ouray, except he acted on his beliefs and joined up after college. We all were in school during the Vietnam War, and I don't think he supported it, but he sure wouldn't protest against it because he thought that was disrespectful."

"Disrespectful? To who?" asks Henry.

Delany hesitates. Patriotic feelings are back in favor since President Reagan called the Soviet Union the Evil Empire and the Korean jet was shot down, but there remains a substantial segment of the country that ridicules all parts of the military. Being a motel manager, she has become milquetoast and politically correct in her public persona. "To America, to what he thought America really stood for at its core. He understood many of the men who were drafted to go to Vietnam were," Delany stops to choose her words carefully, "not a good fit to represent the country." She looks deeply at Henry to see if he approves of her direction. His face tightens, but he doesn't object in words, so she continues. "Sam just has this deep sense of patriotism, like he was born into it, like it runs in his blood. He hated the communists. He and his dad had some pretty heated arguments about the Cold War and all that. Mr. Elkington was such a gentle man, and Sam could be pretty forceful. They weren't much fun to be around when the conversation turned to the military."

"Do you know why Sam chose the Navy?"

"Oh, yeah. It's what broke us up. The Army was in shambles when Vietnam ended, so that was out of the question, and he didn't think the Marines would be used again, since ground war seemed to be discredited then. The Air Force might have been an option, but Sam wasn't going to fly, so he picked the Navy. Thought he could make a difference there."

"How long did the two of you last after he joined?" Henry pauses. "If I might ask?"

"Not long. Two years, off and on. We were young anyway, and I've never been one to be patient, so I wrote him a nasty letter and ended it. He replied in kind, and that was it. We've talked on the phone occasionally, but I wasn't going to be a military wife whose husband was gone for long periods of time. A lifer. He tried to convince me to come with him, but I said no."

Henry nods. "Well, young lady, we all have to make difficult decisions. Being a nice guy and fun doesn't guarantee a good husband or a happy life."

"Everyone likes Sam. I think if I didn't see him for twenty-five years and he walked into my life again, I'd like him immediately."

Henry has lots of questions; he has since the first day he met Sam. "Did you know Sam is pregnant?"

Delany squinches her face. "Do you mean he has a wife or girlfriend?"

"No, he said he was carrying another spirit in his belly, a girl." Henry is purposefully vague.

"Okay, back up. I'm confused. How can Sam be pregnant?" Delany leans forward in her chair, clasping her hands and resting her forearms on her thighs.

"Join the club. He said he felt like he's carrying around some spirit inside him. I laughed—kind of made light of what he said— but he held to it. Told Barkley and me it just popped into him a few months ago, and now it's trying to tell him something. He didn't know what yet."

"First, who's Barkley?"

"Another old guy; older than me. He met Sam before I did. Sam wrote a poem about him." Henry can tell Delany is even more confused.

"God, I can't imagine Sam writing poetry. He's smart and all, but tenderness wasn't a strong suit. So, has he flipped out?"

"No, I don't think so. Something happened in Washington, and he feels guilty, but he won't tell us—Bark and me. A friend of his committed suicide, and now he feels responsible. All of this confuses us too."

Delany's stare blurs the image in front of her. Never did she see this side of Sam. "Sam Elkington. Six-foot one, strong, big fore-arms, dark hair, brown eyes. Are we talking about the same guy?"

"Yep."

Henry and Delany try to make sense of Sam for another half-hour, but they get no closer

to believing they understand. Before Delany leaves, she asks, "Anything else I should know that will shock me?"

Henry nods. "Sam's AWOL. The Navy won't be happy. He talked of going to Canada, but I hope I convinced him to return to base rather than desert."

# Chapter 5

*Hermosillo, Mexico, April 1984*

Mexico provides Samuel with the anonymity he desires. Working for the new Ford Motors company in Hermosillo, he saves a few dollars, grows his hair long, and takes a deep breath. The inner spirit seems to have accepted the move, seems to have found a comfortable spot in his upper abdomen and adjusted to spicy foods. She also seems to be in a holding stage. If Barkley or Henry were to ask Samuel about this, he would not be able to explain it to the old men, but Samuel feels a serenity in his companion, even though he has none. Barkley would accept that, but Henry would just ask more questions. Samuel now talks to the spirit, but it doesn't answer directly. It's more like the half-naked old man's trees that swayed in seeming approval when he read his poetry.

Samuel likes the midnight shift at the Ford plant; his job allows him to do his line work in silence. The Mexican workers' chatter makes no sense to him, so he simply smiles and laughs when they laugh. He returns to his apartment around six-thirty, eats a small breakfast, works out with a series of exercises, and then heads off to the Catholic cathedral. It is a magnificent church, and Samuel sits in a different section each day. He knows no Spanish, but the ritual of the services captivates him. After an hour he goes outside to the cemetery where he picks grass, straightens headstones, and tidies up—much like a caretaker. He started doing this the first day he saw the grounds, and now it's a routine. Each family has a plot, and the marble and granite stones tell their history. Samuel studies the burial rites, with the holy water, candles, and words that he can't translate. He knows the blessing invokes a plea that the souls rest in peace. He remembers a line from his childhood church attendance, "Deliver us, O Lord, from eternal death in that awful day when the heavens and earth shall be shaken, and Thou shalt come to judge the world by fire." Sam delivered the line by memory at his grandfather's funeral, and he often feels like delivering it again. Around noon, he returns to his apartment for his tablets. He has written over two hundred pages in his notebook. On most days he writes at an outdoor café over a beer and lunch, his main meal. He's grown fond of Mexican beers, especially the light cervezas. At three he goes to bed. Like his naval duties, he divides his day into four unequal shifts, with a six-hour sleep before work. The Hermosillo libraries offer no help in his quest for information about Yamantov, and he avoids the American snowbirds in the local restaurants and curio shops. He regained the twenty pounds he lost in the three months after leaving Washington, the months when he was disoriented, and there are no more mood swings. Except that he lives in a silent world, his life has gained some normality. He had not anticipated these things.

§

In early April one of the priests strolls over to Sam while he kneels at a gravesite picking grass. "You do a nice job on each grave, son," the priest says in fluent English. "You're quite meticulous. Do you know any of these people?" The priest knows the answer.

"No, Father. I just sort of see an unkempt plot and straighten it out a little." This is the first time one of the priests has directly addressed him.

"I've watched you for several months now, and you are a puzzle to me." He waits for Sam to respond, but he doesn't, so the priest continues. "Our own gardener worries we have hired someone to take his place. As a result, he has been working harder. You have been a good example for him."

Sam pivots from his knees onto his seat and brushes off his hands. "This gardening, as you call it, is therapeutic for me. I have a lot on my mind, but here, everything goes at a slower pace. My friends here don't seem to be in a particular hurry." Both men smile at that.

"Therapeutic. Yes, I guess I can see where it could be. I have a small vegetable garden of my own, mostly tomatoes, and I suppose that's what it's for." The priest takes two steps over to the headstone for the Diaz family and sits on it. "Is there anything I can do for you, son?"

Sam knows the answer is God, yes, but he defers. "Thanks, Father, but I think I'm working them out okay."

The priest is dressed in a white robe and the sun sits on his shoulder, making Sam squint when he looks at him. "Like most of us, your soul stirs at times, but it appears as if yours is in a bit more turmoil than most. You aren't from here, that's obvious. Where do you call home?"

"The easy answer would be Colorado, but I've been in the service for ten years, so nowhere really seems like home these days. I have plans to return to Colorado soon, but your city has been a welcoming place."

"But not a restful place?"

Sam nods. "In some ways. Your cathedral soothes me for now, but I have some responsibilities elsewhere."

"You could stay. Then instead of running and hiding, you would be living. There's a difference between the two. We could pay you for your work, not much, of course, but a little to supplement your other job. You live the life of a monk, silent and isolated, but it's not your calling. Your hands and eyes give you away."

The priest's powers of observation amaze Sam. He doesn't want to end the conversation, but he's not sure how to answer the priest's questions either. "Can anyone be buried in this cemetery, Father?"

"Oh, no. One has to be dead first." The priest smiles. He appears to be a middle-aged man, as tall as Sam, but slight. His fingers are long and thin with clipped nails. He wears a gaudy ring. Mexican in all appearances. "Generally, those who reside here have been parishioners; they are a part of our flock. This is their domicile. Rich and poor, although most of them are poor, we lay them to rest here. You have watched the burials with great interest."

"I have, Father." Again, he goes silent for a moment. "A friend of mine committed suicide last year. Could he be buried here?"

"Probably not. The church frowns on that, although I personally think people who take their own lives are the most in need of a peaceful place. Under certain conditions, the church will allow it. Where was he laid to rest?"

"His family came for the body and took it back home. Lutherans, I think. His mother told me about it. She had no doubts his soul resides in Heaven."

"Parents should not have to worry about the soul, especially when they're hurting for their child under those circumstances. Why did your friend commit suicide?" The priest has taken a big leap.

Sam hesitates. "He was lied to. He was told to protect our country, but when he thought he did, it turned out to be a lie. I was going to join him, but I got visited by . . . something. I'm not sure how to explain it."

"You speak so generically. What did your parents say about the suicide or your leaving?"

"I haven't told them anything about any of this. I wouldn't tell my stepdad; he divorced my mom and isn't in my life, but my mom doesn't know yet. I never called her. She's probably worried beyond any explanation now." Sam realizes he trusts the priest at this moment. "Father, do you believe that a person can carry another's soul?"

The priest stands and offers his hand to Sam. "Come, son, let's walk." The two men walk in silence for a time. The wind blows through the mesquite trees that border the cemetery, and birds chirp. Finally, the priest answers. "Yes, son, I do. As a priest I have felt it. It's a temporary condition. I like to think of the passage that says, 'In my Father's house, there are many rooms.' You happen to be one of those rooms for this spirit. It will leave you in time, but we don't know when that might be. Is it the soul of your friend?"

The question startles Sam. It has never felt like Greg's spirit. "I don't think so, but it would make sense. I've been calling it a she. Maybe souls are so gentle that they seem feminine."

The priest laughs out loud and lays his hand on Sam's shoulder. "That's a good one. Would you mind if I use it in one of my sermons?" It is a rhetorical question. "I believe that sometimes a soul needs extra time on earth to complete some tasks. I believe God would accept the soul at any time but allows the soul to determine the time. Most are eager to arrive in Heaven, but a few are in denial about death. God understands. Some of my brothers disagree with my view. Do you talk to this passenger?"

"No, we don't speak the same language. She pokes me a lot though. Right now, she seems pretty satisfied with where we are."

"A she for now?"

"I'm not so sure. I'll have to think on that, on what you said about it being my friend."

The priest stops. "You have plenty to think about, son. I have some work to attend to, but you're welcome to stay in the," he smiles, "the garden. There is plenty of work to do here. We'll talk again." He shakes Sam's hand and walks back to the cathedral.

§

Two days later the two men meet again, but this time in a side chapel. Samuel asks about Father Tellez and his cathedral, and the priest is anxious to tell him. In English the name of this church is the Cathedral of the Assumption. "Our Virgin Mary was taken into Heaven complete in body and soul. There is some discussion as to whether she had died or not. I'm of the belief she did not physically die, but God decided her mission on earth was over, and so he took her to be with His Son. Myself, I am descended from the Yaqui tribe. Since the beginning of the Spanish invasion into Mexico, we were changed. Very few of us even speak the Yaqui language anymore." Father Tellez offers Samuel his arm, and they walk out the front doors and across the street to the plaza. There, he continues. "Plaza Zaragoza forms the historical center of Hermosillo, and it is named after our great General Ignacio Zaragoza, the hero of the Battle of Puebla way back in 1857. In that great battle, a smaller Mexican army defeated the French, which began the process of Mexican independence from Europe. It would take many years, but we finally won. Unfortunately, General Zaragoza died shortly after his great victory. He was only thirty-three." The two men sit on a bench in silence for a time.

"I'm thirty-three, Father. Your city is growing rapidly, even though it is in the middle of a desert. I love the orange smells. When I leave work in the early morning, they are especially strong."

"You should have been here fifteen years ago. The city was a town, and the orange groves were everywhere. We are losing our identity; soon we will be a sprawling city like those farther south or along the border with Texas."

"You have been to those cities, Father?" asks Samuel.

"No," laughs the priest, "but I have heard about them, and I don't want Hermosillo to become what I've learned. What is your name?"

"Samuel." He catches himself. "John Samuels. Does it matter?"

Father Tellez thinks it a strange question. "We all have a name. It's a bit easier than saying 'Hey you' to everyone." He arises and motions for John Samuels to come. "I need to return to my chapel. I apologize for doing all the talking today, but I am proud of my church and my city."

"No, Father, it has all been very interesting." They cross the street and shake hands. Samuel asks one more question. "And are you proud of your country too?"

§

Instead of writing the next afternoon, Samuel stays at the café and stews. With his elbows resting on the table and his fists held together in front of his face, he strikes his jaw with short, one-inch jabs. Anger simmers just below the surface in these months since docking at Bangor and learning that the bargain was phony. He keeps this anger off his face, but he can't control it. When Greg committed suicide, Sam drove through Bangor destroying property, especially anything that presented a target for his .45. Public statues in Bangor and Tacoma have gunshot wounds. He was apprehended by the police and turned over to the Navy, who found a way to get the charges dropped—or forgotten, as the master-at-arms said. He was then sent to the psychiatrist, who recommended an extended leave of up to sixty days. Sixty days, six hundred days, six thousand days. Unless someone is able to give him information to completely contradict his senses, six thousand years will not soothe his anger. Living with a second spirit tempers his anger, at least outwardly, but it drives him to find answers.

The café buzzes. Samuel eats his late lunch here frequently because of the activity. He writes in his journal and there are few distractions, as if the café knows he needs quiet, but today he only watches. Father Tellez told Samuel he is safe in Hermosillo, that there are no demons here. What he meant was whoever might be pursuing Samuel won't find him in Mexico. He can be as invisible as he chooses to be in this city. Father Tellez also told him the cathedral would always be his safe house. Samuel wishes he could transfer the spirit in him to Father Tellez; he a good man, a peaceful man. There is no peace in me, thinks Samuel. He watches a woman about his age with a child. She is gentle with the little girl, stroking her hair one moment, bending down to smile and whisper secrets into her ear another. The little girl keeps one hand in contact with her mother, almost like a lifeline, thinks Samuel. An old Mexican also watches. His pleasure glows on his face, where Samuel's visage remains stoic. An observer would conclude the two men are observing completely different occurrences. Maybe they are. Just then, Barkley pops into Samuel's mind, and he manages a slight smile. Samuel seats Barkley next to him. What would the old man have to say about this? What bit of philosophy would Barkley offer to the poet? *Esse est percipi;* "To be is to be perceived." Samuel picks up his beer and toasts Barkley Abbott, finishes the beer, and heads out, leaving Barkley at the table to people watch alone, half-naked.

§

Father Tellez sees John Samuels in the cemetery from afar. He sees the American in a different light today. There was anger in his question from the previous day, anger not directed at the priest, but someone. The Catholic priest sips his coffee and watches as this man with the alias cuts the grass around another headstone. Somewhere he has procured a pair of snippers. He pulls the grass away from the headstone, snips, and then tosses the cut grass into a brown paper sack. This man pays close attention to details. From the family headstone, he moves to the smaller stones in the family plot, those made from pure white limestone, marking the graves of poor children who died too early. The wealthier families have granite or marble stones. Father Tellez knows that fate too well. Catholic Mexican families are large, and too many children die before their fifth birthday. The American seems to understand this.

Samuel reads the inscriptions as he works. Mexican names, crosses, dates, and Spanish words he doesn't know. He is sure there is a gentleness in these words, but it isn't transferred to him. Six children under the age of seven: Frida, Beatriz, Jose, Isabel, Adriana, and Pedro. With his fingers he traces the names. Suddenly, he feels a constriction in his stomach. Ah, there you are. What did I just do to arouse you?

§

Samuel has come to grips with one truth in Hermosillo: he agreed to a bargain, even though he never believed it would happen, but it did. Now he will take responsibility for it. In time he will cross back into America at the border in south-central Arizona, near the Tohono O'odham Indian Reservation, where he believes he can pass without documents, and then drive to Colorado. He will miss Father Tellez and the men on the Ford line, but he must be there for the meeting in the mountains, and the time is coming. He can't return to Ouray, but he wants to be close.

III


# A Foot Soldier in the Cold War

# CHAPTER 6

*Buena Vista, Colorado, late September 1983*

When Walt Kramer concentrates, the Korean War shows on his face, at least that's how his former first sergeant describes it. Facial frostbite from the winter of '50-'51 up near the Chosin Reservoir in Korea left permanent dark circles under his eyes, and a year later, a piece of shrapnel grazed his forehead along the line of his eyebrows. Even when he relaxes, his eyes appear to be squinting. When he actually squints, his visage takes on the image of a man too far away to be reached, possibly in hiding. And that is often the case. Walt's profession as a nuclear trouble-shooter requires a heightened awareness and ability to concentrate.

He studies a series of wind charts intently from the first-class section of the United flight back to Denver, unfazed by the severe air turbulence causing the jet to jerk and spasm. The stewardess has retreated to her seat to ride out the buffeting, leaving a worried old man sitting next to Walt to fend for himself. There has been no small talk between the two men; Walt's full attention is directed to prevailing winds, Westerlies, seasonal anomalies, and latitudes. The State Department librarian printed twenty-two different charts for him, most with colored arrows pointing south, east, west, or northwest. Northwest would be optimal, he thinks. During the Rocky Flats fire in 1957, the winds blew east and showered Denver with radiation. That was a terrible location to build a nuclear weapons facility, next to a metropolitan area. With a six-inch ruler, he calculates distances according to the inset. He makes notes on each chart. Still, Mother Nature laughs at those who make plans.

Fifty-one years old, Walt exudes a forceful presence. When he joined the Army in 1949 at age seventeen, he stood five feet ten and weighed one-forty-five. Skinny. Now, thirty-four years later, he measures a bit over six feet, one-ninety, with Popeye forearms. His hair shows specks of gray, but aside from a slight receding at the temples, he retains a full head of hair. Since the early seventies, he has kept it short.

Reserved by nature, Walt's demeanor could be misinterpreted. Decisions he will soon have to make about his work weigh heavily on his mind, but there is more. The state of the world for a man entering his sixth decade troubles him. His past and his penchant for current events both cause him to wonder what has happened and what may happen. These thoughts seldom entered his mind until a year or two ago, and he wants to know why they now seem to bombard him. He smiles to think maybe his best friend has finally gotten into his head. A week earlier, on September 19, Walt received a phone call from Dean McElroy, the Sarge, inviting him to Buena Vista, to spend a few days with him in the mountains. Despite a very busy schedule, Walt has accepted, knowing the invitation would not have been extended under normal conditions. Best friends often operate this way.

Walt's return flight to Denver from Washington National Airport will not be the end of his current job. This job might never be over, even if the desired results occur. Job. How inadequate this word defines what just transpired. The world reads about the civil war in Lebanon, a piece of the Arab-Israeli conflict. President Reagan orders more Marines into Lebanon, part of the international peacekeeping force there. Walt opposed those actions; he believes Reagan has put American soldiers at risk. The whole situation between the Israelis and its neighbors started badly back in '48 and continues to fester to the present time. Things that start out badly usually end up the same way. If anyone had told Walt early in life how bad balances out good over time or how good comes from bad, he would have shaken his head with a large bit of skepticism. When Bellena implied the same idea to him a decade ago, his reaction was more forceful. He visited Israel after the Yom

Kippur War for the Nuclear Energy Associates and found it to be a unique country, but he can't shake the feeling that Israel survives on borrowed time and land. Still, today, Lebanon is such a minor event. In two days, the President will address the U.N. General Assembly and call for a renewed attempt to limit nuclear weapons. Nice cover.

You're a good soldier, Walt Kramer. Well, you weren't at the time, but now you can certainly follow orders. The President and the Joint Chiefs ask for your expertise, and you give it to them. You don't give them advice or your opinion, you just give the facts. "Can it be done, Walt?" "It's risky, but, yes, sir, it can be done." Walt told the NEA cadre he would not take over the NEA when Foster died, but he would serve as the interim head. Nuclear Energy Associates. Shit! Just the information gathering wing on nuclear energy for the CIA. Lapdogs.

With his return to Denver, Walt will see Bellena for a long weekend. She recharges him. He called to let her know when he was returning, but it wouldn't have mattered. She is always glad to have him, even if he can't tell her about his latest trip, about the details of his work. The drive from the airport to Bellena's condo in south Denver takes a half-hour. He expects to take her to dinner and maybe a movie and then be swallowed up by her physically. She has cracked the door to allow him easy access; a good sign thinks Walt. Bellena comes out from the hallway and greets him with the usual hug and kiss, but she is not dressed for a night out, and a small suitcase sits by the door.

"Dad has had a setback. I got the call just after you called. He's been taken to the hospital in Salida."

§

The drive takes about two hours; Bellena in her Mustang has been known to get a ticket or two. It takes Walt normally a half hour longer. Walt was anxious to tell Bellena about his trip, at least what he's at liberty to tell, but he knows the focus has been transferred to her dad. Three meetings with the President in three months, and Bellena will want as much information as he can tell.

It won't be much, but she knows the crisis has escalated since the Soviets shot down the Korean Air Lines jet nearly four weeks earlier on September 1. Maybe tomorrow they'll talk, but not tonight. No, tonight he'll try to be a civilian out of touch with Washington and totally in touch with Bellena and her father, his best friend.

"Who called you?" asks Walt as he reaches over and rubs the back of Bellena's neck.

"The Bueny sheriff who drove him to the hospital." She rolls her head over to one side to let her cheek touch the back of Walt's hand. Theirs has always been a physical relationship, lasting nearly fourteen years. "You must be tired."

"I will be, but I'm okay right now. I didn't take the NEA job, at least not permanently." Walt had already told Bellena he wasn't going to, but she worries he could be persuaded to do so because of the heightened tension since President Reagan took the verbal offensive against the Soviets. Sense of duty, you know. "I'm not completely out, and General Kelley wants to keep me close as an advisor because of my CIA ties." He stops and laughs. "There's a lesson in life, Bellena. Don't be a smashing success in the one mission the bigwigs are watching, or they'll think you're an expert and keep asking you things you aren't an expert on."

"Poland? Walesa?"

"Yep. The President has sort of tied his kite to Solidarity."

Bellena pulls into the Chaffee County Hospital in Salida shortly after nine, just after visiting hours have ended, but neither she nor Walt will allow the schedule to deter them. The two nurses are not concerned either, and the younger one escorts them to Mac's room. They find him sleeping in the dim room with an I-V attached to his arm and a plastic oxygen tube around his head. The nurse informs them Mac has been asleep for about an hour and can be expected to sleep through the night. She tells them they can stay as long as they want. Bellena leans over her father and kisses him on his forehead, while Walt lifts a wooden chair and sets it down next to the head of the bed so she can sit close. He helps her with her coat and lays it over a movable food tray. He sits on the radiator next to the wall. The only light shines over the sink, and the only sound emanates from the oxygen tube.

"He looks comfortable. When he was here last June, he could never get comfortable." Bellena takes a brush from her purse and straightens her father's hair.

Walt leaves her and walks to the nurses' station. He returns with another chair and a hospital blanket. Bellena hasn't moved except to hold her father's hand, and it looks to Walt like her extended arm is a second I-V. The soft light enhances her beauty, and Walt has to remind himself that Mac deserves to be the center of attention for the next few hours. He thinks about his call to Washington.

"Is he going to be all right?" asks Bellena.

"For tonight and the immediate future. The nurse thinks he'll be released tomorrow afternoon, but he might need oxygen." Walt lays his hand on Bellena's neck. "I spoke with his doctor on the phone. He's cautious about a long-term prognosis. He hasn't determined what caused Mac's breathing problem today. He wants to talk with you and Mac tomorrow about moving to a lower elevation." Walt knows Mac will absolutely refuse.

"It's pretty serious in Washington, isn't it?"

Walt nods. "Yeah, I let them know where I was and how to reach me."

"Ever since he was diagnosed with this damn cancer, I've been dreading the day he leaves me." She speaks in a whisper.

"He's liked his life, most of it, and you've always been the most important part." They sit quietly with their own thoughts for several minutes. "After Korea I lost it. Mac somehow found out and got me a job at Rocky Flats, started me on the way to everything I became. I'm not sure how my life would have turned out without his help, probably a lot like my miserable childhood."

Bellena leans over and kisses her father's hand. "You've never spoken of your childhood in all these years other than to say how rotten a kid you were. Tell me a story from when you were little."

Walt smiles a warm smile. "To do that, I'd have to dig into some ground that hasn't been turned over in many years."

"Plowing's good for the soil, you know. Any old girlfriends?"

"You don't really want to know that, do you?"

"Yes, honey, I do." Bellena teases her longtime lover.

Walt reluctantly accedes. "Colleen. She was my high school girlfriend, I guess you might say, at North High School in Denver. We skipped a lot of classes together and did a lot of daytime drinking. One night we broke into our school, just for the hell of it. Other than breaking a window to get in, we didn't do any damage. No vandalism. She assumed the role of teacher, a history teacher, and I was the student. Quizzed me on World War II, things we all knew because we lived through it as teenagers. She asked me if I was going to join the Army. This is in '49, and no war rages anywhere anymore, so I asked her what good it would do. She said I wasn't making it in school, and it might make a man out of me." Walt smiles. "Might straighten me out."

"I like that you're telling me this," says Bellena. "Go on."

"I asked her if she would write to me if I went away, and she said she would. Later, the school found out it was me who broke in and suspended me. So, I joined the Army."

"How old were you?"

"Seventeen, but my mom signed off for me. She pushed me out the door basically."

"Did Colleen write to you?"

"A few letters, but after the Korean War broke out, she stopped."

"Whatever happened to her?" asks Bellena.

Walt doesn't answer her right away. He doesn't lie to Bellena, but he has kept secrets. He realizes this secret doesn't need to be kept any longer. "I married her when I got back from Korea. She had given birth to my son in 1950. Raised him alone while I was in the service. I didn't know until I came home." He studies Bellena's face waiting for a reaction.

"Huh," she replies with a subtle nod of her head. "Does my dad know any of this?"

"Maybe a part of it. There was a time when I wanted nothing more to do with the Army, with my past, and I avoided everything connected with it, including your dad." Walt takes a second to remember. "The marriage didn't last; less than a year. I was becoming the same guy I had been before the Army, before Korea. Colleen tried to help, but I was just too angry and sullen. She kicked me out, and I never came back. Somewhere, divorce papers were filed. We've seldom spoken since."

Bellena gives Walt a reassuring smile. "You've never told anyone this before, have you?" She leans over and kisses Walt on his cheek. "Thank you for telling me." She won't ask about his child tonight. She'll wait until he's ready to continue. Strangely, she feels a door has opened between them, one more door.

They sit quietly for an undetermined amount of time. Walt wants to talk with General Kelley to see what new information there is, to be in the inner circle without reservations. He knows more about nuclear power plants than any of the men who sat around the table two days ago, but he's now excluded. He wonders if there exists in the Soviet Union his counterpart, someone who can solve problems like this. There would have to be, wouldn't there? In the background from the nurses' station, a radio plays "The Sounds of Silence," and Walt cringes.

Bellena finally speaks. "Dad was born to be a sheriff. He loved Leadville, and it loved him. Three hundred pounds of protection and care. It hurt him when he had to resign because of this damn cancer. At least he could stay close. Buena Vista's been good for him."

They leave just before midnight. At Sarge's house in Buena Vista, they go straight to bed and make love, the first time in nearly a month. When they finish, Bellena falls asleep in the crook of Walt's shoulder. As the night passes, his thoughts about his best friend and his job interconnect. Walt remembers those first days in Korea, those days when he found a will he never believed he possessed. He remembers huddling in a ditch in fear, and he re-fights a battle over some caves north of the 38th Parallel. They are so far removed from this week, but still connected somehow. He gets up and calls Washington; no one is sleeping there tonight, and they fill him in with part of what they know and tell him to stay close to his phone.

§

Back from the hospital, Mac takes the ribbing from his daughter about his drinking habits with good humor. He has never purchased a bottle of wine, so Bellena stockpiles reds in his pantry for herself. She pours Walt a glass, but given the choice, he would opt for beer like Sarge. A light snow falls and the stone fireplace roars. Mac raises his iced tea.

"A toast." He and Walt wait for Bellena to wipe her hands and raise her glass of wine. "To another day of life, because maybe it's what we should always be thankful for."

"To another day," responds Bellena.

"To this day," toasts Walt with his Korean War stare.

"So, tell me, Mr. Big Shot, how'd your meetings in Washington turn out?" asks Mac.

"Not much to say. The NEA needs a new boss, and I gave them some advice."

"Bellena says they offered it to you."

Walt hides behind a laugh. "They did, several times, but I refused. I'll do it for a few months more is all. I'm not much for working closely with a bunch of politicians. Besides, solving local problems with nuclear power plants suits me just fine." He takes a bit of bread and changes the subject. "Doctor says you're going to recover. That means you'll be around to continue to cause me more grief." He smiles at Bellena. "Every problem has its own solution."

Mac laughs. "That's always been your creed, Walt, but I have to disagree. I tried to buy into that same philosophy myself for a long time, but it just ain't so. In real life we do our best, but sometimes we fail. Then you assess and move on. As sheriff I could solve most of my town's problems. I lived by your creed, but in that bigger world, the one you live in, humans fail much of the time. But life goes on; we go on."

Bellena looks to Walt to take the bait. He doesn't, so she pokes him. "Are you going to let this old geezer make light of your life philosophy?"

Walt twirls several strands of spaghetti noodles around his fork and places the large wad into his mouth. Even though the Sarge is a dozen years older, they behave like brothers. The wrestling matches of old have stopped, but the bantering continues. "I have to respectfully disagree, Sarge. A solution can happen if you're persistent, if you're smart enough to see it." He lifts his wine glass to Mac.

Mac turns to his daughter. "He is one stubborn SOB. His creed makes him carry a heavy bag around. Sometimes it's best just to bury that bag. I say do your level best and move forward. Try not to get too lonely or isolated and keep your people close."

"And what if your people don't support you?" asks Walt.

Bellena responds quickly. "Then they weren't really your people, were they?"

The conversation pauses as both Mac and Bellena wait for Walt's response. He keeps his face down, eating another bite of spaghetti. Mac reaches over and touches Bellena's arm. "You can hear his head pounding, Princess, trying to get it around my life's philosophy."

"I get yours, Sarge. Bellena's troubles me though."

"I have no philosophy, remember. I'm a pragmatist." She pours herself another glass of Fess Parker merlot and says casually, "How about if I quit my job in Denver and move up here with you, Dad? I've given it a lot of thought, and this latest episode just convinces me even more."

Her father reaches over for her wine, brings it to his nose, and sniffs. "Davy Crockett brewed himself a mighty strong wine here. You'd have to stay in the smaller, upstairs bedroom, because I'm not going to walk up those stairs every night." He looks to Walt for his opinion.

Walt puts up his hands in defense. "I think you two need to talk it over in the front room, while I clean up the dishes."

"Oh, no," says Bellena, "you're not getting out of this that easy. I want you to live here too."

Walt Kramer seldom gets caught off guard. To buy time, he offers a lame option. "I guess I could sleep in the back room, but it would be a long commute to St. Vrain each morning."

Bellena smiles. "You can clean the dishes up now. I'll take Dad into the front room and talk about what I'm going to do."

§

Walt Kramer's and Dean McElroy's lives intersected in Korea and seldom diverged after that. Mac's first encounter with Walt was at the Chosin Reservoir when Mac reported to the company commander for duty. Standing in a line in the bitter cold, Mac watched a young soldier carry frozen bodies from the side of the road to a protected spot, and then cover them with ponchos. Walt had not been assigned to do this; he did it out of respect for his brothers, known and unknown. All around him, soldiers were huddled in tents and foxholes in futile attempts to ward off the sub-zero temperatures and howling winds, while one man delivered these dead soldiers for transfer and a flight home.

The war revealed another side of Walt too, Mac tells Bellena. "Until he was a teenager, all he knew was the Depression and WWII, basically poverty and war. His mother never nurtured him, so he never understood the real meaning of family. His foray into adulthood was Korea, and the worst of it. He experienced much worse than I ever did, and it still has a hold of him. When I met him, he already had those sunken eyes." Mac likes his daughter with Walt, but he believes that the relationship is best maintained with large chunks of separation as it exists now. "We heard stories, rumors really, about his first weeks in Korea. One of them was he had been a prisoner of the North Koreans for a few days, and maybe he'd been tortured. He's never said, and I never asked." Sarge pauses to compose himself. "You know my feelings for him, Belle, but make sure you go into this thing with your eyes wide open because every day won't be like the ones you're imagining."

§

Bellena returns to the kitchen just as Walt puts the last dishes in the cupboards. She comes up behind her man and hugs him with her head on his back. He reaches his arms around her without turning. They hold each other for a moment before Bellena speaks.

"Did you like the wine?" she asks.

"Yeah, I did. Bellena . . ." Before he can continue, she interrupts.

"I told my dad all about us. I want him to know about the best thing in my life before he dies. He knows, of course, but not all

87

the details." Walt turns around into Bellena's chest and waits for her to continue. "We're expected in the living room. He has some questions for you."

Mac can't resist. "Since 1969, huh? Was my baby old enough?"

"Your 'baby' is only eight years younger than me. Remember?" Walt pauses momentarily. "I'm a good liar, Sarge. I tell people what I think they want to hear."

"Except with me and my daughter," responds Mac. Bellena sits down next to her dad, while Walt settles on a single recliner.

"Sadly, I've fudged with you guys too. I'm sorry."

Bellena breaks in. "Not lies, just omissions. You cover up; you keep your life to yourself. I know you have to with your job. We understand."

Mac waives his hand. "Some people keep secrets because they're afraid of what people might think. Sort of like Bellena all these years. She wasn't worried about what I would think. She was afraid of what you might do, and so she kept a lot secret. Some people keep secrets because they want to forget. Doesn't always work. When I served in the Pacific during the last year of WWII, island hopping, I did some things I'm not particularly proud of. I didn't need to do them, I just sort of got caught up in the brutality of war. Japs did things worse, but it doesn't excuse what we did—of what I did. Anyway, when I came home in '45, I only told about the good stuff, the brave stuff. Kept it a secret for over fifteen years, and it never got better. Knowing what I did helped me in Korea. I was a soldier there, not a depraved young man." Mac's eyes never leave Walt's, and Walt doesn't flinch. He knows what's coming. "Finally, one night I opened up to Bellena's mother. Staring straight into the blackness late one night in bed, I told her everything. I couldn't have done it in daylight, but it was a release. Not that night. Hell, I couldn't sleep that night, but afterwards I let it go."

Walt readies himself. Now here it comes, he thinks. Bellena purses her lips in anticipation.

"You were the best soldier in Korea, Walt, but I wasn't with you during those first few months. Something happened that scarred you, and it's time to let it out. I've wanted to ask you for a long time, but I always figured you'd tell in your own good time." Their eyes don't waiver, but Bellena's dart between the two men. "But your own good time won't be in time for me. Yesterday and today, what Belle said, reminds me of that."

No one speaks while Walt goes digging inside himself for those painful memories. They aren't hard to uncover, but they are nearly impossible to let out. His Korean War stare prevents him from seeing the two people in front of him. Bellena sees the sweat beads on the side of his head, and she senses something in her man that she has never sensed before: terror, in the brief instant of a full body shudder. Somewhere, Walt battles to return. His head falls slightly, and Bellena casts a sideways glance at her father that asks whether this is the right time. Mac takes her hand and nods.

Without looking up and with his fists clenched between his legs, Walt begins to whisper. "We were ordered to hold the road at all costs. If we couldn't, then the whole company would be lost. But there were so many of them, and they were on all sides. Even some of the Koreans who we thought were refugees turned out to be North Koreans." Walt's voice labors. "I could hear the tanks, those treads, but more than that were the screams of the North Korean soldiers as they attacked. Those screams came from everywhere." Walt falls silent again. Bellena's eyes well up and she puts her head on her dad's shoulder. Mac knows Walt isn't done. He hasn't escaped his cave yet.

Walt swallows hard, a gulp really. "We tried to stay, we did, but it was suicide, so we ran. Nobody decided for anyone else. I got up from my foxhole, threw my weapon in the direction of the tanks, and ran. My squad followed me, and they all died. I didn't protect my squad. I couldn't save them. Why did I live?" Walt asks this question in a condemnation of himself. "I should have died with them. I was a coward." He falls silent.

Walt doesn't feel Bellena's hands on his face when she says gently, "Oh, Walt, you're not." He doesn't hear Mac get up from his chair and go to the kitchen or hear the refrigerator open and close. Walt only responds when Sarge takes his hand from between his thighs and forces a beer into it.

"Every soldier in Korea knows what you guys did in those first weeks. You were used as cannon fodder to delay the commies." Mac speaks slowly and deliberately. "You were ordered to die, but the longer you held out, the longer we had to prepare. Those soldiers who died were heroes, but so were all you soldiers who lived. In battle we can't decide who will live and who will die. In Korea by staying alive, by any means and for whatever reason, you saved thousands of the rest of us. America forgot about us when we came home, but none of us forgot. We know we did something important. You and your buddies were on the front lines, and you weren't given a chance, but in the end you guys saved the war." Mac lifts Walt's ashen face with his hand and speaks a command. "Now, let's have a toast to your buddies and move on."

§

Only Mac sleeps well that night. Walt assures Bellena he is all right and sends her to bed, but he doesn't join her upstairs. He allows the flames to die in the fireplace and spends the night staring into the embers—and then into the dark. There has been no release. Instead, he regrets telling about his first weeks in Korea. Everything he accomplished in the last thirty-three years to make up for his dishonorable act has not achieved this purpose. A life-time can't make up for running out on his squad, for letting them die in that ditch while he cowered under a bush only yards away.

Walt is not alone in the darkness. Bellena sits half-way down the stairs, watching and waiting. She sees only the back of his shoulders and head. Sometime between two and three in the morning, he lowers his head slightly, and his hands move slowly over his head. He locks his fingers together, draws in his elbows, and rocks ever so slightly. Bellena hears him say in a muted voice, "God dammit, Walt." She descends the stairs and moves to him, where she kneels at his feet. Walt hovers in that cave where he goes to hide and doesn't hear her come. Instinctively, however, his hands loosen from his head and fall over her shoulders, and he returns.

Bellena speaks. "I guess I set you up a long time ago to be perfect. You've been my fantasy, you know." She talks into the side of his leg where her head lies.

"I'm a phony, Bellena. I've not always been who I am today."

"Being secretive doesn't mean you're a phony. When you're not with me, I hold conversations with you, and you always give me the responses I expect. Dad says if I'm going to ask you to join us here, you might not give me the answer I'm expecting. You've always made me feel beautiful, and because you're perfect, I've always believed you. Tonight, maybe you became real."

"My being real doesn't make you any less beautiful."

Bellena's fingers on her right hand begin to gently scratch Walt's thigh, but the rest of her remains still. "Now I know why you never spoke of your past. That must have been a terrible time. I'm surprised you talked about it tonight. I know you were really telling my dad because he asked, because you thought he deserved to know before he dies." Her voice quiets even more. "When I was young, I used to ask Dad all kinds of questions about you. Once, he told me that you hide yourself; that you block out a whole other life. Now I know why, but for me, only the life that began when I met you after Korea matters."

Walt remains silent for a few moments. On a normal night, there would be sounds from the outside, but the snow has muffled those. Finally, he begins. "Jimmy Mellon was from Waynesville, Missouri. His dad was Army, a drill sergeant. Jimmy wanted to be just like his pop. Talked about him all the time. Artie Gallegos couldn't sit still. Skinny like me, but shorter. Wanted to go home to Los Angeles and be a dancer. Greg Powers was a boxer. He said he was undefeated in Golden Gloves. Artie tested him once and got his nose broke in the first round. Greg was going to go to OCS after Korea. He'd have made a good officer. John Veslek just wanted to please me. He'd do anything I asked, and I took advantage of him sometimes. Had him clean my rifle, get me beers, loan me money when I was short after losing at poker. He was my radioman. Steve Vincent had been in Japan since the surrender in '45, four years before the rest of us arrived. Loved the Japs. Taught them how to play baseball. Taught me how to throw and hit properly. He said he'd go back to Tokyo when the war ended. Gary Johnson." Walt goes quiet for a moment. "I think his real name was Ronnie, but somehow he got stuck with Gary, so he just went with it. Always writing letters to girlfriends back in Illinois. Don't remember him getting any back while we were in Japan at the start. Lance Gilliam was always reading a book. He was the only one of us who read much. Wanted to be a teacher. A high school teacher. All of them were from a different state. All of us joined. Good guys. Just wanted to do our duty and go home." Walt takes a deep breath and lets it out of his mouth. "I took the dog tags off each one of them that night."

Bellena raises her head and slowly traces her right forefinger across Walt's cheek. "After all these years, you still remember each one."

"I promised them I would. I've carried them with me ever since."

§

When Mac awakes the next morning, he finds Walt and Bellena asleep on the couch, wrapped up in each other's arms. He leaves them where they lay, goes to the bathroom, and then to the kitchen to make a pot of coffee. He walks quietly past them to get to the front porch to retrieve the newspaper. Three inches of snow cover the ground, but the road hasn't iced up, and the sun breaks up the remaining clouds. Mac checks the baseball scores. The Yankees are out of it in the AL East, but his Giants are making a charge in the NL West. President Reagan has castigated the Soviet Union over the Korean jet shooting once again. His inflammatory words are pushing the Cold War to a new intensity, and it scares the old veteran.

Mac wants Walt to return to the Korea discussion today somehow, but how to get him there is a concern. Walt certainly won't be anxious about retelling the incident. Incident, he thinks. The start of a war. What the young soldiers who were sent to Korea to hold the line went through was not an incident. It was a tragedy. It had to be done, but that didn't make it any less cruel to the young men who either lost their lives or their souls. War! Those men who survived and stayed in Korea earned them back, but you couldn't tell them that. They didn't believe you when you did, and Walt had not believed Mac last night. Thirty-three years of believing he was at fault for the deaths of his men. Now Mac knows where Walt goes. He goes to a dark cave of shame and isolation.

Bellena gets up and walks upstairs. Mac is proud of his daughter, but at this moment, after what went down last night, his pride reaches a greater level. She flinched, but she didn't leave, and she helped Walt during the night.

Walt strolls into the kitchen trying to tuck in his shirt. "I bet I look like hell. Did you get any sleep?"

"Slept like a baby. Why shouldn't I?" Mac hands Walt a cup of coffee. Sarge decides to jump right back into the previous night. "You exposed yourself pretty good last night, you know. You okay?"

Walt pulls the muslin curtain aside on the east window to check the weather. Outside, a mother pulls her child on a sled through the pure white snow. Walt turns and sits at the counter in silence for a moment. He looks at the newspaper headline, folds his hands in front of his chin, and carefully reads the story. While Mac might think Walt is contemplating an answer to his question, Walt churns. "It's doable" is what he told President Reagan. Maybe he was right, but only time will tell.

Mac asks again. "Are you okay?"

"Yeah. Didn't get much sleep, but I'll find time for a nap today." Mac lays out six strips of bacon in a cast iron frying pan, then pulls down a plate and covers it with paper towels, while he waits for the younger soldier to continue. "What kind of father lets his daughter hang out with an old man with skeletons?"

Mac smiles and tilts his head but says nothing. The daughter in question comes into the kitchen wearing jeans and a dark-blue, hooded sweatshirt. She has washed her face clean of makeup. She goes straight to Walt, puts her arms around his waist, and kisses him. She avoids any talk of Korea, injecting the discussion of Mac's cooking and her plans for the day.

§

After breakfast Bellena walks into town to size up the real estate market, her specialty, and Mac and Walt drive up a wet and bumpy dirt road to Mac's cabin. The snow melts rapidly, leaving only patches in the shady areas behind the pine trees. Winter made an appearance, but it isn't going to arrive on this day. It will be a day to fish on the small pond adjacent to the old cabin. As Mac fits the two parts of his rod together, he asks what Walt thinks is a strange question. "What's a day worth?"

Walt knows where his old friend wants to go, but he hasn't figured out his path yet. He hopes the fish on the small lake will be hungry for bigger flies, so he attaches a small silver hook to his line onto which he can quickly slip size 14 and larger flies. He selects a #14 Gray Hackle Green. "A day, huh? Twenty-four-hour day or just the sunny part?"

"Twenty-four hours."

Walt makes his first cast, pulls out several more yards of line, draws it back, and sends it out into the pond. "Well, let's see. A man could repair a cabin or climb a fourteener. He might spend a day with a beautiful woman or fish with a good friend, but how do I put a dollar figure on any of those?" He strings out another cast. "Do you want a dollar amount?"

"Nah. I just want you to realize that a day can be pretty import-ant. The last two days with you and Bellena have been damn important to me. Just to be alive." The fish aren't hungry.

"Sarge, any day with Bellena is a good day. Most days with you are too, even though you can be a bit of a horse's ass sometimes." Both men smile at that.

"I think my daughter would say the same thing about days with you."

Walt allows his line to drift without tension. "Where are you going with this day's worth thing, Sarge?"

Without turning to look at Walt, Mac continues. "You were with the Twenty-fourth Division out of Japan in those early days, weren't you?"

"Thought that's what you were getting at."

"The Twenty-fourth got chewed up pretty good from what we heard. Outnumbered ten to one most places. Nothing to stop their tanks. Unaware of the terrain. Did you guys do any serious training in Japan before you came over?" Before Walt can answer, Mac has a fish. Small, but the first. He unhooks it and sets it carefully back into the water.

Walt reels in his line and turns to Mac. "No training. No PT. Just beer and smokes. In my squad none of us had ever seen combat. I'll answer your next question before you ask it. We were dumped onto a road between Seoul and Taejon, about four hundred of us at a place called Osan with Task Force Smith and ordered to stop the North Koreans at any cost. Nobody told us how. Just said do it. Ever try to stop a tank with an M1? I don't recommend it."

"How long were you in Korea before you got support?"

Walt lets out a breath. "Seemed like a lifetime. At the time it was."

Mac stops fishing too. "I'll bet it did, but how long?"

"I don't know. Ten, twelve, fourteen days, maybe. We were in constant retreat. Hard to mark your calendar, you know." This anger about Korea has always been a part of Walt's character.

"Two weeks, give or take, huh?" Mac looks at his fly and blows on it. "Pretty expensive when you figure it on a soldier per day basis. Gives you a new perspective on what a day's worth, doesn't it?" Mac lets that sink in for a few moments. Walt knows he isn't supposed to respond just yet. Sarge will let him know when. "You know what those days bought us, us guys who didn't arrive until later in the year?"

Walt has never accepted any explanation for the deaths of his squad other than his own culpability. His men were squandered for nothing because America wasn't prepared.

Very gently and deliberately, Mac answers his own question. "You and your guys bought us ten days. Ten gawdamn days. Ten days that saved Pusan. Ten days that saved the war." He moves a step closer to his buddy and places his left hand on Walt's shoulder. "MacArthur used you to fool the North Koreans. Made them think maybe there were more of you than there really were. They paused in their drive to Pusan. That was all we needed."

Walt's face hardens beyond the squint that is so difficult to penetrate. "But I should have died with my men," he answers with a guttural sound.

"No, Walt. If every American soldier would have died, then the North Koreans would have pushed forward, and we'd have lost the war. Some of you had to survive. Why it was you, we'll never know. All I know is you honored your men over the next three years, and since the war, you've been a good man."

For a moment Walt remains rigid. Then, as if some long-dead Army captain calls "at ease," his body sags. The tenseness in his shoulders falls to the ground and his head drops. His rod falls from his right hand, while his left hand comes up and covers his eyes. A few seconds later, he places his right hand on Mac's left forearm, as if for support. "It's the world I have. It's the one I've chosen to live in. It doesn't much care about me, except when I make a crucial decision or act decisively, and then only for a moment. The Korean War was important only for a few years, and now it's the Forgotten War. The soldiers who fought there are even less regarded. Americans don't want to think about the Korean War, and it hurts. I figure if I work hard enough, and if I stay busy, I won't have to worry about making any sense of this crazy world." The image of a small boy flashes before his eyes, and he retreats behind his stare for a moment before finishing his words to Mac. Walt regains control over his body, and it firms up again. "Don't read so much into me. All Korea taught me was I was neither tough nor brave. War is just a temporary solution to a bigger problem, and not a particularly good solution at that. Things go on in the world that make a person's life pretty insignificant. I know that well."

"No life is insignificant, Walt. You taught me that." Mac narrows his eyes. "Are we going to fish, or are we going to stand here hugging like girls?"

§

Washington calls early the next morning. Before Walt leaves, Bellena reaffirms her decision to move to Buena Vista, to move in with her father. Then she looks at Walt and waits. He asks if the end of October would be a good time for a wedding. Walt drives

Bellena's Mustang back to Platteville, Colorado, to Ft. St. Vrain Nuclear Power Plant, his official job site. Platteville is less than forty miles from metropolitan Denver and over two million people. Yamantov is eight hundred miles from Moscow, nearly a hundred miles from any city of any size. Does it matter? Walt walks around the outer concrete walls of St. Vrain, trailing his hand against those walls. He knows the people who work inside, and he remembers the workers who built it. Good solid people, every one of them.

Five hours later, Walt is back in Washington.

§

In the morning Walt takes a cab from The Watergate to Arlington National Cemetery, to the Memorial Amphitheater, where he stands and stares into the cavern. There is no memorial to the Korean War. His meeting with President Reagan, his advisors, and the Joint Chiefs is an hour and forty-five minutes away. Thirty-four years ago, he stood at the Federal Center in Denver and raised his right hand to get into the Army, to do his part to fight the Cold War. He didn't know it then; he was just running, too young to understand. Now, he does. This month has shaken him to his inner fiber unlike any experience since Korea, maybe even more, but in a different way. Sharing Korea with Bellena forced him back to the beginning of his life's journey, but now he has come here, to the core of the Cold War. He wonders if he should pray. That would be a first in this journey. Maybe he should walk away, not go to the White House. He won't make the decision anyway.

This solitary life that he has meticulously cultivated is what he thought he deserved, and yet now he sees it's been a façade. If the worst occurs, he doesn't want to be alone. He wants Bellena and . . . Walt pauses. He turns and looks back on the gravestones. The war dead. Except for the Hand of Chance, he could be interned here-- the tomb of the unknown dead Korean War kid. But he lived and has journeyed around the world to this place. His life after he died, or nearly died, or should have died. Whatever. He's here. It's come to this. And he doesn't want to be alone any longer.

He turns back to the amphitheater with the Korean War on his face, but he is not hiding this time.  The cavern is simply the stage for solemn ceremonies.  He walks back to the waiting cab, climbs in, and says, "The White House."

# IV

# MOUNTAINS

# CHAPTER 7

*Central Rocky Mountains near Buena Vista, Colorado, April 1986*

Samuel's teeth have not had a cleaning in three years. A lower left molar decided to force him into a visit by going sensitive to both heat and cold. The older, dental assistant is rough, and Samuel's gums are bleeding. The receptionist warned him about her, told him she was good, but the excessive plaque built up over not seeing the dentist regularly would need extra attention. Samuel now knows an additional definition for the word attention. Excruciating pain. Each time the assistant attacks his mouth, Samuel puts the armrests in a death grip. He only releases his grip when she retreats and tells him to spit. Blood swirls into the bowl. Except for the words "open" and "spit," the assistant doesn't speak. At least, thinks Samuel, I don't have to answer questions when the probe and her hand are in my throat. She finishes, pushes her tray off to the side, rings a bell for the dentist, and leaves. The nervousness in Samuel's stomach subsides.

The young dentist, younger than Samuel, studies the chart. "My assistant says you have two cavities. Let me take a look." He's wearing a green bowtie. With his left hand, he pulls Samuel's cheek away from the gum and holds the mouth mirror. Gently and deftly, the dentist pokes Samuel's teeth with the sickle probe. Samuel relaxes his hands on his belly during the procedure. "Let me know if this hurts," and he pushes the probe into the enamel of the left lower molar. Samuel gives out an "unh-huh" that it does. The dentist moves the mirror and probes a tooth on the opposite side. "And this?" "Unh-huh." The dentist removes the two instruments, sets them on the tray, swivels his stool around to the counter, and writes in John Samuels' chart. "Well, Mr. Samuels, you have two cavities that are in need of repair. I'd like to schedule you in soon, maybe next month. I'll give you some pills to alleviate your pain until you come back in. On your way out, meet with the receptionist for another appointment." The dentist doesn't ask for feedback. He stands and leaves the room. A second assistant comes in to take off Samuel's bib and give him the vial of pills. She hands him a small can of dental floss and lowers her head as if to warn him that he needs to use it daily. He doesn't schedule a second appointment.

Outside, Samuel rubs his jaw through his beard. He heads for his car to drive back to Forest City. When he left Hermosillo, Father Tellez switched out cars with him, and now Samuel drives a red Ford sedan. The two men correspond with mail delivered through the Catholic Church. While Samuel is in Buena Vista for the morning, he will stop in at St. Rose, "a congregation of the mountains," to speak with Father Spreewell and give him another letter. The priest will ask, as he always does, when John plans to convert to Catholicism. Through the collaboration of these two Catholic priests, Samuel has returned to Colorado.

Twenty miles southwest of Buena Vista into a crack in the mountains lies Forest City. It is a ghost town for much of the year; during the summer months, about sixty people live in scattered cabins along Chalk Creek, escapees from the Front Range. It is an old gold and silver mining town that flourished in the late-nineteenth century but was mostly shuttered by 1920. A few families stayed, hoping to find a fresh gold vein. A general store survived for another generation, and St. Mary of the Assumption offered mass in the summers until the start of World War II. Then it fell into disrepair and suffered vandalism. Its small cemetery also became dilapidated. Both, however, remain sacred sites but badly in need of repair. Father Tellez wrote to Father Spreewell offering the services of a man in Hermosillo, a conscientious man who needs to live in obscurity.

April Fools' Day, 1986. To Samuel, it seems as though he has achieved his goal of being invisible. Over two years ago, he sought this isolation, but now he wishes he could talk to someone. It could be Barkley or his mom or even Delany. Thank God for his correspondence with Father Tellez. Samuel told him his real name and some of his life. After seventeen months in Hermosillo--Father talked him into staying longer in Mexico than he anticipated--he returned to America, to Colorado. Father continues to offer advice with his naval problems, to encourage him to connect with his family, and to counsel him on the best way to get large, succulent tomatoes. He wants to help Samuel water his garden. When Samuel left Mexico, he turned over much of what he had written to Father Tellez, asked him to keep it just in case, and told him he could read it if he wanted. Father read it all. Samuel isn't writing as much now, but on some nights, he will pump up the kerosene lamp, pull out his red pen, and ask himself what he is seeking. The writing focuses his mind, and the red ink that flows from his hand to the legal pad brings clarity to his journey. He has a difficult trek still ahead of him.

After visiting Father Spreewell, he stops for groceries, a newspaper, a six-pack of beer, and then drives back to Forest City. His cabin rests next to a small creek short of Forest City, surrounded by the pine forest, so the majestic Collegiate peaks can't be seen. The Church owns the cabin and rents or loans it out for its own use. In the summer he can hear his neighbors, but he can't see them. He works each day at restoring the church, a painstakingly, slow process. In the Navy Samuel knew about computers and electricity, not about nails and planes and sandpaper--or boilers. As summer approaches, he will work the cemetery again for part of each day.

In today's letter Father Tellez writes, "You are positive about your Truth, but try to understand the position you are rejecting. Can two opposite things both be true? Get your tomatoes in now. If you plant them in the cemetery, you can water them along with the new grass."

§

Bellena Kramer finishes her power walk, picks up a piece of litter from the gutter in front of the house along with the morning news, and goes inside to have coffee with her dad. Her move has been good: the real estate market is booming in Central Colorado, her dad's cancer is in remission, and her marriage to Walt brings him to her on most weekends. He promises to quit even his position at Ft. St. Vrain soon and retire to the life of odd jobs and sloth. She can't imagine that last part, but she would love to have him around each morning—and go to bed with him every night. Mac warns her to be careful what she wishes for, but she does wish for it.

"Walt called this morning while you were out," yells Mac from his bedroom. "Woke me up. Said to have you call when you got in." It's a little after seven and the days are noticeably longer and warmer. Buena Vista lies in Colorado's banana belt, but winters can still be unpleasant, and the wind through the Arkansas Valley annoys Bellena no end, and the wind in Bueny does blow. She brews coffee, fries four strips of bacon, and puts out a banana for her dad. She makes peanut butter toast and covers it with honey for herself. She dials the wall phone and waits for Walt to pick up.

"Hey, hon, what's up? Beautiful morning up here."

Walt smiles on his end. Bellena exudes confidence and happiness, and with good reasons, he thinks. "Sorry I missed our call last night. The conversion of the plant away from nuclear is taking more persuasion than I thought it would. I had to meet with two guys from the regulatory commission last night, and I didn't get back from Denver until late. It'll happen, but I think I won't be the guy to do the final overseeing on it."

"That's good. You'll get up here sooner. Did you finally get your house listed?"

"Almost. The broker's ready to move on it when I go in and sign off." Walt wishes his wife was selling it, but she's firmly rooted in the mountains now. "Belle, do you know of any motel properties in Bueny or Salida that might be on the market? An old friend of mine has a friend who's interested."

"Not right off hand, but I'll check this morning when I go in. Does it have to be a motel or can it be any small business? Anybody I know?"

"I don't think so. Just a guy from the war. I don't know what his friend does or what the specifics are."

They make small talk. Mac walks into the kitchen, leans into the phone and says hey to Walt, pours himself a coffee, and sits in front of the bacon. Bellena brought in the paper for him and now points out the story about the bombing of the discotheque in Berlin that killed some American soldiers. Her father shakes his head, but she has turned away and doesn't see it. She tells Walt she loves him and will see him soon and then hangs up.

"Is he going to make it up today at all?" asks Mac.

"No. Next weekend for sure though. I think he has more on his mind that just Ft. St. Vrain."

"President Reagan isn't going to be happy about this bombing. He'll respond somewhere when he finds out who's behind it."

"As long as he doesn't ask Walt for advice, he can do what he wants. God, do we need to make war over every incident anywhere in the world?" asks Bellena. "I know you think we need to retaliate or else we'll seem weak, so I'll shut up. Is there anything you need in town today, since I'll be working this morning?"

"No. I'll get out for a walk and maybe start getting the yard in shape. Or I'll drive up to the cabin and see how it wintered."

Bellena smiles at her father. She knows neither of those things will happen. He'll drive over to the golf clubhouse and have a beer with some friends.

§

Samuel no longer follows the news each day, as he once did. He doesn't own a television, gets the paper only when he goes into town for groceries or lumber, and listens to the radio sparingly. He avoids town as much as possible, but he wants a fishing pole like the one he saw at the hardware store two weeks ago. The two creeks near Forest City entice him, and it's not like he doesn't have extra time. What's holding him back is the fishing license. He calculates it's Saturday and that he needs to go into Bueny next Tuesday to meet with Father Spreewell. That would be April eighth. He could buy the pole and fish without a license, and he was never checked in all the times he fished as a kid. Or he could buy the license and add one more piece of evidence that he's John Samuels, caretaker of Catholic cemeteries.

Two suburbans drive up the dirt road, and he recognizes both cars from last summer. Probably just up for the weekend, since both cars are loaded with kids, and schools won't be out for another month. He pulls a sweatshirt from the rack by the front door, puts on his key chain, dons a baseball cap, and heads out for St. Mary, a few hundred yards up the road. Not St. Mary's the possessive, but St. Mary. He asked Father Tellez about that in a letter, but the priest couldn't answer the question. He laughs. Not Samuel Church, but Samuel's Church. He gets that. Today's job includes clearing out the last couple of broken pews and shoring up the floor under them. Thank God for carpentry books. His windows and doors are holding up, and Father Spreewell blessed him for his expertise. If the priest only knew how ignorant he was about jambs and such, he probably wouldn't have taken him in a year ago.

Last night, the spirit tried to communicate again after several months of calm. It doesn't seem like Greg, even though Father Tellez asked if it could be, and Samuel wanted it to be. I'm angry, thinks Samuel, but she's grieving or sad or lost. She has a multitude of personalities. None of those emotions are mine! Anger and guilt, these are my emotions. One thing about Forest City, there are stars and quiet at night. Crystal clear nights where every star in the universe comes out; Samuel even thought he saw Halley's Comet. That's when the spirit stirred. She does seem to have a calming effect on him, but now he will wonder all day. Samuel needs to talk to her; he needs to talk whether she can understand him or not. She has earned this.

A truck drives up behind him and turns off on the Tazwell Creek road that goes to the four-acre pond. At St. Mary the first order of business is to find his hammer. He was so frustrated Friday when the nails holding the pews kept breaking that he tossed his hammer toward the back corner of the church and went back to the cabin. He cooked a can of beef stew and then sat on the porch with a bottle of bourbon. I won't do that again, he vows. Childish. The hammer stands propped against the wall, just like someone put it there for him to find and start working on the church. Samuel has to admit this has been a good job—and so different from his previous life. With the hammer and a new pry bar, the nails offer less resistance, and the morning passes quickly.

The days in April pass quickly; May will arrive soon.

§

Pyotr likes school in America and has grasped English rapidly. His mother began teaching him English as a baby, when Ursula gave birth to him in Canada. Babu's skills are not as good, and she often asks him to translate, especially in stores. She comprehends English fairly well; years of learning English for her science studies is serving her well in America, but she hesitates to speak it, even at her job with the dentist. Her accent is obvious, and she is self-conscious about it. When she gets nervous or excited, she omits the English articles, pronounces "th" sounds with a "z," and substitutes "ds" at the ends of words with a "t." Pyotr's second grade teacher is young and pretty, and she constantly asks him about his life in the Soviet Union. He tells her that he lived near mountains there too. She knows he lives with his grandmother, but doesn't quite understand the circumstances, and Pyotr can't explain it to her. Olga doesn't try. Pyotr walks to school each morning and back to the house in the afternoon, and he finally feels like they won't be moving before the school year ends. Babu has a job, and she no longer writes so many letters back home. She says maybe they aren't meant to find his father, but Pyotr sure looks for someone. It never seems to her as if they are looking for the same man. Pyotr often stops by the high school fields on the way home and watches the baseball team practice. Grampar would like baseball, not so much as hockey, but he would like it. It's a game that allows spectators to talk easily between the action, and Grampar would like that. Babu signed Pyotr up for the baseball league for little kids, and now practices have begun. She bought him a baseball mitt at the hardware store, along with a ball and a bat. It's not difficult to hit the ball when Babu tosses it, but he doesn't think he could hit the one thrown by the high school pitchers. He wants to try though.

Olga longs to return to Pechora and her father. She misses them both, and her memories of Ursula are clouded, harder to form clearly in America. She and Pyotr landed in Toronto, traveled to New York and D.C., and promptly got lost. She knew immediately that Melor could not be found, but Pyotr didn't want to give up and go home. He looked at every man he met, studied him, and never gave in. He has pushed Olga west to Colorado: "He lives in the mountains, Babu." Babu knows better, and she has promised Pyotr they won't give up, but she doesn't know how to end this fruitless search for his father. She doesn't know how to go home, when to go home. Over dinner she asked Pyotr if he wanted to go home, and he told her "Pretty soon, I'll let you know." He was so sincere, so cute, and he had his mother's twinkle, so Olga could do nothing but smile and hug him.

§

"You need a name. You've sat in my gut for all this time riding on the winds with me, and I've never called you anything except *You.* So today, while I work on these front steps, we're going to talk and come up with a name. I don't have my real one anymore, so you don't have to have your real one either." Samuel takes off his shirt and lays it over a pew too broken to restore. He sips water from his jug and begins to pry nails from the steps. He swears frequently over the number of nails used in the construction of this old church. "You're a tough one; you haven't deserted me through all of this. We've traveled a lot of miles, and you haven't complained. You've let me do all the whining. My guess is you came from the Seattle area, since that's where you joined on, but maybe spirits don't have hometowns." Samuel gets the crowbar for some of the more diffi-cult, rusted spikes. The sweat glistens on his muscled back and his brown hair is matted. "Mary's out, since that's what I call this place. Besides, you deserve something more fitting a fellow traveler. I've mostly assumed you are a woman, but if you're not and you have a girl's name, you might be pissed at me. Maybe I'll come up with a non-gender name, like Chris or something." Samuel laughs. "Feel free to jump in for a little guidance. Not like I need any of that in my life." He takes great care so not to splinter the two-by-sixes as he pulls the nails. He decided when he first started on the restoration that he would be slow and meticulous, that time was not an issue. He's been given an open account at the hardware store for lumber and supplies, but he wants to avoid using it unnecessarily. The Church in Rome may have lots of money, but St. Mary of Forest City sure doesn't.

"How about a city name? Seattle? That's non-gender. You liked Hermosillo, didn't you? We could come up with a Mexican name. I had an Indian girlfriend once, and we made up names for ourselves back in high school. Can't remember what they were though." Samuel realizes he's talking aloud and wonders if he's becoming delusional. "See, now this is why you need a name. If I'm just talking to myself, I might be crazy, but if I'm talking to you, then it's okay." He finishes removing all the boards from the porch, about sixty planks, and figures he'll have to build a new foundation for the porch. He still has the steps to remove, but he'll get to those after lunch. He puts his shirt back on, grabs his cooler, and sits on the broken pew for another peanut-butter sandwich.

St. Mary sits on open acreage, closer to the road than Samuel's cabin, and offers spectacular vistas of Mt. Princeton. The aspen have begun to leaf out, and Samuel tries to remember if late April is the normal time. "Maybe an animal name or a bird. Crow? Deer? No, that's too much like my old one. Bear?" He mulls on that while he chews. A tiny creek, Grizzly Creek, runs on the opposite side of the road and flows into Chalk Creek a mile down the path. A few cars pass on the dirt road in front of the church, and a few hands have extended out of the windows to wave. None stop to ask directions or take pictures of St. Mary. He promises to restore the old church to elegance so tourists will stop for photos. It has a nice skeleton, certainly not extravagant, but nice. It needs a bell for its tower, but that will be the final touch, and he might not be around for that.

Bear. Hey Bear. Bear. He says it out loud. "Bear." The spirit doesn't protest. "I don't see you as big as me, so how about Baby Bear? Think it over and let me know if that's okay. I'll use it this afternoon too." He finishes lunch and starts back on the steps. He calculates that he can decrease the size of the landing, and there will be enough boards to make a new foundation. He may need to get a dozen or so new ones, but most of the hundred-year-old ones have weathered well. He sketches the foundation's layout, so he can duplicate it later. When the entire porch has been dismantled, he takes his square and marks the boards in order to cut off the frayed ends. Every board will need some trimming; that will take some time, but it will determine the size of the porch when he reconstructs it. He'll saw tomorrow. He puts his tools in the church before deciding to walk through the trees on the trail to his cabin. "Come on, Baby Bear, let's head back."

§

Baby Bear sticks.

More and more cars pass by St. Mary on their way to St. Elmo. Several of them stop to ask something—directions, the age of the church, will the general store be open, are there fish in the creeks— and it has slowed Samuel's work, so he decides to stop early this afternoon and hike up the slopes of Mt. Princeton. He won't get above timberline, but he'll follow Tazwell Creek as far as the melted snow will allow. Runoff water from those snows follows the trail, making footing a bit slippery. At various spots he pauses to take in the views—the Collegiate peaks, the Arkansas Valley, the fishing pond near his cabin, and even St. Mary. The incline isn't steep, a hike rather than a climb. Samuel remembers the first line from an old camp song, "I love the mountains, I love the rolling hills." He can't recall the rest, but he hums the tune as he walks, and a calm settles over him. He is at home in mountains; he missed them when he served. He pauses at an open spot for water and to gaze at Mt. Princeton. "What do you think, Baby Bear? Beautiful, huh." He removes his cap and wipes his brow. Suddenly, he is struck in his gut and hurled to the ground.

§

Darkness has fallen by the time Samuel regains consciousness;

the trail will be difficult to traverse. He hurts and it's cold. What the hell happened? He sits and tries to clear his head, tries to remember who came up on him. He must have been waiting for him. Samuel looks around to see where the guy could have been hiding. Maybe behind the stand of trees off to his right or behind the rock where he now sits. Why just the one punch? Was there just one? It doesn't matter right now. What matters is that he gets back to the cabin, or at least the church. He'll have to be careful along the trail. He finds a walking stick to swing in front as he walks. He hears voices coming from Forest City, and he walks cautiously toward them. He stumbles and falls, but the trail is not steep, so he doesn't roll any. He cuts the palm of his left hand. He picks up his stick and starts down again. Through the trees he sees a light where he thinks St. Mary should be. Wasn't there a clearing after the first part of the trail when he started up this afternoon? The light illuminates a dozen or so people, and he moves toward them, but then stops. What will he tell the gathering? A ragged, bearded, thirty-six-year-old man out this late? He might scare them, or it might raise questions to the point where they could call the sheriff. Samuel veers off and tries to make out the outline of the church. With no moon to help him, he moves slowly, trying not to make any noise that would attract attention.

Finally, he sees the church. Just as he gets to the cemetery, a car drives past in front of the church. Samuel decides to move through the headstones toward the back of St. Mary and go in the sacristy door. He crawls on his hands and knees so he can feel the markers. He's worked the cemetery so many times he can almost tell whose grave he's crawling over, at least those who have kept their identity. He gets to the back door and reaches up to open it. He smiles at the ease with which it opens. Damn good repair work, he thinks. Inside, he decides to stay for the night. It will be cold, and he won't be able to use the lights, but at least he now has his water jug, so he can get a drink and wash off his hand. He'll sleep and go back to the cabin when the sun comes up. So much for being invisible, for being safe. The circle of time and events is tightening, and while Samuel no longer believes in time anymore, another does and searches for him.

The cut on his hand is deeper than he thought. He feels for a rag to wrap around it. He slides up against the north wall and breathes deeply. For the first time since he left Washington, he's hurt himself physically and may need medical attention. He won't know until tomorrow. His eyes close on him and his head falls to one side. A noise startles him, which he quickly determines to be a small animal under the floor. But he's awake again, and his mind goes to Baby Bear. The punch landed right where she resides.

"Baby Bear. You okay?" He lifts his shirt and lays his right hand over his belly. He waits for an answer, for any movement. He remembers something Delany once told him. "When we're apart, put your hand on your tummy, which I call your yellow, and no matter how far away I am, I'll be there with you." She lifted her shirt, took his hand, and placed his hand on her tummy. It was warm and her eyes were wide open. Her belly warmed his hand. Now, his hand feels that warmth.

§

Samuel senses the sunrise before it begins. He gets up, goes out the back door, and quickly makes it to his cabin. Inside, he examines his wounds. The cut on his hand will need stitches, but no bruising shows on his belly, and the other scrapes can be washed out. In his fatigue during the night, he decided it wasn't a person who hit him, but maybe an animal charged him. The absence of a bruise confuses him. In the kitchen he pours a glass of orange juice, gets the box of cereal, and brews coffee. After breakfast he showers. It will be okay to tell the doctor that he fell on a hike, he thinks. Maybe he ought to see Father Spreewell and let him know. Besides, he can recommend a doctor, just as he did a dentist. He decides to see Father Spreewell and let him work his local magic on this Saturday.

# Chapter 8

*Chernobyl, Ukraine, Soviet Union, April 1986*

Walt gets his call on Monday morning, April 28, at his office in Platteville before he's had his coffee. A Soviet nuclear power station in the Ukraine has had an accident two days earlier and released radioactive contamination into the atmosphere. The Soviets grudgingly reported it only after Sweden and Finland detected radiation and determined that it had come from the Soviet Union. TASS conceals the scale of the accident, as always, but Walt knows it must be bad if the radioactivity can be detected in Scandinavia. He also knows that Soviet reactors don't have containment covers to prevent radiation from escaping in case of a meltdown. Chernobyl. It was built in the late-Sixties, if he remembers correctly, and started up in the Seventies. Near Kiev. The Soviets built a new city just to house the workers. He searches his mind to recall the name. Prypiat: a nuclear city. Have evacuations started? "Walt, we may need your help on this one."

No, he thinks silently, it's too late for that. The Cold War started when I was a boy, and the rush to build nuclear power stations and nuclear weapons occurred without my permission. What can I do anyway? The accident has happened, and the poison released. Put the fire out anyway you can and then cap it. Pour as much cement over the reactor as you can manufacture and do it now. The workers who do this will die, either immediately or within a few years. He tells the voice to get him a ticket to D.C., and he'll be there. He hangs up the phone and gets his coffee. He walks over to Jim Borgardt's office to tell him the news, the very bad news. Jim will soon be the new boss at Ft. St. Vrain, and he'll have to answer the questions from the press that will certainly arise in the wake of a new nuclear accident. Better Jim than me; he handles the press with grace. The Soviet press will delay and downplay the accident. The U.S. press will report the worst-case scenario given to them by the Reagan Administration to gain a Cold War public relations advantage.

Borgardt thinks along the same lines as Walt. He asks, "How will this compare to Three Mile Island or Yamantov?"

"I don't think we can compare them. We were able to contain Three Mile Island, and Yamantov has always been clouded in secrecy. Besides, it was so isolated that it wasn't a threat to civilians. This one could be a disaster, so close to Kiev and central Russia. They've got to get the fire out." Secrecy, thinks Walt. What the world doesn't know.

The phone rings in Borgardt's office. The Nuclear Regulatory Agency is just now getting the information and warns Jim to get ready for a barrage of questions from the local press. He hangs up and looks puzzled. "How do you get this information before the NRA, Walt? You must know some mighty important people."

Walt just raises his eyebrows. "Oh, you know, the President calls me daily just to chat."

The two men go over all the details of Ft. St. Vrain's safety system, do a quick comparison of Chernobyl's specifics with their own, and then call a meeting with the operators at their plant.

Walt gets an update just before noon. Evacuations have begun in Prypiat; fifty thousand people as fast as buses can be arranged, strictly as a precautionary move reports TASS. The U.S. should have immediately evacuated the residents around Three Mile Island back in '79 but didn't want to alarm anyone. Screw that, he says to himself. Voluntary evacuation of pregnant women and school kids! The voice on the phone tells him he will leave out of Warren Air Force base in Cheyenne, Wyoming, at three. Walt tells Borgardt the latest, then he leaves to pack a few things and drive to Cheyenne, an hour up the road. Just enough time to call Bellena. He's glad for the past weekend with her and Mac. That's where he needs to be, Buena Vista, not D.C.

§

The *NY Times* reports on Chernobyl on Tuesday, and the story is quickly picked up by the rest of America's media. Some newspapers report up to 25,000 deaths buried in mass graves, although cautious articles estimate only 2,000 casualties. The Soviets say only two people have died. Access to Chernobyl, Prypiat, and even Kiev is restricted, but Walt knows the morality tale that pits the United States versus the Evil Empire will be ramped up again. He wishes the manipulation by the Administration would stop, especially since the relationship between Reagan and Gorbachev seems to be improving relations between their two countries.

Walt warns Bellena and Mac not to believe initial reports about the casualties of Chernobyl's accident. Most deaths in such an event occur years later when cancer takes over. Still, Walt doesn't know how dangerous the Chernobyl meltdown is, and he won't be consulted by the Soviet nuclear scientist on how to deal with it. He's been flown to D.C. simply to be one of several experts capable of interpreting new information for politicians and journalists, all of whom will swallow the American Cold War position. Walt understands, and he certainly knows the U.S. is more honest than the Soviets have been throughout the conflict. Both of them can tell huge lies, however, and keep even larger secrets. As can I, he says to himself, but he worries Chernobyl will trigger a response from the invisible man, and Walt can't allow that to happen. He leaves the briefing room to find a telephone, a secure line.

§

"Oh God, not again!" gasps Olga, when she hears the TV newsman report about Chernobyl. She brings her hands to her face and sucks in a breath. Pyotr is at baseball practice, and she is home alone. She understands most of what is said, but her English skills can't keep up with the technical jargon. When the news ends, she calls Dr. Kinkade. "Tell me everything, so I can understand. I have an old friend who lives in Kiev, and they showed a map of the radiation that will blow over my home in Komi." She speaks rapidly. The dentist tries to explain without including the death figures, but Olga sees through his compassion.

"Olga, try to relax. This accident was hundreds of miles from Pechora, maybe thousands, and we don't have any reliable facts. Even the Soviet government would tell us if it were a complete meltdown. No one can keep that deep of a secret."

"No! No, they will try. They did once before. I was thirty miles away from the nuclear reactor at Yamantov when it exploded, and no one knows it. My government can keep a secret. The world must demand answers." The dentist has never heard of Yamantov. "I must go get Pyotr." The dentist cautions Olga not to scare him.

Pyotr talks only about baseball: strikes and balls, pop-ups, singles, doubles, and homeruns, pitchers and catchers, infielders and outfielders, and how many hits he had. The coach showed them how to roll their socks under their pants to hold them up allowing the stirrups to show best. His teammates rolled the bill of his cap around a baseball to get the right fold. He goes on and on. Olga decides not to say anything about this place called Chernobyl. Maybe the dentist is correct. Wait for more information. But inside she shudders; she just has a feeling. She listens and cooks dinner.

Finally, Pyotr stops talking about baseball and asks her, "Was it close to Grampar, Babu?"

He has done it again, and Olga shakes violently. How can he know? She rolls her lips inward and bites on them. Tears form at the back of her eyes and then rush to the corners near her nose.

"It's not the same thing, Babu. There was no whiteness." Pyotr's eyes lock onto his grandmother's with such pull, as if it is he who must reassure her. "Soon, we will be able to go home to Grampar. Not yet, but soon." He cocks his head and smiles at her. "He will be all right, Babu."

Olga can barely speak, but she manages to swallow and ask, "When did you know?"

"I felt it when it happened. People are moving today. It will be all right. You'll see." Again, he smiles at his Babu. "Let's go play."

§

In the next days, Pyotr says nothing, but Olga follows the news as closely as she can. It seems to her as if the Soviets are playing a contest with the Americans. The Cold War has been turned inside out, but why can't there be a truce for this accident? Why can't America offer help? Is there no one in America who knows how to help? Why can't my country ask for help? While Pyotr attends school, she works, but more silently than before. An anger grows toward her patients, these Americans. They don't seem to care. An elderly man, a big man, asks her why she came to the United States, and she has no answer anymore. How can she explain such a complicated question? She answers curtly, "Like everyone else." She turns away and rings the bell and leaves the room.

The young dentist tries to help, with pats on her shoulder, with encouraging news from the television, with questions about Pyotr. He only hurts her with his optimistic ignorance. She remembers her practice back in Pechora when she could make idle chatter to her patients. Her world no longer has room for ignorance. She longs to return home.

§

"Walt, the white station wagon is down here in Hermosillo. A local priest here says the church bought it but doesn't have any records about who sold it to them. I'm not sure I believe him. He seems a little smug. He asked me who I was looking for. Nobody recognizes the picture. I'm kind of at a dead end. I've looked at every thirty-six-year-old man that hangs around this church, and none of them could be him."

"Come on back. He's not in Mexico anymore, if he ever was. My guess is he's been gone from there for quite some time. He's not the type to live in another country for the rest of his life." Walt hangs up the phone and hides behind his Korean War stare. Sam Elkington has returned to the states, maybe to Washington, but probably in Colorado. But where? I'll need to talk to the Catholic priest myself.

§

Father Spreewell drives up to St. Mary on Thursday to check on Samuel's health and to bring a newspaper and some supplies. Despite his bandaged hand, he has been able to complete the porch, including the varnish. Now, he is standing on a scaffold, painting the front of the church when the Father pulls up.

"I recall the doctor saying something about taking the week off and recovering. Isn't that what you heard, John?" His black cassock almost touches the ground as he walks closer.

Samuel banters back. "A polite observer might have commented on how nice the porch looks."

Father puts a sack down next to Samuel's shirt. "I brought you some fruit and some treats. Father Tellez told me he could get you to reveal secrets if he fed you cookies. Any truth to that?" A car honks as it passes, and Father waves.

Samuel climbs down and wipes his brow. "Secrets? Don't you hear enough of them from your regular parishioners?" He looks into the sack and smiles. "Oranges. Great protection against scurvy. Thanks. The hand's doing fine, and I don't sit still well. Did Father Tellez tell you that?"

Father hands Samuel another letter from his Mexican counterpart. "He told me a lot about you, but said you were an enigma. He said there was a man down there looking for you." Father looks for a reaction but gets none. "John isn't your real name, is it, son?"

Samuel purses his lips in a half-smile. "How old are you, Father?"

"Fifty-seven."

"I'm thirty-six now and have been going by John Samuels for nearly two and a half years. Only Father Tellez knows my real name or what I did before I left for Mexico. I suspect he hasn't told you any of my secrets. He's a man of his word, a credit to the church."

"Yes, he is."

"Without reading this letter, I think I know what it says. I told him I was thinking about turning myself in, to face up to my demons, to stop being John Samuels. He'll tell me that it's time, that he'll come up here to be with me when I go in, and that he's praying for me. But he'll also say if I'm not sure yet, then to wait.

I wrote down my story, at least as I perceived it that first year, but now it's not quite the same. Oh, the facts are accurate no matter how you perceive things, but perception is key. I'm going to finish this part of the church, and then I'm going looking for some people. I'll surprise them, pop in to say hi, and then head out. I'll need to be careful, but it's time I do that. There have been people looking for me for all the time I've been on the lam, but they won't find me until I want them to." Samuel pauses. "At least, I don't think they will."

"Like my friend in Hermosillo, I'll stand with you too. I've never seen a man work so hard as you. You ask for nothing, live your life like a monk, and see beyond each day. I don't know what you seek or what crime you've committed, but I can tell you that when you're gone from here, St. Mary will mark that you passed through here. If you stay to see its completion, I'll be glad. If you don't, I'll hire a crew to finish it up. You've shown me what can live in the mountains, what can be reborn in the mountains. Your work has been impressive, John."

"Thanks, Father. You can call me Sam. It's time I start ending that lie."

§

After dinner at the cabin, Samuel reads the newspaper the Father left him at the church. Nearly a week after it occurred, he learns of the Chernobyl nuclear accident, which happened on the day he hiked Mt. Princeton. His body contracts, and a guttural moan arises. Baby Bear stirs, but he ignores her. He holds his head with both hands and bites his lower lip. The story says Chernobyl is near large population centers. It can't be the same, can it? He leans forward on the couch, and a single image forms. He sees Greg Benson hanging from the scaffold, but he hears Father Tellez's prayers for the dead.

§

Ft. St. Vrain. Chernobyl. Sam Elkington. The NEA. Walt asked for it all, but tonight he's glad to be back in Buena Vista with

Bellena and her father. Mac's home has become Walt's refuge, even if just the weekends. He arrives late, but Bellena's body makes him forget his fatigue. When they finish making love, they stay awake and talk. "I'm pregnant." She pauses. "And, no, you're not too old to be a daddy." It isn't what first comes to his mind. He stares stupidly at Bellena, but she simply smiles and pulls his face into her breasts.

In the morning they sit at the breakfast table giddy in anticipation of telling Mac. They decided last night to have Walt tell him. "Well, Grampa, what's on the agenda this morning? Mac misses the point, since he has a grandson by his son who lives in Oklahoma. Mac says he'd like to drive up to the cabin and fix the stoop, but aside from that, not much of anything. Walt asks him if there's any baby furniture in the garage that he could get at. Mac looks confused. Bellena gets up and walks behind her dad, leans over, and throws her arms around his shoulders and kisses his cheek from behind. She whispers the same words to him that she whispered to Walt the night before. "I'm pregnant." Mac smiles broadly to Walt and tilts his head into Bellena's soft cheek. "Well, I'll be damned."

They all drive up to the cabin after breakfast. Mac tells Walt that the old church at Forest City is being renovated and looks pretty good. "If I were Catholic, maybe you could bury me there." It sits close to his cabin and favorite fishing hole, even though he and Bellena have talked about selling it, since it mostly goes unused. Small talk. Bellena tells Walt about a motel for sale about five miles south of Bueny, but way over-priced. Walt hasn't heard any new information about the person who was interested. Mac wonders if becoming a father might speed Walt's retirement from Ft. St. Vrain and his life of solving the world's problems. Walt says he might have to find a new job to earn enough money for the child's college education. Bellena says she has that covered. Mac beams, Bellena glows, and Walt churns.

Chernobyl will be handled by the Soviets without foreign help. Walt contacted his counterpart in Moscow but was curtly rebuffed. He and Mac work on the stoop. It's old and needs to be replaced. Mac asks about Chernobyl and then tells Walt of an encounter with a Soviet woman in town. Her son couldn't stop staring at him.

"What's a Russian family doing in Colorado?" asks Walt.

"She didn't say. I just asked if she was lost or something and needed directions. I had the feeling her English wasn't too good. She works as a dental assistant for Dr. Kinkade, the new guy who took over for Dr. Jack when he retired. The office uses more high-tech stuff now."

"What about the boy?"

"Handsome. Penetrating eyes, but not in a foreboding sense. More like," Mac pauses to think of a word. Bellena comes outside and sits on the bench. "More like optimistic eyes, as if he has good news that he wants to share but can't because his mom might disapprove."

"Was he afraid of her?" asks Bellena.

"No. Maybe he was taught not to be so open with strangers. Had a feeling about him though."

"A feeling?" asks Bellena.

"You never had a feeling about others?" says Mac sarcastically.

"All the time. I can sense the moods of my prospective buyers, and I'm sure that's why my husband here is so successful in his profession."

Mac laughs. "Whatever that profession is."

Walt smiles a smile that hides his true thoughts. He has a feeling.

§

A hummingbird crashes into Olga's kitchen window and falls motionless to the deck. She calls to Pyotr who runs out and gently scoops the tiny bird into his hands. He strokes its head and back for several minutes and then puts it into a flowerpot in the shade. Pyotr goes back to his play, but Olga watches the bird. He has done this before, and like before, the small bird eventually flies away.

# Chapter 9

*Colorado, early May 1986*

Barkley misses his friend. Henry has been away for the better part of April, and now May has arrived with its abundance of yard work that he can't do alone. The snow melted, and leaves are developing on the branches of the fallen cottonwood in his back yard. Damn Henry! He calls, but won't tell me where he is or what he's doing? Deflects all questions back on me. Well, at least Lizzie has been responsive, and Delany comes by on her way to Salida and Bueny. Barkley gets up slowly from the kitchen table to answer the knock at the door.

"Your welcome sign is down, Bark."

Barkley smiles a huge grin and extends his big right hand. "Where the hell have you been, son? Come in." His house has not changed, except there are more African violets. "Still carrying around the spirit?"

"Oh, yeah. I don't go anywhere without her." He pats his belly. "Barkley, I need to ask you something. Was it you who gave out some information on where I might have gone when I went AWOL?" Sam doesn't wait for a response. "I think someone from Ouray followed me out of town and then told someone else which direction I was headed." He has asked the question in a non-accusatory manner, but he is direct, and Barkley gets the message.

"You seem to be a little more sure of yourself this time. Any more poetry?" A rhetorical question. "Wasn't me, but after you left, you became pretty popular for a few months. Couple of guys in Navy uniforms stopped by to ask about you. Then, not too long after that, a fellow was asking questions around town. Most important, your old girlfriend stopped in, about a week after you left, if my old brain remembers right. She's stopped by pretty frequently since. I think she's taken a liking to me." Barkley smiles at that. "You okay, son?"

Samuel nods. Hmm. Delany. That surprises him. His eyes stay focused on Barkley. "Was the civilian guy about my height—and good looking like me?" The question breaks the little tension that existed.

The old man shakes his head. "I can't remember. Hell, that was a lifetime ago. I can't even remember if I took a crap two hours ago. I forget things sooner. Have you got time for a coffee?" Sam nods and they move into the kitchen. Barkley taps a glass picture frame just inside the kitchen to draw Sam's attention to it. It's the poem he wrote about the half-naked old man. "You need to sign it sometime." He pours two cups, and they sit at the table.

"You look good, Barkley, real good." It's small talk to become comfortable again. "How's Lizzie?" Barkley tells him that they still talk by phone? "You telling me the truth, or is this just bullshit from a previous era?"

"The truth," swears Barkley. "We've moved past the time of hurt and bluster and reconciled into a warm, albeit distant, friendship." For the first time, Barkley calls Lizzie him. "He's a poet, although he writes a tad more than you. I read him your poem, and he liked it a lot. You know who else likes it? Delany. She never saw this part of you. I think she drops by just to talk about you. She's a grown woman now. How long were the two of you together, son?"

"Oh, shit, let's see. A couple of years in high school, on and off through college, and two years, I think, while I was in the Navy. Eight years or so, maybe." Barkley fills Sam in on the details of Delany's current life that he remembers. Sam slides his chair away from the table and crosses his legs. "It might be interesting to talk with her again, but my current predicament kind of precludes that."

"And that 'predicament' is what exactly?"

"Glad to see you haven't lost your curiosity any as you've aged. I'm not considered AWOL any longer; I'm a deserter. If they catch me, I'm looking at a long jail term." He lets that sit on Barkley's tongue for a moment. "Henry still hanging around?"

"Mostly. He's gone somewhere just now. Never tells me where or when, but he'll leave a message either on my phone or under the door and be gone. Old men do strange things. I think he may have a girlfriend."

"Have you seen Arnold around?" asks Sam.

"Not for a few years, but then, I never did notice him when he was here. He could still be up in Ridgeway, and I'd never know." Barkley understands what his young friend wants and answers his questions as they are asked. There are more. In time they end, and he asks, "Are you ever going to be able to sit around for a coffee without looking over your shoulder?"

Sam shakes his head. "Probably not, Bark, probably not." He pauses. "At least not around here. Absolute silence settles over them for several minutes, and then Sam goes on. "I met a priest on my travels who's helped me a lot. We keep in touch. Maybe someday I'll be able to return to his church and be safe there. There's no guarantee I won't slip up here and get caught. Each day, I'm careful, but when a number of days go by, the odds aren't in my favor."

"Why not just go back to this priest now?"

"That, my old friend, is the million-dollar question. I'm here for a reason, and when I figure out what that reason is, it'll tell me which direction to head next. I need be here. This may sound like crazy talk, but I don't have any alternatives really. That's crazy to me because I've never believed in fate or destiny. Make a choice and move on was my belief, but I'm here for a reason, and I'll see it through. I do know that I'm not here to be caught and thrown in the brig though."

There is an understanding between the two men.

"What can I do for you, Sam?"

The younger man stares into the older man's eyes. "Without asking why, I want you to tell Henry I was here, but not for a couple of days. Delany is another matter. I can't see her now, so I don't know what good it would do to tell her I was here, but if it comes up and you think she can handle it, go ahead. The Navy won't be the ones to find me. I'm lost to them. It's that other guy. I want to meet with him, but on my terms, on my turf. He needs something from me, but I'm not sure what it is, or even if all this is connected."

"I didn't hear you drive up."

"I walked the last few blocks over here. I've seen enough movies to know I can't just drive up to your door." Sam smiles and gets up. "Gotta go—for now. Maybe I'll call, but no guarantees." They walk to the front door and shake hands. "You can tell Delany I said hi, and that I still have her rock."

"I already told her that."

$

Olga sits alone on the wooden bleachers watching Pyotr and his team. He has improved rapidly and been promoted from right field to second base. She didn't know it was a promotion, but two older men watching the practice comment on his improvement and how he has "solidified" the infield. She likes watching these practices every afternoon after school and on Saturday mornings. Here, there is only the sport, and the rest of the world be damned. Games will begin in a week. A coach hits ground balls to the infielders who throw them to the first baseman. A bond has developed among the kids and their coaches, three older boys really, maybe in their early twenties. On this Saturday morning, there are a dozen parents watching, whereas on the weekdays, only two or three others watch.

Pyotr fields several balls cleanly and makes good throws to another player before a "grounder" bounces up and hits his chin. Olga stands protectively, but then sits quickly. He's a boy and will be all right. She can't protect his every move. He never looks to her during practices; he is intent on learning his new trade. She remembers another time when she moved to protect him.

"Excuse me," says the older man sitting nearby. "Is that your boy playing second?"

After a start she smiles. "My grandson is there." Olga doesn't know where second base is located, so she points to Pyotr.

The man feigns great surprise, and Olga understands the compliment on her youthful looks. "He's a natural. He has soft hands and a good arm." She wonders what soft hands has to do with anything about baseball. "It's good you support him every day but stay quiet during the practices."

"I have never played before." She realizes what she has just said and corrects herself. "I mean I have never seen baseball before, and I am learning too. I could say nothing to help him." She stretches out her words, saying each syllable precisely.

The man extends his hand but doesn't give his name. "You don't remember me, but I spoke briefly with you at the dentist's office a while back." Olga vaguely recognizes him. "If I can help explain this game, don't hesitate to ask. Baseball grows on you."

"We are not from your country; hockey is our game. Maybe Pyotr has some abilities from that game to help him with this one. Is that possible?" In her time in America, she has not let down her guard and talked casually with an American. Like most Russians of her generation, Olga believes Americans dislike and fear her country. She has seen it on their faces during these past months, so she avoids mentioning its name when she can avoid it.

The older man chats and the grandmother listens, while Pyotr repeats the action of catch and throw, over and over. Finally, he takes his turn at bat. He sprays line drives to each side of the field, the solid ping sound echoing around the park. The man sits erect with his arms folded and continually nods his head in approval. "I think he'll bat in the first or second slot in the lineup once the games begin. He makes solid contact and can move the runners up." Olga has no idea what that means, but she imagines it is a positive sign. Finally, Pyotr bunts three pitches and goes back into the field for the rest of practice. Olga longs to return to Pechora, but she will wait until the baseball season ends.

The old man stands and extends his hand again. "My name is Mac, short for McElroy. My friend here is Arnie. I guess I'll be seeing you here a lot. You have a fine boy out there." Olga remains seated and nods.

§

Life is not good for Olga; only Pyotr gives her any focus. She sits on the porch with her vodka and stares into the night sky. So tired, so alone, so lost. She pulls the blanket up from her lap to her shoulders. I came in search of a man who bore my daughter a child, but who means nothing to me. Melor. I can barely even remember his last name, and it won't be the same anymore anyway. The mountain range here in Buena Vista runs north to south, so the sky is open to the north, as does her porch. This could be a nice little town, but it is not her town. Soft noises come to her from across the yard, and she makes out the forms of four deer. She sips her vodka. This journey, she thinks, began with the shooting of The Great One. He slumped to the ground in slow motion before her eyes; died with Pyotr's hand on his flank. She remembers now. Pyotr reacted to the gunshot, to the blast, but returned immediately to the reindeer. He knew The Great One had a moment between life and death, and Pyotr seized the life. Then came the whiteness, and she and Pyotr survived, saved by the cave, while the hunter died. Where is her cave now?

The screen door opens behind her, and Pyotr walks out in his pajamas. He says nothing, but climbs into her lap. He is so much bigger than he was when she carried him on her back away from the cave. He takes the glass from her hand and sips the vodka. He coughs and hands it back. They sit in silence. Eventually, he asks what time is it in Pechora where Grampar still lives. Around eight in the morning, but he probably hasn't gotten out of bed yet.

"Do you think he misses us?" Alone, they speak Russian.

"With all his heart. He will be very happy when we return."

Pyotr removes his hand from under the blanket and points up the valley. "The Big Dipper."

"You remember."

"I remember everything."

Pyotr falls asleep, and Olga carries him to bed. In her bed she dreams about her home. All her dreams end in whiteness where no image is clear, and all sounds are muffled. She waits for the whiteness to lift, but she wakes to the blackness of the night and its silence. She longs for color in her dreams again. She gets up and checks on Pyotr, who hasn't moved. She sits on the edge of his bed trying to understand. And cries again for Ursula.

§

It's an old gold mine, probably from the 1880s. When he found it in October, Samuel explored it to a depth of about eighty feet. He determined it was unsafe at any level, so he built a wire cage around the opening and painted no trespassing signs, danger. Once a week or so, however, he goes into the mine and shores up more of the walls. St. Mary holds his passion, but the mine is his hobby, a diversion, and it offers a plan. He is comfortable in the mine, just as he was comfortable in the skin of the submarine at great depths. There are some ore car rails in the mine at the entrance, although most are missing. Forest City has a dilapidated depot, and Sam wonders if the rails of the two were somehow linked. Many of the old mines had an auxiliary opening far from the main opening, but he hasn't found one for this mine.

Tuesdays seem to see less traffic to Forest City than the other days, so today Sam decides to walk from the mine to the depot along a path he thinks may have been that link. The mine lies about equidistant to the church and the depot, which are separated by about a quarter of a mile, the church being closer to his cabin, which sits just in the trees on the road to Buena Vista. There are hills and a gulley to Forest City. He thinks a rail line from the mine would have been laid on level ground, so he walks along a path that heads west first. There are several alternatives on the way, each posing a question for Sam. Trees have grown along the route he has chosen, but he stays to the path that feels most level. At the gulley he finds the remnants of a bridge, broken, but with most of the hewn timbers still in the area. It was not a simple foot bridge. Whoever designed this line had a good feel for the topography. Sam scrambles into the gulley and then up on the other side, where his path turns south. He bends down at one point and brushes the dirt off a timber. Maybe.

With the depot only three-hundred yards away, the path leaves him. Too many years have passed; too many cars have run over this piece of land; too many people have walked between here and the town. Sam can't know for sure, but he is convinced that the mine did connect with the depot at some time. It would only make sense.

Beyond the depot lies Forest City. He turns and retraces his steps to the church.

§

Walt watches the Russian boy watch him. Walt sits in the bleachers at the ballfield wondering, while the boy slugs his mitt as he stares—and doesn't. The man has done his research; the boy and his grandmother came to the United States from Pechora, Komi Republic, Soviet Union, in the remote northern Urals. They arrived in Toronto, Canada, in October 1984. Her daughter, the boy's mother, worked at Yamantov. The boy's father defected and now is protected by the U.S. government, but he lives in the Los Angeles area. Dr. Cherkasova was never close to finding him. The boy's father never knew his son was searching for him. Practice starts and the boy gathers with his teammates around the coaches, but he looks beyond the huddle for a last look at Walt. Walt nods at the boy, but the boy looks down. Walt will not meet with the boy alone; he will arrange a time when the boy and his grandmother are together. Maybe it's just curiosity, but Walt has this feeling, the type of feeling Bellena alluded to during dinner.

Walt expected to meet the boy's grandmother at practice, but she is not in attendance, something that surprises Mac, who sits with Arnie, but not with Walt. "What's going on?" Mac wanted to know at the house.

"CIA stuff," Walt said with a smile, the explanation he always gives Mac when he can't tell him. Walt can't reveal details, and while Mac believes it's not anything big, Walt knows it could be. When he was chasing a Solidarity informant in Gdansk, Poland, several years back, he had solid leads. Now, he chases a ghost on a hunch. How would he explain that to Sarge, even if it was allowed? They all watch to the end of the practice, the last before the first game tomorrow, Saturday. Walt waves to Mac and leaves to meet Bellena for a drink downtown. Mac and Arnie leave for beers at the golf course. Pyotr piles into a blue station wagon with several of his teammates for pizza.

§

The night before, Pyotr told Olga about a sensation he was having. Babu joked with him, asking if it was about hitting a homerun. No, it was about going home to Grampar, he thought, but he needed to talk with a man first. Babu wanted to know what man, and Pyotr couldn't tell her. Does he live here in town, she wanted to know.

"Yeah, sort of. Good night, Babu."

"Yeah? Sort of? I need to get you back to Pechora before you become too much American."

§

Pyotr has three singles in his first baseball game, and his team wins. Olga sits in the bleachers behind home plate and studies the men in attendance, wondering if any of them are the one. Pyotr never looks beyond the field. Arnie watches by himself.

§

Bellena orders her two men to take her to the cabin on Saturday morning. Yes, they can bring their poles, but if Mac is serious about putting the cabin on the market, he needs to spend a day there to be sure. Mac bought the place the year after he moved to Bueny and used it frequently the first few years, but as his cancer progressed and he weakened, it sat idle. He hasn't spent a night there in four years. When they arrive, the first order of business is to open it up for some spring air, sweep out the cobwebs, and set out the lawn chairs. Everything goes at a slower pace at the cabin. Bellena makes coffee while Mac and Walt prepare their fishing gear. Across the pond a man casts a fly against the backdrop of the forest.

"You know, Dad, you can do this without owning the cabin. Bring your coffee and lunch up in a cooler, park by the lake, and fish. You used to do that at other high lakes near Leadville. Maybe someone could actually get some use to this old place." Bellena speaks in her real estate broker's voice, something both men notice.

Mac spins nostalgic for a few minutes, but he decided over the winter. He points at the fisherman across the lake. "That could be you, Walt, except he catches a few fish." They laugh and watch the action in the distance. The sun warms them.

Walt reaches over and takes Bellena's hand. "There's another option. I could buy it."

Mac grunts. "Is this just a way to transfer some money to me for my old age? Charity for the old, sick guy?"

"You hardly need that. Between your pension and your daughter, I'd say you're set for several more years, and if I own this place, you can't tell me when I have to drive up to make repairs." They all laugh at that and then settle into more quiet, each pondering the last option. The man across the lake lands a fish, puts it on his stringer, and vanishes into the forest. Walt has his Korean War face on, something the Sarge notices.

"What's on your mind, Walter?"

Bellena squeezes his hand, and he returns. "Just wondering where that man lives. He must have a place near Forest City, since we didn't see a car or a truck nearby, maybe a summer resident."

"He looks a little like the caretaker at the church over there. I've seen him a couple of times working on the place when I've gone over to the general store. He's got the church looking pretty good. Hard to tell though from this distance."

How long's he been working on the church?" asks Walt.

"I don't know, a couple of summers or so, I guess."

"Anybody know anything about him?" asks Bellena.

"Not that I know of. I've never seen him in town."

"The mountains attract men like that, men who seem to want their isolation, who hole up in some of the old places in the hills. As I drive around looking for places to list, I see lots of cabins that are run down, but with somebody living in them. I wonder if they're happy or have just come to the end of their rope."

"Invisible men," says Walt. "Men with secrets."

Mac laughs. "That guy probably lives in Texas and rents one of the more expensive places in Forest City, and here we are making up a life for him. Let's see, he's a secret spy, which would mean the place where he stays is chalk full of electronic equipment. With all your government connections, Walt, you could find out."

"I could sell the place to him, if he's a rich Texan. There're certainly plenty of them around Bueny and southern Colorado," says Bellena.

"What's the price? We could bring our kid up here and make memories. Grampa here could teach him how to fish. I'm going to need a hobby in my retirement, and there's plenty of work to do on this place."

"Him?" asks Bellena. They all laugh. She takes Walt's hand again. "I think I can get you a good price."

§

Sam watches from the trees. Baby Bear nudged him when they drove up, and now he studies them in search of a reason. He sees nothing strange in their behavior, just a family spending a few hours at their cabin. Why the movement?

§

In town Sam buys starter tomato plants at the greenhouse by the stoplight. May's temperatures have risen enough to put them out, and he will follow Father Tellez's advice and plant them in the cemetery. Plant. Great word for a cemetery, he thinks. From the greenhouse he drives to St. Rose to get his bi-weekly letter from Mexico and to ask Father Spreewell about the direction of his repairs on St. Mary. The Father wants Sam to continue working on the altar, but Sam's a bit apprehensive about his ability to restore the most sacred part of the church. His carpentry skills have improved, but he's still no master craftsman by any means. And there's that time thing. If his hunch about Henry proves correct, the active search for him will intensify.

With Father Spreewell's encouragement on the altar, Samuel stops at the hardware store for more tools, most importantly, a belt sander. In the garden section, he buys some hoses for watering the cemetery and grass seed and fertilizer. Suddenly, he pulls back behind the aisle divider to conceal himself. Arnold! What the hell? Pushing his cart toward the back of the store to keep Arnold's movements in sight, he parks near the electrical supplies, hoping that Arnold won't spot him. Arnold shops from a list and carries a hand basket half-full of garden supplies. He files through the vegetable seeds, selecting four or five packets, puts them in his basket, and then walks to the checkout station. Sam watches him pay and leave. Through the large front windows, Sam sees Arnold drive away in a green and white pickup. He takes a deep breath and unclenches his fists.

"May I help you?"

Sam is startled but composes himself. "Ah, no. No, thank you. I'm finding everything I need." And more, he thinks to himself, as he steps past the young male clerk to retrieve his cart. He has one more stop, at the electric company to have an electrical line repaired from the road to St. Mary, but his mind races past his tasks and appointments. If Arnold is here, and if Henry is talking, who else nearby knows? Bit players. Where would I look? The Man? What would make him think I'm here? Have I been marked? Sam narrows his eyes and tries to recall the family at the lake. What was Baby Bear trying to tell me?

§

Across town in the real estate office of Bellena McElroy-Kramer, a prospective buyer studies the fact sheet of the Wagon Wheel Motel. Twenty-eight units, live-in apartment for the owner, swimming pool, good location close to shops, on Highway 24 for good tourist traffic, built in 1954. The owners are retiring and asking way too much, but Bellena thinks they can be persuaded to lower their price considerably for the right buyer. "It would have to be a lot lower, if I'm going to get it," says the buyer. Neither woman senses a deeper connection for this meeting. The agent is acting on a referral, while the buyer, in her mid-thirties, has waited too long to grab her own life. She has lived too long in a small mountain town under the protective wings of her parents.

§

Olga finishes cleaning another mouth, rings for Dr. Kinkade, and leaves the office for lunch. Across Main Street at the New York

Deli, she orders a black bread sandwich. She sits at a table instead of the counter along the south-facing window, her customary seat this past winter. When a man slides into the seat across from her, her body tenses.

"Excuse me, Dr. Cherkasova. My name is Walt Kramer, and I'd like to talk with you if you don't mind."

She does mind, but she doesn't have the wherewithal to refuse. No one in America has called her Doctor, but surprisingly, it feels good. Is this the man Pyotr referred to?

"You met my father-in-law at the ballfield the other day. Mac. He loves baseball and has lots of time on his hands, so he frequently goes over to watch the boys play. He likes the younger kids better because they have no egos, and they don't swear. He was impressed with your grandson's ability and hussle." Walt walks a fine line with this part of the conversation, trying to relax Olga enough so she doesn't walk out on him. "I've probably made you a little nervous, and I don't mean to." He slows down. "Dr. Cherkasova, I do some work for the government, the U.S. government, and I'm looking for a man who has some confidential information. This may sound crazy to you, but for some strange reasons, I think your grandson may have information about where I can find him." Walt rubs his cheeks with his hands and then interlocks his fingers in front of his face. "I'd like to speak with Pyotr, but I won't do it without your permission and without you present." He stops to allow Olga time to judge all that has been presented to her.

Olga looks down at her sandwich. Is this The Man, and should she allow his proposal? She nods her head unconsciously and looks up. "Pyotr told me he was looking for a man in the mountains. I really do not understand, but I know I need to allow this meeting."

§

Barkley likes to walk, work in his garden, take care of his violets, write about the Colorado saga, reminisce about Western State and Lizzie, and read philosophy. At eighty-five he no longer sees a big picture. He is often confused. His life belongs to those people who call or come by and to the past. When Sam suddenly appeared at his door, Barkley was confronted with a series of images from his past and present that seemed to conflict. Because of the poem, Barkley felt warmth toward Sam, as if he was family or an old friend. Their subsequent talks about Barkley's past only strengthened that feeling. Sam was a good listener. Barkley doesn't recall that Sam only spent three weeks in Ouray back in 1983. He didn't remember much about Sam's leaving or the part Henry played in the escape. He doesn't remember Henry sitting in when he and Sam drank beer and talked big ideas. And now, Barkley forgets Sam's request that he tell Henry about Sam's visit. But Barkley can't wait to tell Delany.

Nobody followed Sam out of town back in December of '83. He and Henry had gone over the route to Canada in such detail, even marking the atlas roads in red ink, and Henry was sure of where Sam was fleeing. The plan was for the authorities to apprehend Sam in one of two places in Montana just before he crossed into Canada. Henry liked Sam, but he was AWOL and that was unacceptable to Henry. He had served honorably, even in difficult times. So should Sam. When Sam didn't arrive at the planned destinations, Henry took it personally. Sam must have lied to him. A deserter and a liar, so for the past twenty-eight months, Henry has been on a mission to catch that son-of-a-bitch.

§

Delany stops by Barkley's on her way home from Buena Vista. She knocks once, pops her head in the door announcing her presence, and walks in. She isn't surprised to find Henry at the kitchen table with Barkley, both drinking a beer.

"Get yourself a beer and make yourself comfortable," says Barkley. "Any luck with the motel?"

Delany leans over and gives both men a brief hug. "No beer. I still have to get back to Durango." She gets a mug from the cupboard and pours herself a coffee, then sits down. "Do either one of you two gentlemen want to invest in a thirty-year old motel in central Colorado? I need investors because I can't afford it on my own."

Barkley puts his hand on Delany's forearm to comfort her. "It'll work itself out. If you're meant to be there, the money will appear."

Henry shakes his head. "What new philosophy is this? Old age optimism? Good things appear out of thin air? Not all things are meant to be, Barkley, even good things."

"Never mind the world's greatest pessimist, darling. More importantly, I had a visitor a couple of days ago who asked about you." Barkley stops, hoping Delany will guess. She doesn't, so he goes on. "Bearded young man about your age. He said he'd met a priest in his travels, but he didn't say where he'd been. Popped in and then quickly left." Both Delany and Henry catch their breath and lean forward.

"Sam came here?" asks Henry.

"Sam? How did he look?" asks Delany.

"Tired."

"Oh my God!" Delany says slowly.

Henry gets up to leave. "I have an appointment, so I'll say good-bye. Good to see you, Delany. See you tomorrow, Bark."

"He didn't say anything about an appointment to me earlier. I swear, that man becomes stranger and stranger as he gets older. Here one minute, gone the next. He'll leave for weeks at a time and not tell me anything. Then he shows up again with no explanation. I think all little men have lots of energy. He needs a hobby." Barkley shakes his head. "Didn't even finish his beer."

Delany reaches over and repeats the action of touching Barkley's arm to enhance his concentration. "What was Sam doing back?"

"He didn't say, missy. I told him you had been coming by, but he was in a hurry too, just like Henry. He said he still had your rock."

"Is he here in town?"

"I walked by his house, but some woman is staying there, although she didn't answer the bell. I don't know the answer to your question. Sam and I only talked for a few minutes. As I said, he left quickly."

§

Henry drives past Sam's house, just to check. He's pretty sure

Sam won't show up there. Why was he in Ouray? Why did he come back? He can't come up with an answer. He rushes back to his house to make a call.

"He's back in Colorado. You might put a watch on Delany Herrera's place in Durango. I'll keep an eye out here. If you need me to go anywhere, I will."

§

Sam cocks the .45, pulls it up to eye level, closes his left eye, and squeezes the trigger. The tin can remains motionless on the tree stump. It's only ten paces away, but Sam prides himself on his skill with the awkward weapon. In training he was told that if anyone pointed a .45 at you, just run, because no one can hit anything with it. Don't aim it; just point and shoot. That's why they give them to the military police. We don't want the MPs to actually shoot someone; just scare them into behaving themselves in bars. He looks again at the can on the log, but this time he holds the weapon at his side. Draw! he silently commands. His hand moves quickly, and the can flies off the stump.

§

The old altar can't be salvaged. It was just a rectangular box nailed into the floor at the front of the church a hundred years ago, but Father Spreewell doesn't want him to just toss it out. "It's sacred, son." Sam proposed that he dismantle the altar and store the wood inside a new one. He can build a similar, simple altar and place the old wood inside before he affixed the top. The Father accepted this idea, so Sam sands oak boards to construct the new altar. He'd like to make it more ornate, maybe bevel the top and bottom edges, but he doesn't have a router. The hardware store said they could order him some trim: "How long until it would arrive?" asks Sam, and he's contemplating that option.

More and more of the summer residents are arriving to fix up their cabins. To keep them away, he's posted a couple of no tres-passing signs in front of St. Mary and his cabin. In another month when summer begins, a dozen people a day will wave or ask for directions or want to see the inside of the church. Signs won't deter them, and he will allow it. "Just be careful around the places where I'm refinishing stuff."

Sam takes a flash picture of the front of the church where the altar will go, record keeping for the church archives, for his own archives. The front part of a church has a name, but he can't remember it. He'll ask Father Spreewell next time. He sets the camera in his backpack and picks up the sandpaper, wraps it around a wood block, and begins the repetitious actions of smoothing the oak. Tedious, but very satisfying. One board at a time; one day at a time. Yeah, "one day at a time" is what Father Tellez told him. It was good advice at the time, but time is running out, and he's no farther away from his crime than he was two and a half years ago. Sam puts the sandpaper down and runs his hand along the grain. It's getting there.

§

Bellena will fix dinner in two days, on Wednesday, but she's promised to make something a second grader will eat, a second grader from Russia. Walt invited Olga and Pyotr over to talk. He knows things are easier over a good meal. Mac will watch Pyotr's practice and then drive them over. In public Walt professes to lots of weaknesses, but Bellena knows it's modesty and a bit of shyness, but he never allows his natural shyness to interfere with the solution of a problem, and she knows he's working on one these days. She watches him move around the house--his pacing, his facial twitches, his hand movements, and that stare. It's not Ft. St. Vrain; it's something much larger, and, she thinks, personal. He'll keep it to himself until it's time for her to know. Then, after Mac has gone to bed and the two them are alone, he'll tell her. Unless it's NEA or CIA.

After dinner Walt goes to his office and shuffles through old notes. He doesn't close the door, an invitation for Bellena to join him, a sign he wants to talk. Some people have unspoken signals for sex, for intimacy, for one thing or another. For Walt the most intimate act he performs is revealing talk, and Bellena has always been receptive. She is a rare wife, a wife who knows her husband had a previous life that didn't always go well, and she both accepts it silently and listens when he sheds his skin just a bit. She hopes to know it all before their lives end, but she knows that if she pushes it, he'll close her off. Trust and patience. Like his Korean War experiences, parts will be exposed with great difficulty, but she will listen and appreciate his apprenticeship for their life together, at least that's how she looks at it.

"What are you looking for, hon?" she asks. She sits in the colonial couch with a cup of hot tea and watches him pretend.

"Some of my notes on the Soviet Union. I spent a brief time in the home of a scientist in Moscow, and I'm trying to get an idea about what to give a Russian boy as a small gift."

"A boy Pyotr's age? How about a book?"

"I don't know if he likes to read. I know he likes baseball and hockey, but I need something that will make him comfortable." Walt is moving toward one of his revelations.

Bellena moves gently to help. "A rough, gruff government guy meeting with a Russian boy and his grandmother who just this year moved into town and that he doesn't know. Intriguing."

Walt pulls a manila folder from the bottom drawer of a metal file. He stands and pushes the drawer shut with his foot, and then walks to the door of his office and closes it too. Laying the folder on his desk, he joins Bellena on the couch. "Not just any Soviet boy or grandmother. They're from Pechora. It's a city about a hundred miles from Yamantov." Walt doesn't have to remind his wife that secrets disclosed in these talks remain theirs, and not even Mac can be told. He has never disclosed classified information to Bellena, but the time has come, and he needs her support. "Pyotr's mother worked there and died in the accident." So far, Walt has been looking straight ahead, but now he turns to Bellena. "The nuclear accident at Yamantov was no accident." His shoulders tense and his nostrils flare. "We launched a single missile and blew it up. It was a Soviet bunker designed to survive a nuclear war. It wasn't complete yet, and we had an opportunity, at least the President thought so, to destroy it and send the message that there is no surviving a general nuclear war, not in the way we view life today. It was a great risk, and without spelling out all the details, he was convinced that the Soviets wouldn't retaliate. They would pause. We could explain our actions, and there would be no war. It worked out even better."

Now, Walt's waits for a response. Tears form in Bellena's eyes, but she holds them there. She places her tea on the end table and takes a tissue to dab her eyes. "Wow," she says very quietly. "You're going to have to explain how it worked out even better. By 'we,' I assume you mean the United States?" She reaches over for his hand, and even here she knows this is harder on him than on her.

"Yeah, the United States of America. From a nuclear sub sitting under the Arctic Ocean. One missile. The Soviet's radar was faulty, and we found out. They never knew it was coming; in fact, because of the remoteness of Yamantov, they really did think it was a nuclear accident for a few days. The Soviets told their people it was an accident, and they've never come off that story. They know now, and Gorbachev seems to want to move past it, if his military will allow it. I can't imagine the pressure and tension that exists in their inner circles. Each day I wait for them to retaliate, even though I don't think they will now. Enough time has passed, and the lie has become the truth."

Bellena breathes in deeply and blows it out with puffy cheeks. "How many people died?" She lifts her tea to her mouth, the rim pulling her lips apart, but doesn't drink.

"We don't know. Probably one or two thousand."

Bellena dabs her eyes again, but her hand shakes. "I have a hundred questions, but they can wait for now. How do Pyotr and Olga fit into this?"

With his free hand, Walt rubs his forehead. "Two members of the submarine crew that launched the missile suffered tremendous guilt over what they had done. One committed suicide, and the other ran off. Long story, but he's still on the lam, and the government fears he'll tell the world. He's been missing the entire time, and the Navy hasn't been able to find him. It's been my job to find him too, and I haven't been able to either. We'd hoped he had decided to stay in hiding and keep the secret, but the accident at

Chernobyl will make him wonder again."

"Was Chernobyl another missile?"

"No. That really was an accident and could help with the original story in the long run. The Soviets will be able to show the world that it can happen. It's a crapshoot though. This is not a rational world when it comes to nuclear weapons."

"No shit! I'm surprised that more of the sailors haven't spoken out."

"It's a web of secrecy, Bellena. The crew was told it was just a test. Only eleven members of the crew know. Nine now, and seven of those are ranking officers who have careers to think about."

Time again. Bellena takes a slow sip of her tea and rests it on the couch arm. "So, you've invited Pyotr over here for what reason?"

"I have a gut feeling he can help me find the missing sailor. I can't explain it, but that's why I invited them over. Olga doesn't know what I want to ask her grandson, but she's so worn out from the ordeal that she consented. Her daughter died in the attack."

"Olga lost her daughter, but doesn't know why?" Her eyes narrow. "No wonder she's worn out, that poor woman."

"Yeah," breathes out Walt.

"And why did the government put you on the case of the missing Navy sailor?"

Walt's eyes are on Bellena, but they aren't focused. He has passed into his past. She waits, all the while holding his hand. He returns. "The sailor's name is Sam Elkington, and he's my son."

She leans into her husband and hugs him. Now the tears fall. She talks into his shoulder. "Does the government know?"

"Oh, yeah. The CIA assigned me the case for exactly that reason."

"Are you buying dad's cabin for him?"

"No. He can't stay here. His life is in danger. They'll try to catch him, but mostly they want him silenced. Any way they can."

"He must be so frightened. Have you been assigned to silence him?"

"No. God, no!" Walt thinks how to say his next words. "For the first time in my life, I hope that he's my son, that he can save himself through his own guile. When Colleen left me, she took him, as she should have. I was a mess after Korea. He was three, and we've never talked since they left. I've sent money, but I've never been his father. From all I've learned, he was a good kid who turned into a good man."

Bellena pulls back and takes Walt's face in her hands. "Genetics, dear."

Walt shakes his head ever so slightly. "If I can take away some of his weight, maybe he can see a way out, see a little bit of a future."

"I can't know of your son's thoughts, but I feel your concern, and there seems to be a bit of guilt. You've exited your cave from Korea, and I pray you can help your son out of his."

"He has no sense of security, for good reason," says Walt.

"How can he ever feel a measure of normalcy in his life again?"

"Maybe if I can give him one day of security, he can build on that."

Bellena smiles and touches Walt's cheek. "What's a day worth, huh."

"Yeah," says Walt. "Yeah."

# V

# The Seam

# Chapter 10

*Before the Attack.  Washington, D.C., early September 1983*

President Reagan leans on his left foot staring at the four by eight-foot wall map of the Soviet Union, a map with white lines stretching from the Arctic Ocean south through the entire country. A single red line runs roughly along the western slopes of the Ural Mountains.  Seven bemedaled military officers stand rigidly next to four men in expensive suits and another civilian who is dressed more casually.  They wait in absolute silence for their President.  He shifts over to his right foot, steps toward the wall in order to touch the map and runs his index finger along the red line.  Without turning around, he asks a question for which he already knows the answer.

"Tell me again, General Vessey, what am I looking at?"

"Mr. President, sir, that red line is what we're calling the seam. Their radar surveillance has a gap, a flaw, probably because it's a new installation with some technical glitches.  In time they'll correct it. The seam extends from the Arctic all the way south to Lemonev, about two hundred and seventy-three miles.  It passes through Yamantov, which is at mile two hundred and eleven."

"How was this seam discovered?"

General Vessey steps forward.  "From the hundreds of Blackbird flights over the past three years, the PSYOPs flights that are meant to jab at Russia's nerve endings.  Those along the red line have gone undetected.  It's a corridor about ninety yards wide, narrow enough so that a Soviet plane flying perpendicular across it would not know it's there, but a plane flying directly down the line—the gun barrel—goes undetected. We discovered it quite by accident, but later flights have confirmed its existence."

President Reagan turns his head slightly, but not his body. "New surveillance system? Its early warning radar?"

"Yes, sir. Their technology is not on a par with ours, but this seam will be fixed eventually. I can't predict when that will be. We keep monitoring it."

"Could our planes fly all the way in?"

"Risky, sir. They would have to flip over and fly out—barrel rolls." The general anticipates the next question.

"Given its mission then, Jack, it couldn't get out, could it?"

"No, sir, it most likely would not."

The President turns slowly to face his staff, but looks past them, into the future. He is asking and answering questions in his head. Hard questions.

"Sir, permission to speak."

"Certainly, Admiral."

Admiral Watkins clears his throat. "We need only send in the package. It doesn't need to be returned. The Navy can do it without detection. *Ohio* could do it."

President Reagan's eyes focus directly on Admiral Watkins, but he says nothing. Every man standing in the Cabinet Room understands the silence. The President's eyes settle on each man's eyes in the room for a moment. "Gentlemen, what we are talking about here is a selective strike. The United States is on record pledging not to use our nukes first, but there are guidelines for first use. President Kennedy and his staff discussed their use in Berlin in Sixty-one. Their first-strike plan was referred to as a flexible option, and we need to proceed cautiously on this path." Reagan pauses. "But, gentlemen, it needs to be discussed. What we say here does not leave this room—not to your aides, not to your wives, not to your diaries. Am I clear?"

Cap Weinberger moves to the map and points to the northern Urals. "Yamantov is not an urban target; there are no population centers within ninety miles. We are talking about a single bomb whose purpose would be to destroy an underground military bunker and to demonstrate the resolve of the United States to use nuclear weapons if we are sure those bastards are moving towards a first strike in the not-too-distant future." The Secretary of Defense steps back and nods to the President. "We may conclude that we are not at that point, but there is plenty of evidence in that direction. Improved rail lines from Inta are carrying huge shipments to Yamantov. The excavations seem to be beyond the scope of a normal nuclear power plant, and housing for as many as ten thousand workers has been constructed. The Soviet Defense Ministry claims all this to be a simple upgrade in bridges, schools, and roads to the area so that they can expand their mining activities. Our satellite photos refute this."

"Are we talking about a launch with no prior warning?" asks the Vice-President.

"Yes, George, I think that is the direction we are heading," answers Reagan.

"Then we damn well better be sure of every last detail. We will assume a grave responsibility, and the world will demand to know why." Mr. Bush heaves a deep sigh. "The diplomacy after the fact will need to be first-rate."

The room goes quiet again. Walt Kramer, the only man in the room not wearing a tie, speaks. "Mr. President, let me throw out a few things to consider based on intelligence. Mind you, nothing we do can be one hundred percent guaranteed. I refer you to my memo of August 27, six days before the Korean Air Lines shoot-down."

"Go on, Walt," says the President. Walt Kramer serves as the interim chief of the NEA, the nuclear research arm of the CIA, and is well-respected by the men in the room. He gained President Reagan's confidence while working behind the scenes with the Polish Solidarity movement.

"Yamantov just might be a sacrificable target for the Russians. By that, I mean if it can be destroyed without warning and without substantial civilian casualties, the Russians may be reluctant to retaliate immediately, and that's the key here. We believe—our best information from satellites and from Soviet defectors and double agents—that Yamantov is a deep underground bunker designed to survive an all-out nuclear war. It's not the only command post in the Soviet Union; this one just seems to be a planned survivable bunker if the rest of their country is destroyed under the MAD scenario. The Soviets have a network of underground bunkers, but Yamantov will be the largest, and at the moment it is vulnerable. Because of its location in the extreme north, permafrost may destroy the bunker over time. As Admiral Vessey said, the Navy should be able to drop the package in without any warning, and our intelligence seems to concur. Andropov is a former KGB head, but he's in a caretaker position. He's not well, and that may be to our advantage. This isn't Hiroshima. There, we were trying to end the war quickly so as to avoid a land invasion of the Japanese mainland, and casualties were a part of the shock effect. Yamantov's completion would make nuclear war more likely, especially given the current tense relations between our two countries. Our intelligence tells us Andropov and his military don't want war at this moment because they don't believe they can win it, i.e., survive. Despite their massive military buildup over the past two decades, their technology lags years behind ours. The CIA believes a first strike is in the Soviet plan, but they don't want to go until Yamantov is completed and their surveillance is reliable. They're scared shitless of NATO deployment of Pershing missiles in Europe and your strategic defense initiative. SDI would make them the losers. The CIA believes that the Soviets plan to launch in the next three to four years."

General Paul Kelley, the Marine commandant, responds. "What are you saying, you old grunt? Are you saying we can fly in a nuke, blast their new bunker all to hell, and not have them retaliate? Are you sure you didn't take one in the head up at the Chosin?" The group laughs, all except the President.

Kramer tilts his head. "No guarantees, Paul, but that's one scenario. It's doable, at least on the military part. Still, for now, we must consider that Yamantov may be just what the Soviets say it is--a massive nuclear power station. Soviet standing in the international community is at an all-time low now. They're scared of the future." Kramer looks to the Vice-President. "In this administration's time, much of the world will never accept a pre-emptive strike; you could never justify it. You have to make the decision as to whether you can keep the Soviets from retaliating immediately and then whether you can convince them that nuclear war is unwinnable under any scenario. Andropov and his gang have to know we're not bluffing." Walt looks directly at the President, but his stern words are for all the men in the room. "Mr. President, one bomb on a target that seems to be somewhat controversial within their own cadre would send a clear message. Two bombs would send an entirely different message. That would indicate a general war, and they would retaliate."

President Reagan moves just enough to get everyone's attention. "Gentlemen, let's all take a seat." Several of the men remove their coats and hang them on the back of their chairs. When they are all settled, President Reagan leans forward in his seat and begins. "We can't be indecisive on this, and we cannot be wrong in our intelligence. I want complete information, updated daily, on that seam, Admiral." He turns to his Secretary of State, George Shultz. "George, I need to have your staff provide us with the best guess about what the Russians are planning on the diplomatic scene for the next three years. Is their diplomacy a ruse for a military strike, or are Andropov and his cronies up to something? Walt, dig your sources at the CIA for anything new. What exactly is Yamantov? Be discrete and work with Bob McFarlane on this.

If things remain as they are, then we may be able to work through this with the Soviets. As we continue our military build-up, they will get even more nervous. We will need to monitor the progress toward completion of the bunker at Yamantov. If they truly believe a nuclear war is winnable, then I think we all agree our country is more vulnerable. Yamantov is the key here. Our best guess is that it's at least a few years from completion, maybe more."

George Shultz speaks. "Right now, Mr. President, I agree with Mr. Kramer; I don't think our allies would support us in a first strike. Maybe Mrs. Thatcher would, and Israel, but no one else. The Soviet's denial of KAL 007 does give us some time, however."

"Thank you, George. Let's hope this is all talk, but I want each man in here to work through every possible scenario and provide

Cap with your conclusions. Since my evil empire speech, I think we have their attention. George is receiving some back-channel information that the Soviets are uncomfortable with my SDI proposal, and if that brings them to a more amenable position, we need to push it. But if they stay away, then we have to know our options." The President pauses, "All of our options!"

Secretary Weinberger slides papers across the table to each man. "It's September 7. Let's see if I can get your ideas by the fifteenth. I'm sure you don't have anything else on your agendas."

As the group stands to leave, the President asks Admiral Vessey, Admiral MeDonald, and Admiral Crowe to stay for a few extra minutes. Walt Kramer lingers just outside the door. "Gentleman," asks the President, "where is the *Ohio*?"

Bill Crowe answers. "It's on a little cruise in the Pacific, sir. Do you want me to keep it close to port?"

"I think that would be a good idea. Don't let them know anything of what we're talking about but keep them ready."

Walt Kramer sits in the anteroom with the President's secretary waiting for Mr. Reagan. Walt knows he is a part of something larger than himself; he is caught in a force of history that is forging its own end. Is this the climax to the Cold War, and will that label be accurate in generations to come? During the meeting he watched the President, trying to see into his skin. Walt is pretty sure the United States won't launch a first-strike nuclear missile, but the idea of contemplating its use with the most powerful men in the world sobers him. And what if Yamantov is only a nuclear power plant? Another thought crosses his mind. Diplomacy be damned. The American people and the Soviet people can never know. The world can't know of Yamantov.

# VI

# THE MINE

# Chapter 11

*Central Rocky Mountains, May 1986*

Walt buys Pyotr a fishing pole, a great gift for a young boy, think both Bellena and Mac. "If I'm right, you and I are going to have to teach him how to use it," Mac says to Walt. "I wonder if he ever went fishing back in the Soviet Union."

"Being from Siberia, you'd think so," says Walt.

"Yeah," says Bellena, "but he didn't have a dad like I did, and I don't know if Olga fishes."

Walt recalls sitting opposite her in the sandwich shop, noticing her broad shoulders and muscled arms. Those didn't develop in a dental office, but in the outdoors. He wonders if she plans on making the United States her permanent home or whether she and Pyotr will return to the Soviet Union. He knows roots run deep in most people, and despite its frigid temperatures, the Northern Urals are beautiful country. "What are you cooking for dinner?" he asks Bellena.

"Dad will barbeque some burgers, and I'll make some French fries, macaroni and cheese, and corn on the cob. Pretty basic, but pretty standard for a little boy. Would you like anything else?" asks Bellena.

"No, that sounds good. Do we have any vodka?" Walt notices that Bellena looks puzzled. "Seriously, we ought to have a bottle of vodka around. I know it's a stereotype we Americans have, but I found it quite accurate. Mac, could you pick up a bottle this afternoon." He kisses Bellena on his way upstairs to his office. "Don't let your nap last so long that you forget to pick them up, Mac."

When Walt closes his door, Bellena takes her father's arm and walks him to the kitchen. She wants to answer his silent thoughts, but she won't reveal secrets. "You'll have to absorb it as it goes along. You're the one who told me to be careful what I wish for."

Upstairs, Walt filters through the bottom drawer of his desk in a haphazard way. There must be something here, a junk drawer where he puts stuff difficult to throw away. Pocket knives, old photos, used keys, his Army medals, an old wallet. A biographer could concoct a life from the contents. Walt pulls out the entire drawer and sets it on his lap. What am I looking for? Hunches? Remember your basic CIA training.

§

Olga draws blood from the lady who sits in the dental chair, but the woman just flinches without complaining. Olga's thoughts are not on her work; she thinks about dinner with the American family, with the man who has questions for Pyotr. She knows the questions will be for her also, and she has no idea what her answers will be. He said he works for the government, but what would the government want from her and Pyotr. Do American agents interrogate all Soviets in their country? If he's looking for someone that Pyotr can help with, would that be Melor? That makes a little sense.

Last night, she thought about taking Pyotr and leaving, to return to Pechora and her father, to go home. End the search, end Pyotr's imaginings, and go home. Getting back to the Soviet Union would require procedures. Like she frequently does, she sat on the porch and looked to the heavens for any answer. She drank her one glass of vodka and found none.

She will bring a photo of Gora Narodnaya to the Americans as a gift for their kindness in having them in their home. She is reluctant to part with it, but she has nothing else to give them. She finishes cleaning the lady's mouth, swivels in her chair to ring the bell, and bumps the vase with the flowers. Flowers. If she has time after work, she will buy flowers and take them to the man's house and keep her beloved mountain.

Olga wonders about the man's wife. Could she be an agent of the government too?  Did she serve in the military like Soviet female agents?  Now you're just being silly, Olga, she tells herself.  Focus on Pyotr; he's at the center of this.  She knows it has something to do with his abilities to sense the future, to see the invisible, to answer questions for which others have no answers.  Where did Pyotr get this ability?  After his bednight story last night, he hugged her and said he was excited to be going to dinner with the American family.  He fears nothing, and she fears so much.

Dr. Kinkade comes in and Olga leaves.  She has two more sets of teeth to clean before she goes to baseball practice to watch Pyotr become more Americanized.  Maybe after dinner she and Pyotr can go home.

§

Henry persists in his questioning.  Did Sam say where he had been living for the missing two years?  What kind of priest?  What kind of work did he do?  Had he been back to Ouray at any other time?  Is he staying in the States now?  What kind of car was he driving?  Was he going to contact Delany?  Did he give you anything?  Where did he cross into Canada the first time?

Barkley has no answers, but he doesn't get angry.  He knows Henry has concerns about their friend, and he wishes he could be of more help, but his memory is failing, and he knows it.  "I gave him my sign though.  He always did like it."

"What the hell are you talking about, Barkley?"

§

Sam wants no visitors, nothing to arouse curiosity, so he hangs the sign on the inside of his front door, where he can read it whenever he walks out.  *Esse est percipi.*  He thinks about what Father Tellez would say if he saw it, or the Church itself.  After all, this cabin is church property.  Sam taps the sign, "I like it, and that's all that matters."

§

Pyotr, Mac, and Walt talk baseball on the back deck, while Olga and Bellena work on "all the fixins" in the kitchen. When Mac gets the burgers on the grill, Walt suggests they play catch, and Pyotr readily agrees. He has brought his glove. The women bring out some of the food and sit at the table with their drinks and watch. Mac, wearing his Master of the Barbeque apron, joins them.

"You're pretty good, Pyotr," says Walt. The boy has not missed a single toss. He pulls the ball out of his glove and drops his throwing arm straight down to begin his throw back to Walt. Perfect form, thinks Walt. "I learned to play when I was a kid too, but never got very good until a friend taught me the right way in the Army."

Bellena eases the glass to her mouth and smiles to herself. Mac taught her and her brother the elements of baseball when they were about Pyotr's age, and catch is the quintessential American father and son game. She loved the repetitive activity, being face-to-face with her dad, the banter. She was a tomboy without reservation. She understands why her husband chose it for tonight—the perfect game to set the stage, to put Pyotr at ease for questions. This is Walt at his gentlest, a part of him she loves so much, but seldom gets to see in company. Is it an intellectual gentility, a desire to be what never was afforded him as a boy? Her dad isn't particularly gentle either, but he too has his moments. Is this a soldier thing, men who have participated in violence seeking shelter in life's best trait?

Pyotr's throw flies over Walt's head, and the acting father has to chase it back to the fence. "Sorry, Walt," says the boy. At introductions Walt told Pyotr to call him Walt and to call Mac Sarge. Only Bellena retains her title as Mrs. Kramer to Pyotr.

Walt tosses a grounder to Pyotr, who scoops it up and makes a sidearm throw back to Walt. "Nice." He then throws the ball high in the air to simulate a fly ball. Pyotr drifts to his right and catches it easily. "Your coach has taught you well, young fella. Way to use two hands. Sarge tells me you had three hits on Saturday and your team won."

"Yeah, we did, and I didn't make any errors. My third hit was the best. If I wouldn't have tripped on the base, I would have had a double."

"What was the final score?"

"We scored eight, and they only made two."

"Well, congratulations. I'll bet you played hockey back in Russia, didn't you?"

"Yeah, it's my favorite sport so far. I've got a Tretiak sweater that my uncle gave me. Grampar keeps it for me until I get home."

"I'll bet you miss your grandfather a lot."

"Yeah, but we'll be going back soon."

"How soon?" asks Walt.

"Well, since I'm meeting you, it won't be long." Pyotr makes this statement without any pretension, but all four adults tune in.

Walt doesn't press for an explanation yet. He waits. "Do you have a favorite major league team yet? Sarge likes the Giants and the Yankees, but I've always been a Braves fan." From Walt's childhood, he remembers Warren Spahn, Del Crandall, and Henry Aaron, especially "Hammerin' Hank," but Pyotr wouldn't recognize those names.

Pyotr smiles broadly. "I like the Reds." He looks to his grandmother and laughs out loud. Olga smiles back and nods. "Did you get it, Walt, I like the Reds."

"You're pretty clever, son. I like that." It is pretty clever for a seven-year-old to connect the Cincinnati baseball club to the political term for the Soviet Union. Walt throws the ball back to Pyotr with a little more velocity. "Was your grandad ever a Red?"

"He never played baseball, Walt."

Good, thinks Walt. His family hasn't burdened him with events from another era, from a terrible period in Russian history. Pyotr remains a little boy, though Olga understands where Walt is coming from.

Mac stands and calls time-out. The burgers are done. Walt puts his arm around Pyotr's shoulders as they walk to the picnic table. Olga notices. Bellena stands to take the aluminum foil off the mac-and-cheese and to dish up the rest. She seats herself next to Olga at the table. The talk is about spring, school, and more baseball. Olga remains mostly silent, but Walt knows it's not just her limited English skills keeping her quiet. She measures him, judging where he might be heading, and protecting Pyotr.

"What brought you to Colorado," asks Walt to Olga.

Now it starts, she thinks. Now comes the reason we are having dinner with these people. They are very nice, but he needs an answer. "The mountains. Pyotr wanted to come to the mountains." She longs for some answers too. Her grandson has held them for so long, and she hasn't found a way to get him to reveal them to her. "Is that not right, Pyotr?"

When Pyotr arrived for dinner, there was no stare at Walt like he had given at the ballfield. Now, he looks to his grandmother and slowly turns to Walt. "I thought my father would be here, but I can't feel him." Pyotr is not done. Mac starts to speak, but Walt halts him. Bellena reaches out and takes Olga's hand. Instead of pulling away, Olga senses something and squeezes Bellena's hand. "Somewhere here is the man I'm looking for." Pyotr tilts his head and examines Walt so intensely that Mac, Bellena, and Olga are uncomfortable. But not Walt. He relaxes his face, trying to let Pyotr in. The boy's eyes trace the outline of Walt's face. They avoid the man's eyes at first, working their way around the face: the chin, the mouth, the nose, the dark circles around the eyes. Pyotr studies the scar line through Walt's eyebrows and wonders if the blood ran into his eyes at the time. When Pyotr finally gets into Walt's eyes, he knows that it did, that the blood blinded him for a while. Pyotr blinks, but his face does not reveal his thoughts. Walt keeps his eyes open. The boy puts a fry in his mouth but doesn't take his eyes from Walt. "What did he do?" asks Pyotr, a question that only Walt understands.

"He was a sailor in my country's Navy, and he followed orders. He thought my country was in danger, and he acted to protect it. He found out later that maybe it wasn't, and he's having a very difficult time accepting his actions. He's run away, and like you, he's searching for answers."

"He is in danger, isn't he?"

"Yes, Pyotr, he is."

Olga watches her grandson, her eyes trying to protect him. Bellena's eyes stay on her husband. The two women hold on to one another firmly. Mac's eyes flit from Pyotr to Walt to the women, and then back again.

"Does he like baseball?" asks Pyotr.

"I don't know," answers Walt.

"Are we the only ones looking for him?"

"No, Pyotr, we aren't. There are others."

"Do they want the same thing from him that we do?"

"I don't think so," answers Walt. Bellena slides her jaw to one side and bites the outside of her lower lip.

"Then you need to find him before they do."

"Yes, I do. Can you help me with that, Pyotr?"

Pyotr moves his eyes off Walt to his grandmother. "Can I, Babu?" It is not a question of ability but of permission. Olga understands this and nods. Pyotr smiles and returns his eyes to Walt. "He doesn't want to be found for himself, but he's looking for someone too." The boy turns his eyes down and breathes in heavily. When he looks up, he's smiling. "These hamburgers are sure good."

§

Walt carries a sleeping Pyotr into his grandmother's house and lays him in his bed. Olga thanks Walt and kisses him on the cheek when he leaves. She watches the man drive away in his truck, not knowing what to think about their evening. She brushes Pyotr's hair off his forehead and leans over to kiss him. "Why do you know these things, my dear one? How do you know these things?" she whispers in her native language. She sits and looks closely at him.

Pyotr opens his eyes. "Babu, are you sad?"

"I thought you were asleep."

"I was, but I have to wet." Olga pulls the covers off her grandson, allowing him to go to the bathroom. When he returns, he jumps under the covers and pulls them up to his chin. "Mrs. Kramer isn't sad; she likes you, but Walt is, sort of. He's a lot of things."

"You notice a lot of things, Pyotr, things that I don't. Where does this come from?" She strokes his hair.

"I don't know; things just come to me." He pulls the covers over his head and giggles.

"Come back out here, my little mystery." Pyotr giggles again and stays hidden. "Would you like to go outside and look at the stars?"

§

They sit in the dark in the quiet of a small mountain town, watching the stars to the north. "Do you miss your telescope?"

"No, Babu, the stars were still just small dots. I miss Grampar, though."

"I miss him too. Will we be going home soon to be with him?"

Pyotr turns sideways into his grandmother's chest, and she pulls the blanket around his shoulders. They sit together in the wicker rocker, and Olga hums a Komi lullaby. She waits for his answer and thinks of her father. In his last letter, he sounded sad and ready for them to come home.

"I think maybe this summer, Babu."

§

"What a special boy!" says Mac when Walt returns from taking Pyotr and Olga home. "I was the only one out of the loop, wasn't I?"

Bellena gets up off a kitchen stool to hug her dad, goes to the refrigerator for two beers, and places one in front of her dad. "Tonight, you get to break your diet." She takes a single drink from the other before handing it to Walt.

"Mac, all hell has broken loose for me over these past three years, and I've kept it a secret. I'm going to let you in on a lot of it, the part that I've already told Belle." He purses his lips and sips his beer. For the rest of the evening, he tells his father-in-law all that he told his wife, answering questions as honestly as he can, warning him about ever revealing this secret, telling a tale Mac would not have believed if he'd read it in the newspaper. But he knows it's true because Walt told him.

"Are you all right, Dad?" asks Bellena.

"Never better, Belle, never better. I'm sharing a beer with my two favorite people in the world, and I'm hearing secrets about the Cold War. What could be better than this? I've had a delicious dinner, met a nice Soviet family, and learned that Pyotr," Mac pauses for a word, "that Pyotr has feelings." He turns to Walt. "You forgot to give him the fishing pole."

"After our little talk, he pretty much shut down. He finished his meal and just about fell asleep."

"Well, Walt, I'm going to let you in on a little secret. I've always known you had a son. After Colleen left you, she called me. You must have told her about me, and she was looking for support. I met her in Denver a few weeks after that, and we stayed in touch for several years. Your little boy was a cutie. When she remarried, we stopped communicating, but every few years, I'd get a card, but I haven't heard from her since I moved down here. She appreciated the money you sent her; it paid for Sam's college." Mac lifts his beer to his lips for a last sip, and Walt raises his as a toast.

"Well, what do we do now?" asks Bellena.

"I'm going to have another beer," says Mac. "Either of you?"

Bellena refuses but gets two more beers. "I'm so confused by all this. Shouldn't we be worried about a nuclear war?"

Walt hugs her around the waist when she puts the beer in front of him. "Let me do that worrying. I've been doing it every day since Yamantov. Somehow, Chernobyl may give us a little space, but only if Sam sees the opportunity. If he'll stay quiet about Yamantov, and if those who served on his sub do too, maybe the President and Mr. Gorbachev can work something out."

§

In bed Bellena quickly realizes Walt's emotions are not on sex. She snuggles into his shoulder and runs her fingers over his chest. "Where are you, dear?"

"I'm sorry. We can make love if you want."

"We've never made love that way, and we aren't going to start now. Tell me your thoughts."

Walt breathes deeply. "I'm missing something. I traced Colleen's station wagon to Mexico, but the trail went dead. The car ends up in use by an old Catholic church," he doesn't end his sentence.

"How did the church get it?"

"For all I could find out, they bought it from a parishioner who wanted to get rid of it. The priest didn't have any records. How the parishioner got it, I couldn't find out. Sam drove to Mexico from Ouray instead of to Canada. His movements after he crossed the border bewilder me. He was pretty smart there."

"You've probably thought of this already, but what if Sam was the parishioner who sold the car to the church? Maybe he and the priest there formed a bond." Bellena hasn't lifted her head from Walt's shoulder, and she feels his body tense.

In a moment, he replies. "God. Right under my nose. When I spoke with the priest there, he never let on that he knew Sam. He was protecting him. For all I know, Sam could still have been there. He's here now though."

"And that's where Pyotr comes in, huh?"

"Yeah." He turns to her, kisses her gently on the nose, and gets up. "I need to make a call to Washington. There's some info I need."

"I'll be right here when you get done. Waiting."

§

It's past midnight, and Sam hasn't moved from the table since ten. He's written a few thoughts and scribbled a plan for the altar on his legal pad, but mostly he's been immobile. His pistol and Delany's rock lay on the table along with an empty plate and his cold cup of coffee. A .45 magazine lies next to the rock. People close by are stirring.

§

On Saturday afternoon, after Pyotr's second baseball game, they all drive up to Mac's cabin. After lunch Walt presents Pyotr with his fishing pole, which is already set up for his first cast. The boys walk to the shore, and Bellena laughs at her dad's forever line, "First, biggest, most." She touches Olga's shoulder and motions to the chairs where they can watch Pyotr catch his first fish.

Mac bends over to show Pyotr how to flip the bale on his reel and cast far out into the pond. He cradles the fly in the palm of his hand. "This is a caddis fly." Pyotr touches it with his finger to move it around and examine it more closely. "The body is yellow. The part you're touching is the hackle, and the other part is the wing. It's made from elk hair." Pyotr takes it from Mac's hand, holding it up close to his eyes. "Well, don't just stare at it, son. Fling it out there to the hungry trout."

Pyotr's first cast smacks the water hard about ten feet from shore. He looks to Walt. "Reel it in and try again, or else I'm going to catch that first fish." Pyotr does as Walt directs, but with greater success. "Reel it slowly and watch the fly as it trails behind the bubble. If you see or feel anything, make a quick jerk on your rod."

Mac catches the first fish, a small rainbow. "That's not big enough to count, Sarge. Come on, Pyotr, we can't let Grampa beat us." Three casts later, Pyotr catches his first trout. While Walt takes the hook out of the fish's mouth, Pyotr surveys the tree line on the opposite side of the lake.

Olga runs to Pyotr and gives him a hug. "So beautiful!" She touches his fish as tenderly as he had touched the caddis fly.

"We need to put it back in the water before it dies," says Walt. "Put it in gently." Pyotr uses both hands and lays the trout in the pond. Olga kisses him on the forehead and returns to her chair next to Bellena.

"Tell me about your daughter," says Bellena.

"Your husband must be a powerful man to know so much about me and Pyotr." Olga's eyes tell Bellena she is stalling, gathering herself, but she will tell as much as she can. Bellena waits. "Ursula was a beautiful girl, much prettier than me. She was working as a welder at Yamantov when the accident happened." Bellena holds her truths inside at this remark. "We had just spent the night with her in Yamantov." She pauses again. "Ursula was my baby, my only child, and I did not get to tell her goodbye." Olga tilts her head. "Can we walk?"

The two women, so similar in body shapes that they could be sisters, move away from the fishermen and the cabin. Bellena gently takes hold of Olga's arm, and they stroll in silence for a few moments. Eventually, Olga continues with her story.

A ways down the path, Olga speaks. "This land reminds me of my mountain. When Ursula was a baby, we moved from Moscow, where I first started working, to Pechora where she grew up. Her father was a soldier, gone a lot, so we lived with my parents. They raised my daughter as much as I did. In Pechora I was a dentist; that is how I was able to get work here in America. We spent lots of time on Gora Narodnaya, my mountain. When Ursula got her job at Yamantov, she was so happy because she said it felt like home. As a young girl, she caught her first fish in a small stream that feeds into the great Pechora River. Her father died in Afghanistan when she was in her last year of school. Ursula took it hard, as any girl would if her father died in war. After that, she met Melor, a man just a little younger than me, and fell in love. He took her to Canada, but she was pregnant, and he did not want that, so he sent her back."

Olga and Bellena walk down the road that leads to the main dirt road to Forest City. A red sedan passes them at the intersection on its way to Buena Vista. They walk in the direction of Forest City. "This whole area was a mining town a hundred years ago, but as you can see, there are just a few buildings left. Quite a few people live here in the summer, but only a handful stay year-round." Bellena squeezes Olga's arm and points to the old church. "The church is a hundred years old. Around here, we think that's pretty ancient, but where you come from, it's probably not." She smiles, and Olga smiles back.

"It has a fresh coat of paint. Could we go in?" The two women walk up the steps and into the unlocked church. The afternoon sun brightens the entire building. "It is being rebuilt," says Olga. They walk to the front of the church, careful of the pews which are scattered haphazardly around the floor. "Pyotr and I came to America to search for Melor, at least that is who I believed we were searching for. Now, I am not so sure that is who Pyotr wants to find. It was a silly trip."

Bellena and Olga turn abruptly to the front door when it opens. Pyotr stands just inside. "He's here."

# CHAPTER 12

*Ouray, Colorado, May 1986*

Sam stops in Buena Vista to speak with Father Spreewell. He has been angry again, much like he was in those months after he returned from the mission against the Soviet Union. Unresolved anger! He spends as much time in the mine bracing the walls as in the church working on the altar. When he lived in Hermosillo, life developed a pattern and a feeling. He was safe, and Father Tellez gave him somewhat of a purpose, some perspective on his life as a fugitive. Father showed him he didn't have to be angry, and a calm settled over him. He finished the account of the mission and put it aside. He worked at his own pace.

Father Spreewell tells him that he'll get a hold of Father Tellez as quickly as possible and arrange for a time they can talk. Sam thanks him, briefs him on the progress of the altar, and leaves. In the car he checks off the first name on his list. There are two more above the line and two below. Sam feels more vulnerable recently, sensing something has changed, and that time is collapsing. He reaches under the seat of his car and touches the box.

§

Except for the numerous four-wheel drive roads through the canyons, the only way in or out of Ouray is the highway, and as Sam returns to his hometown, he knows of his exposure. He turns on the first street past the hot springs in order to get off the highway and lessen his chances of being seen by one of his pursuers. You are paranoid, he tells himself. You see Arnold in the hardware, you see a family at the lake, Baby Bear turns, and you make the case that the FBI or Navy or The Man will capture you. And I start referring to myself as "you." Still, he knows the need for caution. He parks in the alley two blocks from Barkley's house, takes out a sandwich and a pop, and waits. He has a half-hour before dark, enough time to walk to the philosopher's house.

§

Henry makes small talk with the two men inside the restaurant across from the Broken Arrow Motel in Durango. For eight hours he sits staring out the window, nursing a coffee, wishing his shift would not end. His disguise consists of a pair of cowboy boots with two-inch lifts, which makes him a little clumsy, a bolo tie, and a cowboy hat. He watched Delany come and go three times today, but each time, she left and returned by herself and wasn't gone more than forty minutes.

§

Sam takes the .45 from the box, slips it into his jacket pocket, and walks to Barkley's house. He peers in the window and sees Barkley watching television by himself. No Henry. A good sign. Sam knocks on the door, hears the old man shuffle over, and puts his hand on a small, wrapped box in his other jacket pocket.

"Just a minute," Barkley yells from inside the closed door. He opens it with the same wide smile that greeted Sam the last time. "You again! Well, come in and sit a bit. What brings you home this time?"

Sam learns Henry has left again, off to see the phantom girl-friend who, Barkley now believes, lives in Grand Junction. Sam relaxes and tells Barkley about his recent line of work as a carpenter. He tells him he wrote a book, but no more poetry. Barkley asks about the book's topic and when it might be published. "It's a Cold War, suspense story, non-fiction," he says, but laughs about the publishing date. "Others will decide that." They talk and laugh, and Sam wonders if this will be the last time the two of them will be able to enjoy such camaraderie. He takes the box from his pocket.

"I brought you a gift, my old friend. Well, actually, two gifts, but they're in the same box." He hands it across to Barkley, who unties the ribbon and opens the box. Inside are a small piece of wood and a rock with specks of gold.

Barkley empties the contents into his hand and contemplates their meaning. "Okay, I give up. What the hell are these?"

"My new hobby. I'm a gold miner. The wood I cut from a beam in the mine; thought you might want a tangible piece of evidence that mining once took place in Colorado. Maybe you can put it on your desk for inspiration as you plow through your book. It could inspire you to finish the damn thing. I'd like to read it someday." Sam smiles and Barkley harrumphs, understanding the sarcasm, but pretending disdain. "The rock contains a negligible amount of real gold from the mine. When I found it and examined it in the light of day, it reminded me of you. Shining bits of light in a dark world. Thought you might like it."

While Barkley examines the rock, Sam gets up and goes to the framed poem on the wall. He takes it down, returns to his chair, pulls out his pocketknife, and pries off the back piece of cardboard. He takes out the poem, reads it, and autographs it. He puts it back in the frame and hangs it up again. He waits.

"Thank you, son." A tear glistens in the old man's eye. Barkley reaches over with an extended hand and the two men shake. "First the poem and now these. What might I expect the next time I see you?"

Sam shakes his head once. "You promise you'll still be here in a few years?"

"Nope. I take it one day at a time now, and I can't promise a thousand days from now. What about you? Are you going to be around here in three years?" Their eyes meet and hold, and Sam sees a more focused Barkley. "By the way, someone's been living in your place."

They talk for only a few more minutes before Barkley begins to nod off. He's an old man who tires easily, and when that happens, his head falls to one side, and he will sleep for the rest of the night. Sam studies him for a few minutes. This was a fortunate friendship, he thinks. He gets up, takes the box from Barkley's hand, and puts it on the table. He covers the old man with his afghan, stands over him for a few seconds, and then puts his hand on Barkley's shoulder. On his way out, Sam turns off the television and the living room light.

§

Sam drives past his house and notices the black sedan parked across the street—still running—with a man behind the wheel. Sam suspects his mother has returned, but he can't see her yet. Soon, but not tonight. He would stay too long and be discovered. They have so much to catch up on; he has so much to tell her. So unfair. He turns away and parks several blocks away. He checks Barkley's name from his list, circles one of the names below the line and draws an arrow to put it above the line. He drives the ten miles north to Ridgeway, checks into the spa where he set up his tent three hours earlier, undresses, puts on a robe, and goes for a soak. The water is over a hundred degrees and the sky is clear. He finds a spot where he can look to the western skies and maybe see a shooting star. He and Delany came here often, soaked naked, watched the stars in amazement, and then made love. Those were the best times.

§

On Sunday morning after hearing from Washington, Walt returns to St. Mary. The carpenter did not install a lock on the new door, a heavy door designed to give dignity to the entrance of the old church. Inside, where pews and lumber are scattered around the nave, Walt walks slowly, trying to get a feel for the man doing the remodeling. Eight pews have been rebuilt, sanded, and varnished, but they have not been attached to the floor. Is his plan to permanently affix them or to have them freestanding? Sawdust covers the floor, but it too, has been refinished. Clear stain everywhere gives the church a bright tone. He senses the Church decided to spend a pretty penny to restore St. Mary, and he wonders why. Why allow it to stand idle and decay for so many years and then thrust so much money into it? Are they thinking Forest City will support such a church? Anderson wood windows. One man's mission?

From the nave up to the apse, there are two steps. The communion rail has been fixed in place, and a pulpit leans against the west wall. Old lumber lies stacked against the back of the church, and Walt wonders why it is being kept. Maybe Sam hasn't had the opportunity to toss it out yet. Two oak planks ready for sanding sit on sawhorses. Several more finished oak boards rest on the floor next to the old boards. Walt bends to a knee and touches the chalk line in the center of the apse. The new altar will rest here, and the oak boards will make that altar. The weathered boards are the old altar, and they will be stored inside the new one. The old sacred inside the new sacred. At the right front of the church is an add-on room, not part of the original structure, probably built in the years just before the town closed down, maybe just after World War I. This sacristy measures about ten-by-ten. Except for the window and a door, no work has been done here, but there is a chair and small desk with crude blueprints on it. Walt tests the chair and then sits to look at the plans. They are not of the church, but of a mine shaft, the Mollie Miller. He jots the name on his pad, stands, and exits the back entrance into the cemetery. Every stone and grave marker has been restored. The wire fence has been straightened, and there are tomato plants growing in random spots throughout the cemetery. Watering cans lie near the back fence, close to the creek. Whatever else can be said, Sam has taken great care of St. Mary; he has shown great respect for the dead.

Walt returns to the church. On the lone chair in the apse, he sits down to think about his son. The Navy wasn't much help in the psychological profile. Stable, efficient, honorable, responsible. Nothing to indicate that he would desert, and yet after the mission to launch a missile on the Soviet Union, he bolted. The psychiatrist's report cleared him. Early signs of guilt; he talked of spirits living within him, but he denied that quickly. A note paper-clipped to the psych report warns that the doctor might not have been too thorough with Sam. No shit, thinks Walt.

Spirits within? He wonders about that. He gets up and walks

back to the sacristy to look at the mine plans. He turns the paper over and sees several names and a phrase: Father Tellez, Barkley, Delany, Henry, Arnold. "To be is to be perceived." Mom, The Man. Baby Bear. Walt understands: the players in the game, in Sam's game. But how? Walt doesn't know who The Man is, or Baby Bear. Is The Man the government? Arnold? That doesn't make sense. Walt writes the names down and then the phrase. I need to talk with Father Spreewell and Father Tellez, especially Father Tellez.

Walt leaves the church to call Washington again to get a plane reservation for Hermosillo for Monday, no layover. He calls Bellena and asks her to invite Olga and Pyotr over to dinner again for Tuesday. Bellena suggests they go out to dinner. Ouray information lists a Henry Taluse. Walt calls Bellena again and asks for Mac. "Hey, Mac, when did you meet Arnie?"

§

Sam drives through Ouray and over the pass before the sun rises. Just after nine he parks a half-block from the Broken Arrow Motel and watches. After twenty minutes he climbs out and walks to the nearby café. From the restaurant across the street, he calls the motel office and asks for Delany Herrera.

"Hello, this is Delany. How can I help you?"

"Oh, maybe you could meet me for breakfast, so we could catch up on old times."

"Sam! Where are you?"

"Hi, Delany. How are you?"

"Sam, there are people watching me to find you. They sit in the restaurant across the street and look through binoculars at the motel all day. Where are you?"

Sam turns slowly to survey the restaurant. "Delany, let me call you right back."

Ten minutes later Sam calls from a pay phone four blocks away. "Is there a back room available where we can talk?" He leaves his car on a side street two blocks away and walks to the rear of the Broken Arrow, where Delany waits in room 112 with the door open. She shuts the door behind him, turns and stares, and then steps forward and throws her arms around his waist, burying her head into his chest.

"What the hell have you gotten yourself into?  I'm being watched.  Your friend, Henry, sits across the street, disguised like a fool, watching the motel, and you sneak here to see me this way. What's going on?" She pulls back and looks to his face. "That beard is really ugly. The sketch they showed me has you in this beard."

Sam strokes the back of her hair. "I've missed you, not just these past three years, but since we broke up." He reaches into his pocket for the rock and shows it to her. "You're with me every day, at least for a few minutes." He takes her hand and puts the rock into it, closing her fingers around it. "Hard to know where to start. I'm a deserter. I didn't start out to be one, but that's what I am. If I'm taken in, by any one of those agencies who are searching for me, then I'll spend a lot of time in jail. I don't want to do that, but to stay hidden, I've had to stay away from you and my mom and several others who I care for." He tries to convince her with his gaze. "Let's sit."

They continue to hold hands while they sit on the foot of the queen-sized bed. Delany smiles, "Just so you know, I'm not seeing anyone, and I haven't really had a serious boyfriend since we broke up. I'm not saying that I've been waiting for you, but I am saying that you kind of spoiled me for anyone else. We were pretty good together, I think."

"We were." Sam isn't here to talk about the past. "Delany, I came because I want you to know I'm not a bad guy. I had begun to believe I was, and then I met a guy who gave me a little bit of confidence in myself again." Suddenly, he laughs out loud. "He's a Mexican."

Delany understands and laughs too. She smiles warmly. "I'm Hopi, and my tribal name is Cha'Risa. Remember?"

"I remember my fight with that guy over you, but I'd forgotten our Indian names. What does Cha'Risa mean?"

"Something like elk lover. And you were my spiritual guide. At least my name was correct," says Delany. "What else should I know?"

"The people watching you are probably FBI. Henry tipped them off, and I think he thinks it's his patriotic duty to help bring me in. Barkley is a good guy, though. A real good guy." Now, comes the kicker, thinks Sam. "There's someone else trying to find me too. I don't know who he's associated with, either. I've never seen him, but I have inside information." He laughs at what he's just said. "Okay, Delany, you might start to think I'm crazy, but I guess I am some kind of spiritual guide."

They talk for nearly a half-hour, never moving from the bed, Delany occasionally interrupting to understand. Sam makes no mention of the specific attack on Yamantov, but she is more fascinated by the spirit within. When he finishes, he's sweating.

"You must trust me, don't you," she says, not really as a question. She leans into him and kisses him with her eyes wide open. "You've gone way too long without sex, and so have I."

§

"I've been away from the office quite a while," says a naked Delany, "so I better call down and check in." She makes her call, then sits up with a start and listens. She turns to Sam but says nothing. To the woman on the other end of the phone, she asks, "Would you bring me one of the complementary personal kits, a pair of scissors, and a worker's shirt, one of the white ones?" She hangs up and turns to Sam. "A man is in the office asking about someone who looks like you who was seen in the restaurant. He wants to talk to me."

"Go. Just tell him you haven't seen me, that you were cleaning rooms. Keep him in the office." They go silent and lock onto each other's eyes. "We'd better get dressed."

She buttons her last blouse button and starts crying. "You can't do that, Delany. The man will suspect." He steps to her, and they hug, broken only by a knock on the door. Delany answers it and takes the shirt and kit from the housekeeper.

"Cut your beard off. Put this on and go north. The back fence ends at the end of the motel, where you'll find a ditch. Stay in the ditch for a block and then go to your car." She opens the door, but then closes it and steps back to Sam, into his arms. "I'm not going to see you again soon, am I?"

§

Sam drives out of Durango the same way he came in, towards Ouray. He stops on the far side of Durango for gas and a truck pulls up behind him. He knows the truck. Henry Taluse steps out. Sam continues to pump gas as the little man walks awkwardly toward him.

"What the hell are you doing, Henry? Get in your truck and go home. Go back to being an old man with Barkley."

"Put the hose back in the pump and step away from your car. I'm going to call the FBI, so they can come and get you."

Sam holds the handle down, so gas will continue to flow into his red sedan. He turns away from Henry to buy time. He'll fill the tank, get in his car, and speed away. He'll outrace Henry to Ouray and then lose him for good.

"Sam, I'm not kidding."

The pump turns off automatically, and Sam places the hose away carefully. "Okay, Henry, okay. Do you even know what this is about? It's not about me being a deserter." He rolls his head away and steps to his open door. He hears the pistol being cocked.

"Put your hands on the car, Sam! I'm not kidding." The gun is pointed at his stomach.

"Put your weapon down, Henry, you little toad! I'll do what you say, but I need my wallet to pay for the gas." Without asking, he sticks his head into the front seat, takes his .45 from under the seat, whirls, and shoots Henry. Samuel's aim is true; the slug strikes Henry in the shoulder. Bloody, but not fatal. He steps to check on Henry's condition, but the station attendant is already on the phone. The wound looks bad, but Sam has to go. He gets in his car and drives away; east toward Pagosa Springs, and a faster way to Buena Vista. He knows the FBI guys are not following yet, but they will be, along with the local cops. The red sedan has been identified. He wishes he'd paid for the gas, and he knows he won't be seeing his mother tonight. Stupid Henry! I didn't want to shoot you.

§

"There are several old mine shafts in the Forest City area," says Mac. "Even more up the road as you get near St. Elmo. The railroad built a tunnel through the mountain to Gunnison, but it never was as profitable as they hoped. I think the gold petered out quickly, and the silver became worthless in the 1890s when the government passed the Sherman Silver Purchase Act. After that, those towns died slow deaths."

Bellena claps three times. "I'm impressed. My dad, the historian."

Mac nods in appreciation. "The Mollie Miller mine was the most profitable, as I recall. It's closer to St. Elmo, a mile or two from the church. The general store has maps of the area, but the Mollie Miller was the most famous."

Walt has his chin resting on his fists, listening and wondering. He hasn't been able to make a connection to Sam and his work at the church or with the mine. He asked Mac about Arnold earlier. "One of those guys who knows everybody, talks to anyone, and generally likes everyone. A Will Rogers type of guy. He's lived all over the southern part of Colorado. Served in the Army in both World War II and Korea, tells a heck of a good story, and has worked a hundred different jobs just to get by. That and his disability pension. I met him on the golf course several years back." Walt doesn't tell Mac that Arnie's name was on the list at the church. He pushes away from the dinner table and informs Mac that he's in charge of the dishes tonight.

"I've got to go down to Denver and catch a plane."

Bellena has been informed of the schedule. Denver to Houston before the sun comes up, and then on to Hermosillo. She rises and tells her dad that she'll help him just as soon as Walt leaves. She walks with him upstairs to pack and to touch him before he goes. She has never been comfortable with flying, either for herself or him. "Can you get him to open up?"

"I'll do what I can; torture if necessary."

"You're worried."

Walt zips shut his duffle bag and turns to Bellena. "It's personal. You know that. Sam's in danger of going to jail for being a good soldier and having a conscience. He lost a good friend—he found him hanging in a storeroom—and he doesn't seem to have anyone except this Father Tellez. I'd like to find him and talk to him, help him if I can."

"What can you do for him in the long run? It doesn't seem like there are any options for him."

Walt nods in agreement. "I know. Other people would have acted differently. Maybe I can get some ideas from Father Tellez." He hugs Bellena tightly and speaks gently. "Thanks for caring for my son. You didn't have to, but I really appreciate it."

"He's a part of you, which makes him a part of me. He sounds like a fascinating young man. I hope to meet him soon."

\#

Pyotr comes into the living room wearing his pajamas. Olga dozes on the couch with the television on. "Babu, are you awake?" he asks in his mixture of Russian and Komi. He touches her cheek.

She smiles. "Can't you sleep? Do you need a drink or a story?" She lifts him onto the couch where he snuggles in close. "Is that better?"

"Babu, he's back."

§

The Russian grandmother, more like a babushka now than she was three years ago, walks her grandson to school, kisses him in front of the flagpole, and watches him run into the building. Soon, school will end and summer will begin. Pyotr will miss it; he loves his teacher and fellow classmates, even if he doesn't bring any of them home. Home. By home, Olga means back to the house in Buena Vista. Their real home waits ten thousand miles away, and summer is coming there too. The joyous season; the end to the long, difficult winter. Families became happier then, after being cooped up for eight months in so much darkness, so much snow. Olga wonders if she will ever again feel that family experience, if she will ever have what her mother and father had. Not here she won't, not here in America. She must help find him, whoever him is, so she can return to Pechora.

Today, she will talk with Walt and Bellena and tell them what Pyotr said last night. She will trust Walt, whoever he represents, and believe in Bellena, who seems to understand her man and care about Pyotr. Bellena could be from Komi. Olga called Dr. Kinkade to tell him she wouldn't be working, that she had a meeting with an agent. If he would have asked what kind of agent, she would have told him a real estate agent, but he didn't ask. The doctor is a nice man too. America has so many nice men who are kind and responsible. She hopes Pyotr's man is one of those men.

Mac answers when Olga calls. She can find Bellena at her office on Main Street, and it won't cause an interruption. Walt is out of town on business. Olga takes her picture of Gora Narodnaya, feeling in some way that it is part of the puzzle. Main Street and her house are on the east side of Bueny, the treeless side of town. Not as pretty as the west side, on the other side of U.S. 24 that divides the city, but with better vistas, certainly a better view of Mt. Princeton and Mt. Yale. Strange names for mountains, she thinks. The sign on Bellena's door says, Welcome, Come In.

Bellena acts surprised, but she stands from her desk and hugs Olga. It's genuine, and her fears of disrupting Bellena's work evaporate. Still, Olga apologizes for coming in unannounced and thanks Bellena for their trip to the cabin. Bellena pours coffee for Olga and refreshes her own.

"Bellena, so much seems to be swirling around us, but this wind leaves me tired and confused. Last night, Pyotr told me the man was here. I do not know who this man is, but I know he exists at the center of our wind. We came to find Pyotr's father, but this man is not him. This man, though, can answer some questions?" Olga frames this last statement as a question, and she waits for an answer.

Bellena wonders what she can tell Olga, what she would accept and what Walt would consider acceptable. "I, too, don't know any of the answers, and I have many questions. You and Pyotr are connected to Walt in an unanswerable way, and it began with Yamantov, I think." Bellena gets up from behind her desk, takes Olga's hand, and leads her to the brown leather couch that sits against the opposite wall. She continues to hold Olga's hand. Olga remembers the dinner and the comfort she felt by Bellena's touch. "This may be painful, but would you tell me what you remember about that moment when the accident happened?"

Olga looks down and away for a moment. "Pyotr and I were packing up from our picnic after visiting my daughter. He stood next to a reindeer when I heard the shot. A hunter shot the largest of the reindeer, the one closest to Pyotr. Almost immediately there was the great whiteness; the forest turned completely white." She corrects herself. "No, there was a short moment between the shot and the whiteness, enough time for me to run to Pyotr and bring him back to the cave. Then, then there was the whiteness . . . and I felt my Ursula was gone." Olga looks up for approval of her story.

"It must have been horrible. Do you remember if Pyotr said anything to you at that moment?"

Olga is stunned, but not offended. He did say something, and she hadn't remembered until just this moment. "Yes. He said, 'I got him, Babu, I got him.' He slumped into my body and did not speak again until later that evening when we were rescued. What does that mean, Bellena?"

"I don't know, but maybe Pyotr can tell us. Something occurred that connects us, your family and mine." They sit quietly for several moments. Bellena silently asks her husband for his trust with what she is about to do. "Olga, I'm going to tell you things that I really don't completely know. That makes no sense but try to understand." Bellena shakes her head, mostly to herself, and begins. "My dad almost died that week. He had to be taken to the hospital in Salida. Walt was in Washington in important meetings, but for some unexplained reason, he returned home early. I could tell you everything that happened that day to me to the exact detail." She pauses, about to reveal a tidbit of confidential information. "My dear friend, Yamantov wasn't an accident. It was part of something much larger, and its consequences are still to be determined."

"I do not understand."

"Neither do I, really, but for the first time in my life, I'm beginning to wonder about fate. My faith tells me one thing, Olga, but all of this has made me wonder about the great lies we tell ourselves or that are told to us . . . *for our own good.*" Bellena curls her lips inward as if she has just told a lie, the lie of omission. "We're going to need to trust each other for a while so we can get to the bottom of this. Walt will be home late tonight, at least he plans to. He's off trying to get more information on this mysterious man that Pyotr channels, and maybe a religious man in Mexico can help"

"Yamantov was not an accident? What are you saying?" Olga latched onto that part of Bellena's explanation and didn't hear much that came after.

"As I said, I don't know much. Can I let Walt tell you tomorrow?" Bellena realizes Olga will stress over this until it's further explained, but she can't tell her.

"At dinner then?"

"Yes, and hopefully he'll be able to tell you much more." Who am I kidding, Bellena says to herself, tell *us* much more.

# Chapter 13

*Forest City, Colorado, May 1986*

The cops will descend on Samuel's mother in Ouray and stay close. That hurts. He lucked out in one respect though; the highway patrol didn't stop him on his way to Buena Vista. He knows they were concentrating on the highway between Durango and Ouray for his red sedan, but he also knows his luck will run out soon. He arrives in Bueny after dark and passes no cars on the drive up to Forest City. Someone, though, will recall seeing a red sedan up near the church cabin. Someone will recall seeing the red sedan in town at the hardware store. Someone will recall. His planning will now have to pay off. When he gets to the cabin, he loads the last of his things into the red sedan and transfers them to the mine. He won't be staying at the cabin any longer, but he still has one task to complete at St. Mary, even if it does put him at risk. The altar. He'll start early and work all day, fourteen hours or more, until it's done. Monday and maybe Tuesday, and then he disappears again.

Four feet by two and a half feet by three feet high. A glorified cabinet. The altar will have an easily removable top and doors that face the apse. Sam has altered his plans because of time; he won't be able to glue the oak boards together, and he will now arrange them horizontally rather than vertically. His first task is to sand the last two boards and varnish them and then to fasten a skeletal frame to the floor. He arrives at St. Mary at six and hangs a Closed for Repairs sign on the door and bolts himself inside. He should be tired, since he slept only a few hours, but his mind races. He sets to work immediately, and his concerns are not shown in his demeanor, but he has concerns. Father Tellez, The Man, and Baby Bear. Sam has no idea how he will meet those people or under what conditions. Now, he thinks, I'm referring to Baby Bear as a person; are spirits souls? He hopes he has the time to find out.

§

On the phone on Sunday afternoon, Walt speaks bluntly to Father Tellez. "His life is in danger, Father. He's going to be taken in, and the government only cares about keeping his secret. They'll bury him so deep and isolate him. I need your help."

Walt arrives in Hermosillo at nine in the morning. Father Tellez has a car waiting to pick him up at the airport. Walt doesn't miss the joke by the priest when the white, Chevy station wagon Sam escaped in back in December of '83, pulls up. Now, it's a dusty, well-worn, church taxi. The driver speaks no English and holds a sign on white cardboard: Agent Walt Kramer. Father Tellez has coffee and warm biscuits waiting when Walt arrives.

"I trust you had a comfortable flight, Mr. Kramer?"

"I did, thank you." Walt is preparing to size up the priest, since he got so little information from him the last time they met, and left believing that he didn't know anything about Sam. He had been fooled, something that seldom happens to him, but he has a feeling the priest wants to help. "You deceived me the last time I was here, Father."

"Oh, you must have asked the wrong questions then. I told you a parishioner had given us the car, and you accepted that. There was no paperwork, and if I recall, you only asked about that." Father raises his eyebrows and his cup as if saying touché. "How can I help?"

"Sam, or did he go by John?"

"John, at first, but when I gained his trust, it was Samuel."

"Sam needs a place, and it can't be the United States. He also needs a friend, and I'm going to put that responsibility on you, you and this church." Walt looks to the priest for confirmation.

"Go on."

"I don't know what he told you about running, about fleeing

from the Navy and the United States . . ."

"Let me stop you, Mr. Kramer, and save some time. I know pretty much everything about that, and I know that he feels an overwhelming amount of grief and sadness for his part. Part. He feels completely responsible for the deaths of the people at Yamantov. And, yes, he understands that he could unlock a lot of secrets if he was to tell his story to the press, and that would cause a bit of consternation for the United States . . . and the Soviet Union." He stares directly into Walt's eyes. "Let me ask you a simple question. Did you come down here to do harm to me?"

Walt tightens his jaw. He has stretched his authority and reputation with the CIA to the limits in coming here, since he has kept secrets even from them. He anticipated Father Tellez's apprehension about this. "No, I did not. My people do not even know that I know the connection between you and Sam; they think I'm here following another lead. It's a distorted web of information I've given them." Walt pulls a small envelope from his sports jacket pocket and lays it on the priest's desk. "Sam," and here Walt stalls, and Father Tellez waits. "Sam was put in the position he was because of his character. The men who serve on our nuclear submarines are the finest our nation has." Outside, the church bells toll eleven o'clock. Walt knows Father Tellez has the upper hand, but he doesn't want it to be a contest. He needs the Mexican priest's assistance to help Sam out of this international mess, but Father Tellez will make him spell it out, just as he should. "I can't ask you to do this thing, unless you know for certain it will end this." He pushes the envelope across the table and removes his hand. "Sam lives and works in the Buena Vista area, about fifteen miles from where I live. I've never seen him, but I know he's there. I spent several hours in St. Mary examining his work, just two days ago, and I will tell you that he's become an amazing carpenter. You can trace his development over the past year by looking at the work he did last summer and compare it with his work now. The essentials are nearly complete. He's building a beautiful altar out of oak. Let's hope he gets the opportunity to finish it. Simple, but beautiful." Walt always knows his audience. If he was relating this story to members of the CIA cadre, they wouldn't care. Father Tellez cares, and he already knows this information.

"I hope to visit St. Mary someday and see his work firsthand. His letters have told me about his struggles with carpentry, and I've had many good laughs. Tell me, Mr. Kramer . . ."

"You can call me Walt."

"No, not yet. Tell me, how did you find out that Samuel was in your area if you've never seen him?"

"A boy, a seven-year-old boy from the Soviet Union told me. I don't know how, but he feels him, senses his presence. His name is Pyotr, and his mother was killed at Yamantov on that day. He and his grandmother came to my town, to Buena Vista, last fall looking for someone. Olga thought it was the boy's father, but it wasn't. It was Sam. Don't ask me to explain all this because I can't. Frankly, I never believed in this kind of stuff, but Pyotr led me to St. Mary. My father and I were fishing with Pyotr, and he just took off running down the road towards St. Mary. I chased him, and when he got there, he told me." Walt stops and waits.

Father Tellez doesn't speak, but he doesn't show disbelief on his face. He reaches for the envelope, unhooks the clasp, and opens it. He slides out the two photographs but doesn't look at them immediately. "Yesterday evening, while I was listening to prayers from two of my fellow priests, I had a feeling, a sensation come over me. Would you know anything about that, Walt?"

"No, Father, I don't."

"Hmm." He looks at the first photo. "And what do I see as I view this picture?"

"That was taken in 1953. It's me in my Army uniform with my son."

Father Tellez studies it. He nods but doesn't look up. "This story just gets more intriguing by the minute, doesn't it?" He turns it over to read the faded writing on the back. "Does Samuel know?"

"Yes and no. He knows his father was a loser who deserted him when he was a child, but his mother told him small lies about me to make me sound like a good man. He doesn't know that I'm looking for him or what I've been doing for the last thirty years."

"When did you start looking for him?"

"When the Navy informed me that he didn't return to duty. They had alerted the CIA that one of their men from the *U.S.S. Ohio* was agitated." Walt shakes his head once. "Agitated! What a fucking word to describe his emotions."

Father Tellez smiles. "I'm the only one God allows to use that word in this room."

Walt appreciates the Father's humor.

The priest studies the second photo. "And this one?"

"My wife took that one a week ago with my dad's Polaroid camera. It's of Pyotr and his grandmother."

"She's a nice-looking woman, but very worried. Did you notice how tightly she holds onto Pyotr?" Walt doesn't answer. "Did the boy move as the picture was being taken? He's very blurry."

"I don't think so, Father."

The two men have their own thoughts. Finally, Father Tellez speaks. "And what do you wish for me to do, Walt?"

"I hope to meet Sam this week. He'll be suspicious of my intentions, to say the least. I want two things. I want a brief letter from you that I can give him, and then I want to send him to you for protection. This church is a sanctuary, and maybe he can find a life here that he can never have in America again."

§

When he wakes after surgery, Henry demands to use the telephone, demands to be released, and demands his truck be brought to the hospital so he can drive back to Ouray. The doctors won't release him. When he arrived in the ambulance, he had lost a lot of blood. A nurse comes in, plugs a phone into the wall, and asks how the other guy in the fight looks. He finds nothing funny in her remark and screams at her to leave. Two FBI agents enter his room just as the nurse leaves.

They want any information he can recall, anything that might help them find Sam Elkington. Henry's memory remains cloudy, less than twenty-four hours after being shot at the gas station. He can't remember the new Sam, "but he was still scraggly, like a damned hippie."

§

Yamantov was not an accident? Of course it was. How could it not have been? Olga can't wrap herself around any other concept, the idea she has been carrying for nearly three years. Everyone knows what happened; a reactor blew up. What did Bellena mean? Chernobyl was an accident, but it is a meltdown, not an explosion? Its location, near Kiev in the heart of Soviet Russia, cannot be hidden. But Yamantov was in the far north, so far from Moscow or Leningrad, so far from anything except former gulag prisoners and the Arctic Circle: it can be denied, and those who died remain hidden. Ursula can be explained away.

Olga needs the extra time that baseball practice provides on this Monday. She isn't ready to listen to all of Pyotr's adventures yet, all of his math and geography questions, or any of his new insights into America. At three o'clock he will walk to practice where he will spend two more hours. Maybe then she will be ready, but probably not. Yamantov. No accident? Did Bellena say there was no accident or that it was no accident? If there was no accident, maybe Ursula and the others are still alive somewhere, hidden by the government. Did they suffer radiation poisoning and now are being kept at a hospital somewhere? Olga, do not be silly. She would have gotten word to me somehow. Even my government cannot be so cruel as to keep a secret like that for so long. Some reports about Chernobyl say no one died, but that there will be extensive radiation illnesses. Those early reports about 25,000 deaths are wrong; maybe just a few dozen. Olga continues to pace the small kitchen. Maybe Yamantov was like Chernobyl. She has to get control of her emotions before she faces Pyotr; she can't alarm him or raise his hopes. Come now, Olga, she warns herself. She wants to call Bellena and ask her when Walt will return. Or maybe Bellena could tell her more of what she does not know. Where did Bellena say Walt went? It does not matter; he will be home for dinner and then he will tell me. Mac said to be ready around six. Oh, I will be ready.

§

Previous work on the altar has gone smoothly. Since much of the preparation has already been done, it's more a matter of assembling the parts. Sam uses screws to fasten the oak boards to the frame, driving them in from the inside, so they won't show when the altar is completed. Another carpenter will have to attach the doors that open to the apse where materials are accessible, and the entire altar will need a final coat of varnish. He hopes those who worship at St. Mary in the future keep it up and not allow it to deteriorate again. Premade trim for the corners and base make it easier—and faster—to complete. Simple church, simple altar. Father Tellez recommended that. But Sam has taken great care to make the altar one the congregation can be proud of for many years. He will finish it before dark, and then he will be done. St. Mary will still need a bit more work, work that he had planned to complete during the summer, but his time is over here, and people are closing in. Shooting Henry sealed the deal, and he can't stay any longer. Tonight, and then . . .

Sam pushes those thoughts away and drills the holes for the wooden pegs that will secure the top of the altar to the base. Eight pegs. Father Spreewell allowed him to rent wonderful tools for this job, right down to the drill bits. Sharp, for precise work. Each time he stops to allow stain to dry, he cleans a portion of the church. He hopes to get the altar table attached before the sun goes down. Then he will place the old altar wood inside the new altar, pull the pews into place, kneel at the communion rail and say the Lord's Prayer. It matters to him that he says the first prayer in the restored church. He will turn off the lights and go to the mine.

And wait.

§

Bellena fixes fried chicken and mashed potatoes for dinner, her dad's favorite. Walt thinks her shrimp dishes are better. It turns out that Pyotr likes this dish better than last week's burgers. Of course, he concentrates on the legs and potatoes and ignores the corn and salad. Olga concentrates on Walt, eager to hear any information that will answer her multitude of questions. Aware of her anticipation, he talks openly at the table, trusting that Pyotr can accept the information too.

"Olga, we're glad you and Pyotr could share another meal with us. As you've probably noticed, we aren't real formal or elaborate around here. Mac likes to call us plain folks, but Bellena bristles at that tag. She has a bit of sophistication. We're not sure where she obtained it though." Walt smiles at his wife. "She tells me the two of you talked this morning and you might have a few questions for me. Let me start by telling you where I was today. I flew to Mexico, to a city just a little south of the border called Hermosillo, to meet with a Catholic priest named Father Tellez. It seems as if the person we're looking for, the man that Pyotr talks about, lived down there for about a year and a half, until about a year ago when he came back here. Father Tellez speaks very highly about this person. He says he's honest, caring, and of good character. He worries about this person too, just as we do." He pauses with a forkful of potatoes at his mouth. "Father Tellez said he carries a heavy heart, that he carries a secret too big for one person to manage. Because of this secret, he isolates himself, trying to understand what purpose, why exactly he was chosen to hold onto it."

The adults are locked into what Walt says, but Pyotr seems only interested in the chicken and potatoes. He finishes his first helping and points to the plates in the middle of the table holding more. Bellena dishes him up another round.

"Does this man have a name?" asks Olga.

"Yes, he does, Olga. His name is Samuel Elkington." Pyotr looks up to his grandmother when he hears this name, but quickly returns to his food.

"Does he know anything about Yamantov?" asks Olga.

"Yes, a great deal, it seems. What I'm hoping is that we can talk to him and let him tell us, but first we need to find him. He needs our protection too."

Mac and Bellena understand what Walt means by protection, but Olga doesn't. "Why would he need our protection, Walt? What can I possibly do?"

Walt leans even farther into the table. "The secret he carries might cause my country and your country to go to war. They don't want to, but if he reveals what he knows, it might be impossible to avoid. My country's authorities are trying to find him and prevent him from telling anyone. If they find him first, we won't be allowed to talk to him."

The phone in the kitchen rings, and Bellena gets up to answer it. "Walt, it's for you."

While Walt talks quietly, Mac engages Pyotr in baseball talk. Bellena tries to reassure Olga. "My husband does this for a living. By that, I mean he solves problems for the government. He manages a power plant, a nuclear power plant, in northern Colorado, but none of this has anything to do with that. The government has him working on finding Sam. Anything you or Pyotr can do to help him will make it easier. If Walt finds him before any of the other agencies do, then he thinks we can get some answers." She pauses. "And maybe we can help Sam too."

Olga's thoughts race forward. "Why do you call him Sam instead of Samuel? Do you know him?"

Walt calls Bellena into the kitchen, and she excuses herself by touching Olga's forearm. He has hung up the phone, but he rests his hand on the receiver. When Bellena gets close, he whispers, "That was Washington. It seems as though Sam shot a man in Durango. The police didn't catch him, but this means his time is limited." They stare at each other. "I'll need to go up to St. Mary now. Maybe he's returned. You guys can finish dinner and then decide whether to follow me or take Olga and Pyotr home." Walt and Bellena return to the table, but only Bellena sits. Walt apologizes and explains that he needs to make a quick trip.

Pyotr looks up. "I could go with you to help find him. He's hiding."

Olga isn't surprised this time. "Where Pyotr?"

"In the dark. In his dark."

While Olga talks gently with her grandson, Walt goes to the garage to get flashlights.

§

It's nearly nine when Bellena pulls her new minivan up to St. Mary carrying Walt, Mac, Olga, and Pyotr. Bellena points the van directly at the front door and leaves the lights on, which creates a surrealistic scene. Olga looks to Pyotr, but he has nothing to say, looking more like a small boy out on an adventure. Walt steps out, switches on his flashlight, and climbs the steps up to the church door. The new door has no locking system, but it seems to be secured from the inside. He can't tell for sure; the door fits tightly in the jamb preventing him from shining his light through a crack to determine. If it's bolted from the inside, maybe Sam is still here, thinks Walt. He reaches back with his left hand to his back pocket to reassure himself that he has Father Tellez's letter, then motions for the others to stay in the van.

Walt jumps off the side of the porch and walks around to the sacristy. Duct tape covers the keyhole, and he pulls open the door cautiously. When he steps, in he calls out. "Sam. Are you in here, Sam?" The silence outlasts his question. Walt flashes his light quickly through the small room into each corner, but it remains as empty as when he examined it just a few days earlier. Still on guard he walks cautiously into the church apse. "Sam. I'm not here to hurt you. I have a letter from Father Tellez for you. My name is Walt Kramer." He waits. "I'm going to turn on the lights when I find the switch, okay?" His flashlight scans the walls. He finds a switch just behind him next to the sacristy door. He flips up three switches and the church illuminates. It has been put together for a service, with the pulpit and pews arranged for a minister to deliver a sermon. Walt walks slowly to the front of the church, removes a two-by-four that holds the door shut, opens it, and waves the others to come in.

Pyotr bolts in first followed by his grandmother, Bellena, and Mac. "Anything? asks Olga.

"Just a beautiful church and lots of silence. He's been here, though, because it's done, or at least almost done." Walt runs his hand over the back of a pew. "The man does excellent work." Olga looks to ask another question, but Walt understands and says, "I was here this weekend looking for him. The pews were moved against the walls and there was no altar."

Bellena scans the ceiling, looking for any place Sam might hide. Pyotr has climbed over the communion rail and stands behind the altar waving at his grandmother. Mac remains at the door but looks back to the road. He turns to Walt and motions for him to approach. "Where did Sam live this past year? I mean, he didn't live in this church, so he must have had a cabin near here. From what you've told us, he wasn't living in town, or he would have been seen. Arnie would have known."

Walt points to the east. "The Church maintains a cabin in the trees. I just had a hunch, based on Pyotr's remarks, that Sam would be here. Maybe he saw our lights and high-tailed it out of here. We'll drive up, but I'll bet he won't be there when we arrive. He's been warned now."

Olga and Bellena have walked to the apse where Pyotr plays and are standing together in front of the altar. "It's beautiful," says Bellena.

Pyotr comes around to them. Olga kneels to talk to Pyotr at his level. "Are you tired?" The boy shakes his head. Olga rubs his hair and stands. She looks to Bellena and then steps into her body and hugs her. Olga uses Bellena as her support and allows her head to lay on Bellena's shoulder. Bellena wraps her arms around Olga's waist and feels her weight sag. Bellena wonders if Olga will collapse, but she doesn't.

"Let me take you home," she whispers. "You've had a trying day." Bellena looks up to see Walt just a few feet away, and she motions that they must go. He understands.

§

A quarter of a mile back towards Buena Vista, Walt gets out of the van, telling Bellena to take everyone home and then come back for him. She blows him a small kiss and nods. "Be careful," she says and drives away. Walt turns away from the vehicle's headlights, waits to allow his eyes to acclimate to the moonless night, and then switches on his flashlight. On Saturday he had located the church cabin. Arnie told him where it was. Arnie, thinks Walt, the walking encyclopedia of southern Colorado. He walks down the road, knowing that if Sam hides in the cabin, he will be watching him approach. No sense concealing his movements; walk right up to the front door and knock.

Another unlocked door. Walt cautiously pushes it in and calls out for his son, but there is no answer. A one room cabin with a bathroom. The bedding has been stripped and folded. There are no dirty dishes, no food in the small refrigerator, no clothes hanging anywhere. No sign that anyone has been living here recently. Walt pulls out one of the two chairs at the kitchen table and sits. He rubs his eyes and tries to put the pieces together. Sam must have been here to have completed the church. Where's the car? Did he come back to finish the church, and when he did, did he bolt again? That makes the most sense, but where would he have gone? Why did Pyotr say what he did? Maybe that's why Pyotr behaved as he did at St. Mary. He stands again, turns slowly, finds the light switch, and flips it on. Walt's eyes scan the small cabin, trying to imagine his son living so close to him for over a year. He wonders if Sam ever had a feeling, wonders what he was trying to accomplish here. Was he just hiding? There has to be more. Walt notices an envelope tacked to a sign over the door. He reaches up and reads the writing on the outside.

"This sign belongs to Barkley Abbott in Ouray, Colorado. Please return it to him and give him this note." Walt reads the sign, *Esse est percipi*. He knows its meaning but wonders why Sam would have it. He opens the envelope, unfolds the paper, and reads it. "Hey Bark. I didn't want this sign to get lost or misplaced where either you or I wouldn't have it. Put it back over your door or hang it next to my poem. I need a couple of favors. First, I want you to go over and meet my mother. Tell her what you can about me. I was planning on seeing her the last time I saw you, but Henry got in my way. Sit and talk with her and tell her I love her and that I am deeply sorry for hurting her. Try to get in touch with Delany. I was able to see her in Durango. I gave her back the rock. Remember what I told you about half-lives, because that's how I've lived for the past three years. Maybe you too? Apologize to Henry for me but tell him not to pull a gun on a desperate man. Thank you for your kindness and concern. Know that you helped me beyond what I can repay."

Walt sees Bellena's van driving slowly up the dirt road. He folds the note, puts it carefully back in the envelope, takes down the sign, and flips off the light.

§

Returning to the dark entrance of his mine, Sam watches the lights at his cabin. Baby Bear seems excited, and Sam senses the time has come.

§

Olga puts Pyotr to bed, even though he's wired from the night's adventure. She lays down, exhausted, and falls asleep next to him. He gets up for his drawing pad and colored pencils, turns on his reading lamp, and pulls the covers over his legs. He wishes Grampar was here to draw with him. He sketches the church in great detail: first, the outside entrance with its tiny steeple, then the inside in all its splendor with the pews and the pulpit and the altar. He turns the pad of paper to a fresh page and begins to sketch just the altar. He's very good with inanimate objects, but the person hiding inside the altar proves more difficult. Pyotr wanted to tell Babu, but the man put his finger to his lips in a plea to stay silent, to not give him away. They had smiled at each other, as if they shared a secret, and then Pyotr reached down, touched the man's cheek, and whispered, "I got you, Great One."

§

Mac brews a fresh pot of coffee in anticipation of a long night. He'll stay up with Walt and Bellena for as long as it takes. They seem close to their goal, if their goal includes meeting with Sam, but goals usually are toughest to achieve as one gets closer. Walt said, almost under his breath at the church, that he was missing something, some clue. Mac will review things with him, ask questions to make him reconsider his movements, hopefully clearing away an assumption that was in error. They have been doing this since Korea, although Bellena has become more his sounding board since their marriage. As it should be, Mac thinks. He likes Olga and Pyotr, but he knows they will be leaving soon. Walt will help them return to Pechora. Olga has said as much, even though this journey confuses her about life. She devotes every minute now to Pyotr, but it's a symbiotic relationship. Mac pours himself a cup and sits at the table. He's attracted to Olga, and she stirred sexual feelings in him when he held her up as he walked her into her house. You're an old man, Mac, so don't go stupid on yourself, he says to himself with a smile.

Both Bellena and Walt are glad for the coffee. She asks if anyone wants anything to eat, but they refuse. Coffee will be enough. Mac loves these two people dearly and would do anything for them. Tonight, just working through the recent events will be enough. He's seen Walt in action: hyper-active, up and down, pacing, the stare, a gallon of coffee. Mac remembers that day up at the Chosin Reservoir when Walt's determination saved a hundred men who only wanted to stay warm. His son-in-law is a remarkable force, and he'll solve this problem too.

"What I don't get," says Bellena, "is Pyotr's change. At dinner he couldn't wait to get to the church, but when he got there, he was just a playful boy without a care in the world."

Walt noticed that too. "Pyotr wasn't wrong, and he didn't change, I don't think. His excitement was because Sam was there . . . at least somewhere close." Walt pauses. "He didn't want to be found tonight."

"Why do you think that is?" asks Mac.

Bellena gives a feminine grunt. "Scared to death probably. Law enforcement is closing in, and the shooting makes it even harder."

"Walt, what if you sent just Olga and Pyotr up there? Maybe you could be close, but me and Belle wouldn't go?" Bellena nods and looks to Walt.

Walt stands and walks to the far end of the kitchen, stops at the back door, and stares into the darkness. Neither Bellena nor Mac speaks. They know not to interject anything yet. Three minutes later he turns back, takes Sam's note from his pocket, walks to the table, and gives it to Bellena.  "Read this."  He goes to the living room.  He returns with the plan for the Mollie Miller Mine and unfolds it on the kitchen table.

"What's this?" asks Mac.

"A temporary hiding place, I think."

"Where did you get it?" asks Bellena.

"From the sacristy at the church.  When I first saw it, I didn't know what I had; I thought it was just note paper for him.  There's a list of people on the back, which is important, but he had plenty of paper he could have used for that.  The note you just read tells me that he's trying to contact these people for some reason before he's caught.  The problem is the shooting.  It limits his time."

"Which means it limits your time," says Bellena.

"Yeah."  Walt goes inside himself again.

# CHAPTER 14

*The Mine near Forest City, late May 1986*

The telephone rings five times at Olga's house. It's almost midnight. Pyotr answers it.

"She's asleep."

"I'll need you to wake her up, so I can speak with her. Why are you still awake?" asks Walt.

"I'm drawing. I'll get her."

Olga picks up a few moments later. "What is wrong?" she asks.

"Nothing Olga. I want to go back to the church tomorrow; but I want to take you and Pyotr with me. Just the three of us. I think the man wants to talk to you . . . and Pyotr. It's important for all of us. Can you be ready before daylight?"

Walt doesn't sleep. He sends Mac to bed around one, and Bellena stays with him until two. She knows he won't sleep until this is resolved.

§

Sam sleeps well. Barkley, Delany, Henry, finishing the altar, and watching the family have worn him out. But it's more than that. Knowing he won't be running much longer relaxes him. What remains in Forest City can probably be accomplished tomorrow. He lies down on the cot in the mine and puts his hand on his belly, on Delany's yellow. Funny. "Settle down, Baby Bear, I need some sleep."

§

Walt, Olga, and Pyotr drive the bumpy, rutted road to Forest City before the sun rises. They pass the hot springs, the horse stables, and Sam's cabin without pausing. As Walt drives past St. Mary, he slows, but doesn't stop. The truck swerves gently toward the church on its own.

"What do you think, Pyotr?" he asks.

Pyotr points to the edge of the forest near another abandoned mine shaft. "Look, Babu, reindeer!"

Neither Olga nor Walt had seen them and they smile. "No, Pyotr, those are elk," says Walt.

"They are much larger than the reindeer we have in Komi, Pyotr, but they are very similar," says Olga. Pyotr presses his nose against the truck's window and watches them turn back into the trees.

Walt continues another mile up the road toward the Mollie Miller. He stops a hundred yards from the entrance, but doesn't get out, which seems to confuse Olga. She looks at him, puts her right hand to her lips, but waits. Pyotr bounces on the seat between them. Walt puts his hand on the boy's thigh. "Settle down, young fella, we'll see him soon."

"Any instructions?" asks Olga.

"No. We aren't in charge here; we aren't in control of the meeting." He drives closer before stopping and getting out. He walks around his truck and opens the passenger door for Olga and Pyotr. They walk to the mine entrance, each adult holding one of Pyotr's hands. No Admittance, says the sign. The entrance is boarded up, and the mine looks deserted. Walt knows it isn't safe for Olga or Pyotr. "Wait here," he says.

He lets go of Pyotr's hand, steps to the chain-link fence and pulls part of it away from its post so he can slip through. He knocks on the wood, giving Sam warning. Sam watched their arrival, but he waits. They have to come to him. My terms, not theirs, he thinks. Walt glances back to Olga and Pyotr and reminds them to stay back, to wait for him to call them, and he opens the crude door on the mine and steps in. Walt switches on his flashlight.

"Sam. My name is Walt Kramer. I'm not here to hurt you." He waits for a response. He calls again and waits again. Silence. He explores the mine with his light. It doesn't look like anyone has been in the mine recently. Dust hasn't been disturbed and there are no footprints. His eyes narrow, because he was so sure just minutes ago. He walks a few steps deeper into the mine tunnel. According to the plans, the entrance staging area extends about twenty feet in length, and then the mine drops down several hundred feet. Sam won't be there. He's got to be in this part of the mine. Walt moves cautiously. He calls out again. "Sam, I've brought two people along who want to help."

Walt hears a noise and turns suddenly. "Why are you in this mine, Walt? He's back there," says Pyotr.

"Where Pyotr?" Walt resists the urge to take the little boy out of the mine to safety.

"With the reindeer."

Olga comes in with both a look of anxiety and concern. "A car drove up with two men inside. They are wearing suits, and they asked if you were in here. I told them no, but they are sitting in the car. Did I do right?"

Walt shakes his head yes. He puts his arm around Pyotr and steps closer to Olga. "Let me give you my keys. I want you and Pyotr to walk out and drive away. Drive up to St. Elmo and buy something from the general store, maybe something for Pyotr. If the store hasn't opened yet, just walk the streets and look at the buildings. If the men follow you or ask you any questions, just tell them you're visiting from the Soviet Union and heard that St. Elmo was an interesting ghost town. Tell them I loaned you my truck this morning; that I met your family on one of my trips there, and you're just visiting." He realizes he's probably given them too much to remember, but Olga nods her head. "You can drive, can't you?"

She takes his keys. "Yes, of course. Where will we meet up with you?"

"When the men leave, go to the church. I'll meet you back there."

Walt bends over to check on Pyotr. "Are you all right, son?" The little boy nods. "Take care of your grandmother, and don't talk to the men unless they ask you a direct question. If they ask why you came in here, just tell them you were curious, that you hoped to find some gold." Walt checks for Pyotr's comprehension. "Good boy." He stands and hugs Olga. "I'll find him. This will work out . . . today."

He watches them leave the mine and walk to the truck, while concealing himself from the FBI agents. Olga lifts Pyotr into the truck, gets in, and starts it up. The men let them pass, but they follow the truck as it heads to St. Elmo. He waits until they're out of sight of the mine, and then he slips out and runs back toward the ruins where Pyotr saw the elk. He slows when he gets to the tree line where he can quickly hide himself if any cars drive by. Sweat runs down his back; it's been too many years since he's run this hard. A sound ahead of him in the trees makes him stop. Walt walks cautiously along an old railroad path to a small clearing that is well-hidden from the road. The elk graze peacefully next to a red sedan. A few look up to notice Walt, but don't run away.

He looks around. He wonders what Sam must be feeling. Walt moves back to the tree line and starts walking toward the church. He passes the ruins of the mine they drove past earlier.

"I'm in here."

§

Olga and Pyotr walk the dusty streets of old St. Elmo. They peer into windows of shacks and dilapidated buildings. The general store will open at ten, so they have about a half hour to wait. To the north, across the creek and up a slight incline, lies an old school that has been refurbished for tourists. Pyotr scampers up the steps, but a plexiglas barrier prevents him from examining it closely. The two men sit in their car and watch. A few of the wooden cabins remind Olga of her childhood home in Inta. Homes were built of wood to withstand the frigid winters. All the families were once prisoners in the Gulag, suspicious of strangers. She stops in front of one cabin and stares. From behind a muslin curtain, a shadow looks out. Pyotr comes up and takes her hand. "You aren't afraid anymore, are you?" he says. She shakes her head, bends over, and picks him up. "You're warm," he says. She kisses his cheek. She turns back and looks to the ghost town. The men are pulling out and heading toward Buena Vista. She sets Pyotr down and they walk to the general store.

§

"I'm not here to hurt you," Walt calls out. "Can I come in?"

"Yeah. Be careful of the chicken wire."

Walt maneuvers around the wire, lifts an old door aside, and steps into the mine's staging area. It takes a moment for his eyes to adjust to the dim light. "Can I turn on my flashlight?" he asks.

"No." Sam sits behind a makeshift desk. He switches on his flashlight and uses it to show Walt a chair. "You can sit there. Move real slowly; I've got a gun."

Walt sits. "You won't need it; I'm not here to do you any harm. My name is Walt Kramer."

"We'll see. Are you FBI?"

"No." Walt wishes it was lighter so he could see the facial expressions of Sam. "I have a letter for you from Father Tellez. I asked him to write one so that I could have a little credibility at the start." Walt shifts slightly to take the letter from his back pocket. He leans forward and slides the letter across the desk to Sam. "I'll put my hands on top of my head and sit real still while you read it."

Sam opens the envelope and shines his flashlight on the note. Dust particles float aimlessly in the flashlight's beam. Walt sees a shadowed torture on his son's face as Sam reads the note. Walt is positive Father Tellez's words are gentle. When Sam finishes, he asks Walt, "Have you read this?"

"No, but I do know Father Tellez worries for you."

"I still have a few people who do. He wants me to go back to Hermosillo and live there. He thinks he can protect me from ... whoever ... my fate." The two men sit in silence for a few minutes before Sam speaks again. "Why have you been searching for me?"

"To explain why we did what we did."

"I doubt you can. Are you Navy?"

"No." Walt speaks slowly, measuring his words. "I'm kind of a contractor for the government. Officially, I'm the supervisor for the nuclear power plant in northern Colorado. Ft. St. Vrain. But I have ties to the CIA. A few times over the years, I've done some work for them in foreign countries, and I've gained a reputation for success. During the summer of '83, I was invited to sit in on some very high-level discussions about Yamantov." He pauses to let that sink in to Sam. "I wasn't a policy maker; they just wanted my expertise on nuclear power plants, but maybe I gave them a little more input than they asked. Anyway, when your sub returned from its mission and you went AWOL, they called me to see if I could find you. Obviously, I wasn't immediately successful."

"That doesn't explain why."

"The United States, and by that I mean the President, his advisors, and the Joint Chiefs, all believed the Soviet Union was preparing a first-strike on America within the next few years. By now, by 1986. Yamantov was to be a massive, fortified, underground military bunker. It was to be a survivable underground city. The political climate at the time between our two countries was more tense than it had been at any time during the Cold War, even more so than during the Cuban Missile Crisis, although the general public doesn't know. You knew, and that's why you were serving. You bought into that scenario, to protect our country. Anyway, the decision was made to launch a single nuke on Yamantov, to send a message that we would never sit by and allow them to prepare for our annihilation."

"How many died?"

"Too many."

Sam slams his hand down on the desk forcefully. "How many?" he demands.

Walt breathes out. "Nearly two thousand. We can never give an exact figure. It could have been much worse, but the winds blew the radiation to the northeast, away from the population."

They sit silent again, Sam in guilt and Walt in contemplation.

"Why was I selected to turn the key, to launch the missile?" asks Sam.

"Training. You were one of several who had been trained to do the mission. Then, chance. We had several subs that could have been sent, but yours was chosen by the Navy, and you and Greg turned the keys."

"Yeah," says Sam quietly. With his left hand, he takes a chain from around his neck with two copper keys whose code he filed off and flings it to Walt. "Next time you see President Reagan, give him these." Sam remembers clearly the moment after the missile left the *Ohio*. He turned to Greg in triumph but saw his partner in distress. Greg looked as though something had passed through him, and he said he wasn't strong enough. He wasn't speaking to Sam. Then, he felt something passed into him. Sam refocuses on Walt. "So, Walt Kramer, one bomb to prevent a thousand others, huh?"

"We accomplished what we set out to." There is no bluster in his words, no challenge to the key man.

Sam leans forward and lifts his pistol from his lap. "You don't know that. You don't know for sure they were planning a first strike. They were more afraid of us than we were of them. You couldn't have known." The two men go silent for several minutes. "This was wrong, sir. This was the wrong way. We seem to have learned nothing from history."

"Best intelligence," says Walt.

"Bull shit!"

Walt begins to respond but stops. Even in the dim light, he notices a change in Sam's visage. "What is it, son?"

"There comes a time when you're not much use to anyone. You'll be missed by a few people, but not many, and they'll get over it. People died because of me, lots of people. Someone has to be responsible for the men and women of Yamantov. You? President Reagan? The Soviet government? No." Sam pauses. "No, you've all justified it as necessary. You prevented something worse. Maybe you did, but who's responsible for those who weren't a part of all this? Me, that's who. Me."

"I can get you back to Mexico, back to Father Tellez."

"Thanks, but I doubt that will work. I would always have to lie about myself. I've been doing that for too long, and it's no way to live." Sam's eyes suddenly squint and his body convulses inward as if in pain. He pulls the .45 back into his lap, hidden to Walt.

The action repeats itself more forcefully, and Sam utters a guttural moan. Walt stands and takes a step forward, but Sam raises his pistol from his lap, and Walt sits again. "Bear?"

From the front of the mine, Walt hears Pyotr. "Walt, come quick! Babu is down!"

With his pistol Sam motions for Walt to go.

Outside, Walt finds Pyotr leaning over his mother. "What happened, Pyotr?"

"We waited at the church, but I had to come here. The deliverer is here. You found him. We were standing outside, and Babu fell over. I came to get you."

Walt kneels to Olga and turns her over. She's breathing heavily, but there are no apparent injuries. Her eyes are tightly closed. "Olga, can you hear me?" She opens her eyes, but they're far away, as if in a trance. Walt asks Pyotr if his grandmother said anything.

Pyotr shakes his head.

Walt hears the wooden door to the mine slide shut, and what sounds like a beam being dropped across it. He's locked himself in, thinks Walt. "Go to my truck, Pyotr, and get the canteen from under the front seat. Your grandmother will be fine; she just needs some water." He wishes Bellena was here to watch over Olga and Pyotr, so he could give his full attention to Sam. Like most important events, more is going on here than just Sam's immediate future, more is at stake than keeping a secret. "Pyotr, there's a leather pouch under the seat. Bring that to me too." Pyotr nods, smiles, and runs off.

"Olga. Olga! Can you hear me?" Walt sits her up, propping up her body with his left arm, and taking hold of her chin with his right hand. He shakes it gently. "Olga, come back to me." Her eyes begin to focus, and they blink. She turns her face to Walt.

"Pyotr?"

"He went to get you some water. Are you okay?"

"I think so. Did you see them?"

"See who, Olga? I was in the mine with Sam."

She looks confused and mumbles to herself, and her cheeks feel warm. "There were so many of them." She stops looking at

Walt and begins rubbing her sides, almost, thinks Walt, like she's massaging something inside her. She moves her eyes to Walt again. "Pyotr?"

"He went to get you some water, Olga. He'll be right back. He went to my truck at the church." She doesn't look hurt in any way, just confused. "I'm going to lay you back down, Olga. I need to check on Sam."

"Sam?" she asks.

"The man Pyotr has been looking for."

"Oh," she says, but it doesn't seem to matter to her. He gently guides her to the ground, brushing a small stone from beneath her head.

"Pyotr will be back in a minute. Just stay here." He looks for Pyotr, but he can't see him yet. Walt stands and moves to the front of the mine. "Sam, let me in." He gets no response, so he tries to move the wooden door. Just as he thought, Sam has secured it from the inside. "Sam, you can't stay inside forever." He looks back to Olga, who has not moved, but he sees Pyotr skipping up the road. "Sam, I have to tend to Olga for a minute. Pyotr is here too, but no one else. Come out and let me take you into town to Father Spreewell's church. You'll be safe there."

"I brought the water, Walt," yells Pyotr. He sets the leather pouch down near his grandmother and tries to open the canteen but can't.

Walt climbs through the wire again but snags his shirt. "Damn it." He kneels and unscrews the cap to the canteen. "Help me sit your Babu up so she can drink." It's the first time Walt has called Olga "Babu." After Olga drinks, Walt pours a small amount of water into his cupped hand and puts it on Olga's neck. He looks at her closely. "Better?" She nods. She seems, to Walt, to be better. He takes the pouch, loosens the draw string, and takes out a metal box with a phone attached to it. Pyotr's eyes widen. "It's a mobile phone, Pyotr, one of the presents that my government gave me. He dials Bellena at work, hoping she will be there and pick up.

"Bellena, I need your help." He explains what he needs and then says, "If you have any inkling that you're being followed, elude them. Don't take any chances on this. I don't think you will be; I think the FBI will be watching the house, but don't chance it." He puts the phone in the secure carriage and slips it back into the pouch. Pyotr reaches out and touches it. "I'll let you use it later, but I can't just now." Pyotr smiles. "I need you to stay here and watch your grandma, okay? She's a little woozy, so she'll need you to stay with her. She's going to be okay."

"Where are you going, Walt?"

"I have to help Sam, the man you've been searching for, out of the mine. When he comes out, he'll want to meet you." Walt checks for assurance, and when he gets it, he rubs the boy's head. "This is quite an adventure, isn't it?"

As he stands at the entrance to the mine, Walt wonders if this particular mine has a name. It certainly didn't produce as much gold as the Mollie Miller. "Sam, open the door." It's not a command so much as a request, spoken respectfully. He hears some shuffling inside, a hopeful noise. He waits. A thousand thoughts race through his head, none of them particularly helpful at the moment. He's not a good waiter, too impatient, but he has to endure it now. "Sam, open the door, son."

"I turned out the light for now, Mr. Kramer, sir. I do some good thinking in the dark. Being on a submarine trains one for that. I'm sitting down. You might want to get comfortable too. After you've been at sea for a few months, when you first exit the boat, the sun shines super-bright, almost too bright. Look up at the sun real quickly with your eyes wide open, and you'll see what I mean." Another pause. "Did you do that, sir?"

"I did. I probably haven't done that since I was a kid. It's like a white flash."

"Yeah, kind of like that. It takes a few minutes for your eyes to adjust again. Sir, I committed a terrible, unspeakable deed." Walt wants to say that he didn't, but remains silent, allowing Sam to continue. "I wanted to kill myself after Greg did, but I couldn't. This may sound nuts, but someone jumped inside me and wouldn't let me. At first, I thought I was just a coward, but she convinced me that I had an important thing to do, that I needed to go on. It's kind of cowardly to hide in a submarine and kill people from thousands of miles away, to let them die without warning. Hell, I didn't let them, I killed them." Sam goes silent again.

Behind him, Walt hears Pyotr singing a lullaby to his grandmother in Russian.

"Are you still there, sir?"

"Yes, Sam. I'm not going to leave you again." Walt hears Sam sniffle.

"What advice did you give the President back in '83, if I might ask?"

"I told him it was doable, that launching a missile on Yamantov could be done, and the Soviets wouldn't suspect it until hours later. That a single nuke could completely destroy a bunker. They might even pause, thinking it was a reactor accident."

"Were you right?"

Walt swallows hard. "Yeah, I was." He waits. They sit quietly for several minutes.

"You said you gave them more than they might have asked for. What did you mean?"

"After the meeting with all the advisers, I talked to the President alone, just for a minute. I told him I thought the Soviets would never forget this, and that if they didn't retaliate immediately, someday they would. I told him they would do exactly as we would if they bombed Cheyenne Mountain. I cautioned him against the launch."

"What did he say?"

"He said he thought if we gained time, maybe there would be a sensible Soviet leader."

"Is Gorbachev sensible?"

"He seems to be. The President wants to get rid of all of our nukes and Gorbachev seems to agree."

"There's no chance of that. Reagan is being naïve." Sam goes quiet again and Walt waits. "If I go with you, what will happen?" asks Sam.

Walt wants to reassure him, but he can't. "I don't honestly know. A lot will depend on today, on whether or not you decide to stay in America or go to Mexico. If you stay, well, you'll probably end up in jail or a psych ward. If I can get you to Father Tellez, the government just might allow you to remain there—as long as you don't come back."

"No guarantees, huh?"

"Sorry, no." Walt waits again. "Tell me about this person who jumped inside you."

"I'm sure you know about Henry Taluse. What a dumb jerk he turned out to be. Anyway, he called me a shaman. Do you know what that is, sir?"

"Yeah, a little."

"Well, that's what it felt like, like I was carrying around this soul."

"How did the two of you communicate? Did it talk to you?"

Walt hears Sam let out a little laugh, a sarcastic laugh. "No, sir. She just kind of constricts my insides occasionally. When I was about to do something dumb, I think." He pauses and Walt waits, unable to think of an adequate response. "Father Tellez told me that my own soul is in turmoil, but I've never felt my soul. He asked if this spirit was Greg's, but I didn't think so. I've been calling her Baby Bear for the past few weeks. She didn't have a name for the first two years."

When Sam goes quiet, Walt asks, "What's she telling you now?"

"She's being real quiet, like she's not there. When you were in here with me, she might have left." Walt remembers that Sam doubled over in seeming pain just before he went out with Pyotr. Sam speaks softly, "When I came back from the mission, I thought I would be coming back to war, that much of America would be destroyed. But there was no war."

"Sam, maybe what you did prevented war. About five weeks after your mission, NATO held exercises to test our international communications. It was called Able Archer. The Soviets misinterpreted its purpose and went back on full alert. We had to convince them that this was only a practice event, a scheduled exercise with our European allies, and they eventually stood down. The Joint Chiefs will never say this publically, hell, we've never said anything about Yamantov, but to a man, they believe that the Soviets hesitated because of our success at Yamantov."

"We have a different definition of success, sir," says Sam.

"Yeah, we do."

"Did you ever serve in the military, sir? I suspect you did since you work for the government."

"I was a grunt in the Korean War. I joined when I was seventeen and stupid, hadn't even finished high school," answers Walt.

"How did you get to be in charge of a nuclear power plant without a high school diploma?"

"I went back to school on the GI Bill. More importantly, I had a friend who believed in me and wouldn't let me become the stupid shit I was becoming. I married his daughter, and he continually reminds me how indebted to him I am."

"He sounds like a good friend." Sam goes quiet again. "Sir, I'm going to do a little thinking for a while. Tell that little boy that I said thanks for not telling on me at the church. I'll bet he didn't tell you that I was hiding in the altar."

"You were in the church?" asks Walt.

"Yeah. Is he your grandson?"

"No, I just met him a few days ago. His mother worked at Yamantov. We both like baseball. My son doesn't have children yet."

"We all lost something at Yamantov. Well, go check on him and his mother. I'm not going anywhere just yet."

Walt has been standing throughout the entire conversation and during the long pauses. He turns back to Olga and Pyotr just as Bellena pulls onto the path driving her secretary's old Dodge Dart. He waves at his wife and then checks on Olga. Her eyes remain confused, but her temperature has lowered. Pyotr talks to her about the mine, about the deep hole behind the desk, and about the man called Sam who he first met in the church. Babu responds with a single sentence in Russian. "Into the earth, underneath the ground, back to the mountain," which she repeats to each of Pyotr's comments or questions.

Bellena stops just a few feet behind Olga and Pyotr. She tells Walt that Mac got the axe and crowbar like he asked, and then he brought lunch over to the office, where he now shares it with her secretary. She talked to Father Spreewell, and he promised to contact Father Tellez as soon as possible. "What can I do now?" she asks as Walt takes the tools from the car's trunk.

"I need you to take Olga away from here, maybe drive her over to the church. Something came over her, and she's incoherent. Take Pyotr too. I need to focus all my attention on getting Sam out of the mine as fast as I can and on the road to Mexico. We're living on borrowed time." He lays the tools off to the side, bends to Olga, and tells her to go with Bellena. He turns to Pyotr. "I'm going to need you to be a Cossack here, Pyotr. You need to help take care of your grandma for now. Do what Mrs. Kramer tells you to and hold on to Babu. You can do this, okay?"

Pyotr nods and helps his grandmother stand. "Come on, Babu, we need to leave, so Walt can get the man out of the mine. We'll go to the church and pray." Olga stands and continues to repeat the same words as before. Bellena leans into her husband, kisses him on the cheek, and then helps Olga walk to the car.

Walt watches them drive away and then picks up the tools and walks to the mine's entrance. "Are you still thinking, Sam?"

"Yeah, but we can talk if you'd like. Tell me your plan."

"I'd like to help you get out of Colorado, get you back to Mexico. You said that's not where you want to go, but you could go for a little while. Talk with Father Tellez until you got things worked out. I can help you on this end. I can get the FBI to stop pursuing you, to let you be."

"Sounds like a good plan, except for one thing. The FBI won't forget me forever. One day, I'll look up and somebody will be standing over me with a weapon, and I'll be gone. Nobody will know what happened to me. My mom won't know. Delany won't know. A few others."

"Sam, I know you're having a hard time looking forward because of all that's happened. I want you to talk with Father Tellez. He cares about you. I care about you."

Sam interrupts Walt. "Why do you care? Are you feeling a little bit guilty because of your part in the decision to drop the bomb on

Yamantov? By helping me, will it atone for your past behavior?"

Walt knows he can't say, at least right now. The man in the mine has enough on his plate without me adding anything else, thinks Walt. "Atonement isn't my goal at this moment. That's out of my hands anyway. Too big of a question. Right now, I only want to get you away from here and give you a chance."

Sam's voice changes. "Big of you. Forget the past; you're only worried about my future."

The two men go quiet for a moment. Then Sam speaks again. His voice has returned to the tone before his last accusation. "Sorry about that. Maybe you are trying to help. I appreciate that. I'd like to ask you a favor though, if I could. I've put in a good amount of time on the church and the cemetery, and I don't want it to go to waste. Could you see that Father Spreewell keeps it up, maybe finds somebody to finish the work on the church? I think the altar needs a little more trim and another coat of varnish."

"Yeah, I'll do that. I'll do it myself, if I have to. Anything else before we go?"

"I've got a box of things with me in here, a couple of things of value that I want to give away. Guess there won't be time for me to do it. Some of them are labeled, but the most important thing is my submarine pin. It's a dolphin, and I want my mom to have it. She was pretty proud of me in my Navy uniform."

"Your dad is too," says Walt.

"I wouldn't know about that." He pauses. "Would you do that?"

"Yeah. Anything I can do for your extra spirit?"

"No. Gone," Sam says with a different voice.

§

Bellena and Pyotr assist Olga into St. Mary and seat her in one of the back pews. Bellena sits with her, but Pyotr goes back to exploring, checking out the altar first. For several minutes at a time, he can't be seen. Bellena talks gently to Olga.

"It's quiet in here. Nice to be out of the sun for a while, isn't it? May has been warmer than normal for us. It doesn't usually get this warm until the first of June, but this has been a strange year."

Bellena asks about Russia, about how soon summer comes in the Northern Urals, about how long the snows last on her mountains.

Olga begins to respond. "We are approaching the long days, the days without much night, the days of extended light. Narodnaya never loses its snow. It keeps more than yours do. These Fourteeners, as you call them, are higher than my mountains, but they do not seem so. I guess it is because yours start at such a high altitude to begin with. Still, I imagine you love your mountains as much as the Komi love our Urals." She pauses to look for Pyotr. "Pyotr. Pyotr. Where are you?"

The little boy peeks around the sacristy door. "Here, Babu. I'm here."

Olga relaxes again. "In the small villages of Komi, in the places away from Pechora, there are many small churches such as this, churches that are kept up by a single caretaker. They are sacred places where simple people try to understand a bigger world and pray to pass through it gently. When the communists came to power, they tried to destroy the churches, but in Komi they failed. We hid our faiths, but we saved our churches for another time. They have loosened their restrictions some, and more Komi are returning to church." For the first time, Olga looks directly at Bellena. "Do you attend church, Bellena?"

"Yes, I do. Neither my dad nor Walt go, but I do."

"It is the same in Russia. Most of the people who attend church are women, old women. They keep the traditions alive."

"Does Pyotr go with you?"

"I have to admit that I have not attended for several years, but I have a feeling just now." Olga pauses. "Would you mind if I went to the communion rail to pray?"

§

Sam's last comment alarms Walt. That spirit, thinks Walt, has kept Sam going, has kept him searching for something. "Sam, we need to go now. You need to come out."

"You and your people have spent considerable time, it seems, trying to help me, but now you can stop. If you do what you say, you're the one who will end up in trouble. You've been trying to catch me for your government, so they could keep the secret, but you've had a change of heart. You can keep the secret for them; all my notes are in here with me, and you can do with them what you want."

"Open the door, Sam. We'll find a way. There's another reason for my search."

"Go away, sir. Thanks for trying. Don't forget your promises." Behind the door, in the dark mine, a chair slides back.

Walt grabs the axe and swings hard at the barn wood door. It shatters, but the beam still blocks his way. In the dim light at the back of the staging area, he sees Sam raise his gun.

§

Kneeling at the communion rail, Olga prays. "The white light trapped you, all of you. It destroyed your bodies and prevented you from traveling to that place beyond our world. Now you have been restored after so many months. Your vessel has released you in a safer place, into me, and now I release you to that place . . . to that world out of reach of worldly senses. Back I send you to the place of no return, but to this place of serenity. Back to the mother mountain, the creator of our mountain, for the last leg of your journey." Olga crosses herself, sways, and looks to the altar. "Go in peace. Amen."

She turns with a radiant smile to Bellena. "That was beautiful," says Bellena who understands. "Did you see your daughter?"

"Yes, Ursula was there. She was inside me for a short while. She will be fine now."

Pyotr crawls out from behind the altar. "Let's go home, Babu."

§

Walt slowly lays the axe on the ground. "Don't, Sam."

Sam's lips purse and he nods an acknowledgement. He turns the gun inward to his temple and squeezes the trigger. The violent explosion sends him backward into the mine's shaft.

Walt shudders and drops to his knees, his shoulders hunched

forward, his forearm shielding his eyes. He quickly stands, picks up the axe, and crashes it into the door, using it as a battering ram, destroying the remains to the barrier. He steps into the mine, throws the chair aside, and looks into the shaft. It is pitch black. He steps back, looking for the flashlight, and finds it near the door. He kneels and shines it into the shaft, but there is no sign of Sam. Walt listens for any sound.

# VII

# The Return

# Chapter 15

*Laments for the Dead*

How do we remember our past? How will we remember Samuel Elkington? Father Tellez is secure in his mind and heart, but he wants to deliver a few words of comfort and encouragement to Samuel's family and friends. Samuel's hometown newspaper, *The Ouray News*, called his death "accidental," resulting from a fall, and the U.S. Government granted Ensign Elkington a posthumous honorable discharge. Ah, keep the secret. Back in Hermosillo Father Tellez told Samuel to find a reason to live, that he had so much to live for. Samuel replied that he had taken too many lives, and that someone needed to be held accountable. He kept coming back to that personal responsibility excuse, and the two of them would argue—gently, but argue, nonetheless. Father Tellez understood the transformation in Samuel after the tragedy, that he became a gentle man, although he might have been something else earlier in life. It didn't matter. Father Tellez would suggest they pray together, but Samuel wouldn't participate. "Prayer won't help me, but don't let that stop you. Pray for the dead, for the innocents of Yamantov and the Cold War." Samuel was correct about one thing. Not many people would miss him, but those who did would hold him so dear. Father Tellez will use this in his words to them at St Mary.

Father Tellez stands at the pulpit. He will not allow the small gathering to be sad, even though a life has passed too soon. It will be a short and simple service delivered in a small, simple, and beautiful church. "It is fitting," begins the priest, "that we remember

Samuel in this setting, in this restored church and cemetery he so meticulously cared for. Look up here," Father Tellez commands, "not down into your laps. Be like Pyotr, who continues to smile and see Samuel in the altar." The priest has not seen Pyotr do anything but smile, laugh, and bounce around these past three days. Father Tellez has spoken privately with each of the eight people gathered in front of him. Samuel's mother and father, Colleen and Walt, are struggling the most. Colleen Elkington does not know of Samuel's role in the destruction of Yamantov, knows only that her son went silent and never returned. Walt showed remarkable understanding of his son's guilt, but that understanding does not temper his own guilt for a lifetime of abandonment and his failure to save him in the mine. Because of the depth and disrepair of the shaft, Walt has not been able to recover Sam's body. So far, nothing the priest has said has consoled Walt. It will take time. Bellena and Mac have been rocks for him, and because of their strength, Father believes Walt will recover. Despite the age difference, Barkley was Samuel's friend, and the only one in the gathering who can rightfully claim that title. Such an important role in life—being a friend. The old man brought Sam's poem to Buena Vista and shared it at last night's dinner. He shared much of his life's philosophy too and made everyone laugh.

Father Tellez walks around the pulpit to the communion rail, nods across to Father Spreewell, and continues. "There is no lock on the front door, and I suspect this will allow for a few acts of vandalism in the future, although I hope not, but Samuel made that decision. He seemed bent on unlocking secrets." Walt fingers a necklace in his pocket that holds a single key. He gave the second key to Colleen, saying he would explain its meaning someday in the future. Father Tellez unhooks the communion gate and walks to Delany. He takes her hand, and she stands. "I pray you will find peace in all of this, young lady." He holds her close while he beseeches the others to remain in contact with Delany. She is most vulnerable, he knows, because in all ways, she and Samuel were kindred souls. Father Tellez kisses Delany on the forehead and sits her down.

He turns to Olga and Pyotr. "And you will be returning to your home in Russia very soon. God be with you on your journey." Olga nods. "We can't know in this life about the forces that send us on our journeys, but they are mysterious indeed. We are directed by unseen winds. Some may say that our Lord works in strange ways." The priest smiles warmly, takes Pyotr's hand, and leads him to the altar. He lifts the boy onto a high-backed wooden chair next to the altar to face the gathering. "From what I can glean, you led us all back to Forest City, back to this setting where we could celebrate Samuel's life. I thank you, Pyotr, for making us all laugh last night at dinner. I thank you, Bellena, for the wonderful meal." Father Tellez moves around the altar and addresses the congregation. "Let us pray. Lord, we thank you for the life of Samuel Elkington. I ask that you hold the people in this beautiful Church of St. Mary in the palm of your hand, nurturing and protecting them as they come to terms with their loss. Give us comfort as we grieve for Samuel. But Father, I ask that you make the grieving time short and show us the path back to appreciation and laughter for Samuel. Amen." Father Tellez makes the sign of the cross, lifts Pyotr off the chair to return to his grandmother and takes four small boxes from inside the altar.

"I've filled these four containers with dirt from the cemetery that Sam restored so carefully, so thoughtfully. I hope each of you will find a mountain on which to place this dirt because Samuel so loved his mountains. Delany, maybe you and Barkley can do this together." Father Tellez hands the boxes to Delany, Walt, Colleen, and Olga. He steps back, raises both hands, and says, "Peace be with you."

§

As Father Tellez crosses into Arizona on his return to Mexico, he makes a sudden, unplanned diversion onto the Hopi Reservation. The wind gusts up behind him, blowing toward the west, toward the setting sun. He looks out the passenger window, past his invisible rider, toward the Sacred Mountain of the West. The priest had first thought about spreading his portion of dirt onto the Hermosillo cemetery that Samuel so carefully cultivated, but this seems better.

No one should rest forever in a foreign place, and now the Voices of Nature tell Father Tellez that this is Samuel's place. Samuel might argue, saying he has no place, but Father Tellez knows he must deliver the soul deliverer's soul to its natural affinity. Taking the can of soil from the seat, the priest walks to a nearby arroyo, unscrews the lid, and gently pours out the contents. The wind knows this dirt and blows it up and out in several directions.

§

Walt attaches two cabinet doors to the altar, then swings them open and closed to make sure they don't rub against each other. Satisfied, he gets the premade trim that he varnished two days earlier and applies wood glue to the underside. He tucks the key that dangles from the metal chain back under his shirt. There is still work to be completed at the church, but Walt has time now. He clamps the trim in place and realizes he is on his knees in front of the altar. He shakes his head slightly, looks up at the newly raised cross, and says, "Don't start getting any ideas."

In the cemetery Walt sets the hoses. The July sun is drying out the grass in some areas. He has been contemplating the parts of his conversation with his son from that last day. What is owed the dead? Bellena is pulling him out of his shell; it was she who drove him up to St. Mary and dropped him off in early June. "Get to work." Then she drove away. It's been his routine since. What do we owe the dead? Walt clips the grass along the fence line. A decent burial plot and fond memories if nothing else. He is coming to grips with not being able to know everything about Yamantov, accepting the notion that Sam carried its dead. Walt moves to Sam's stone. "You did good, son. I'm proud of you."

§

Olga waits until the first snows have blanketed the Northern Urals before she returns near to Uralansk. Autumn was Ursula's favorite time of the year, and Olga wants to celebrate that memory. The road is still blocked to Yamantov; the site will be contaminated for a hundred years, but at least this time, Olga will know. She and Pyotr climb the same bluff from where she and her father last viewed Yamantov on the slopes of Gora Narodnaya. They stand in awe of the great mountain; stand in silence of what awful tragedy occurred here three years earlier. Pyotr takes one box of dirt from his pack and hands it to his grandmother. Olga takes a brown paper sack of dirt from her pocket, and she sets them both on the rock where they stand. Pyotr looks to her with anticipation, while she stares at the packages. She moves off the rock to softer ground where she kneels, opens both containers, and mixes them together on the ground. She looks to Narodnaya and says, "I return you to the spot from where we departed, but this time you are joined by the one who carried you safely through the storm. Pyotr and I now send you to the place where the road is not becoming shorter, to the place of which our ears and your ears have not heard of." Then Pyotr repeats the last sentence. She smiles at him, takes his hand, and they begin the walk home.

215

The End